Monster Allergy 1

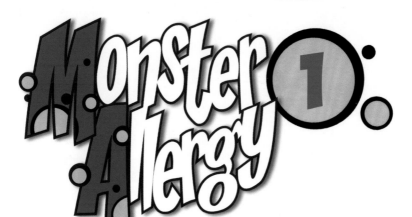

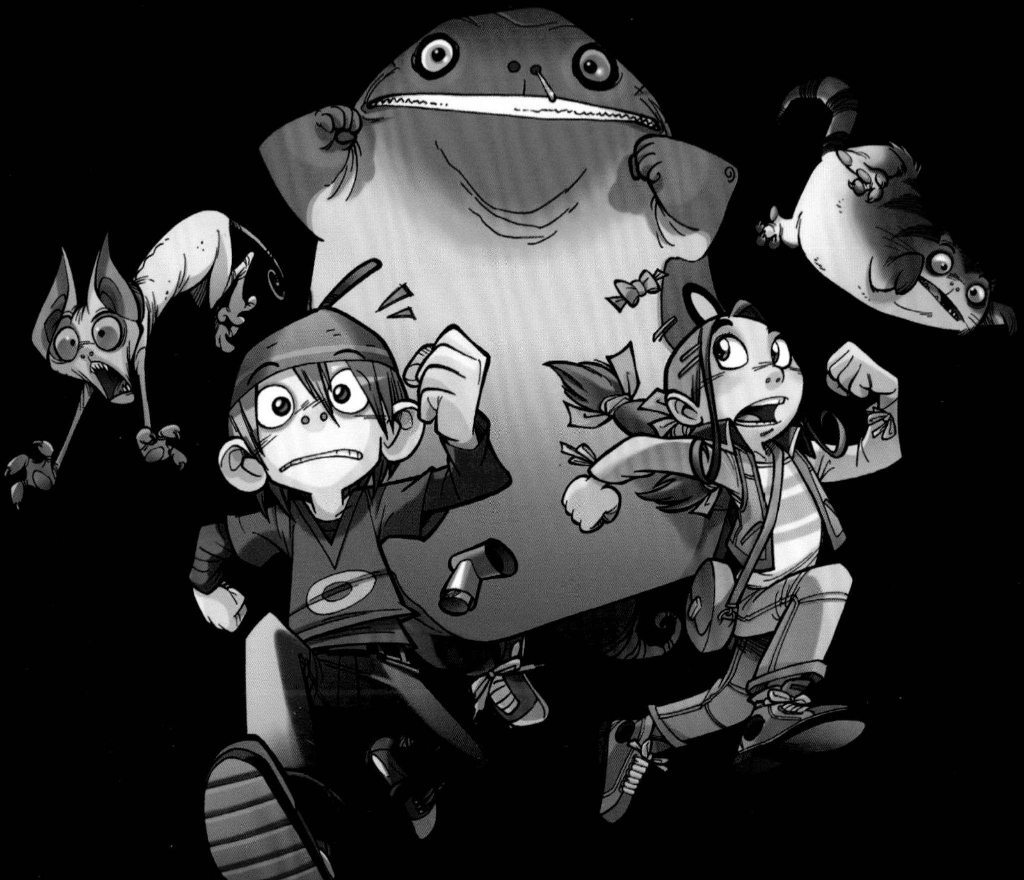
BARBUCCI
+ CANEPA
2003

Monster Allergy 1 — HOUSE OF MONSTERS

CENTOMO - ARTIBANI - BARBUCCI - CANEPA

INSIGHT COMICS

San Rafael, California

PART 1

THE HOUSE OF MONSTERS

Plot: Katja Centomo
Script: Francesco Artibani
Illustrations: Alessandro Barbucci
Colors: Barbara Canepa
and Paolo Lamanna

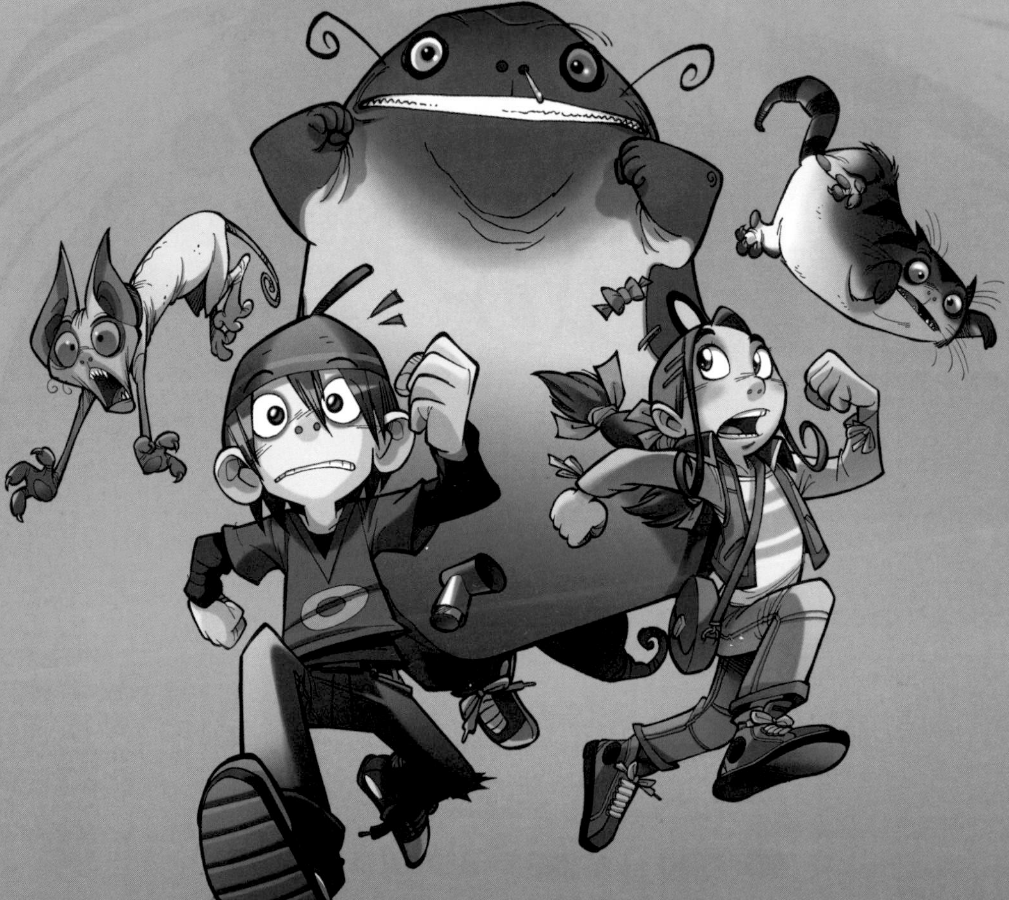
BARBUCCI + CANEPA 2003

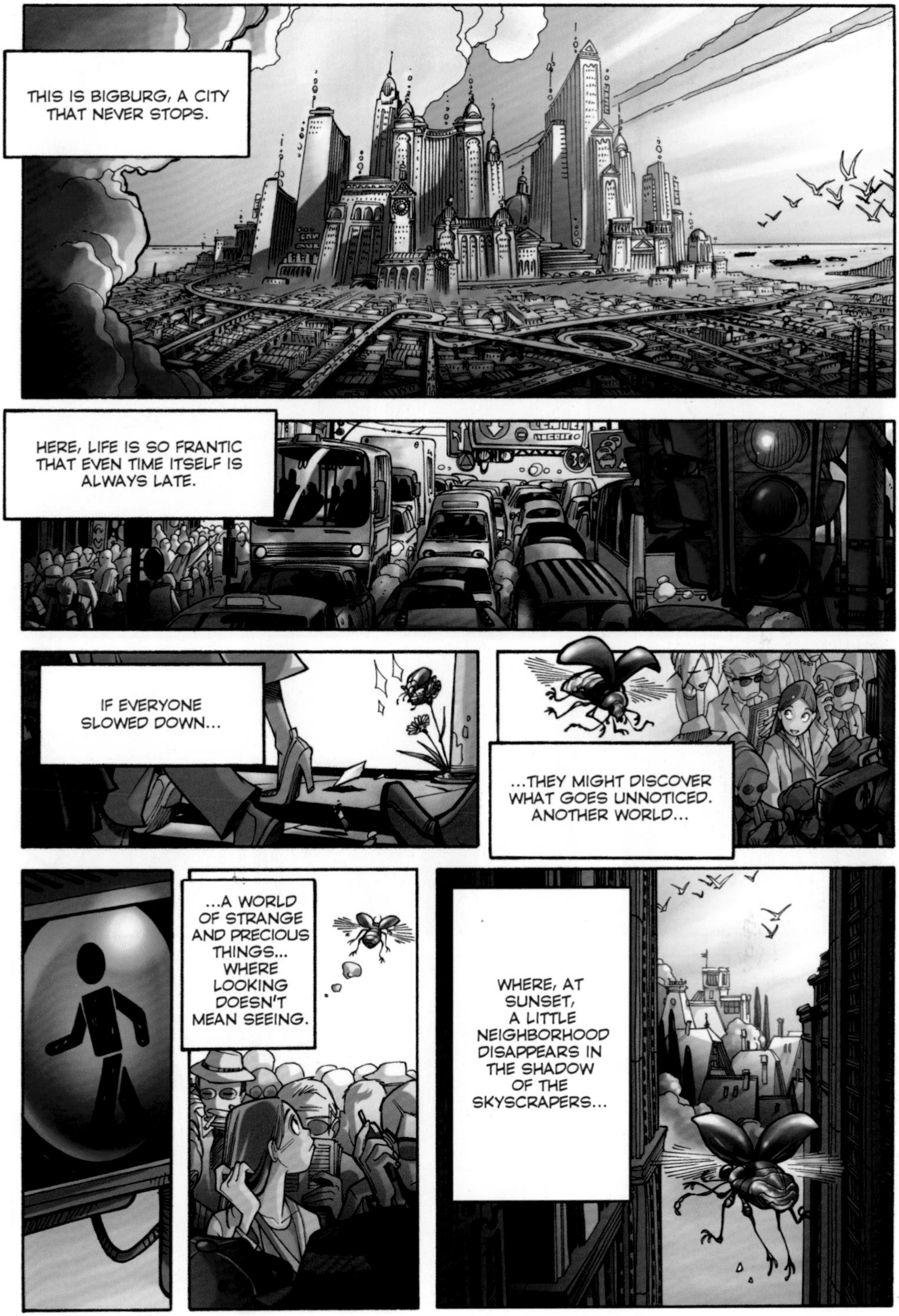
THIS IS BIGBURG, A CITY THAT NEVER STOPS.
HERE, LIFE IS SO FRANTIC THAT EVEN TIME ITSELF IS ALWAYS LATE.
IF EVERYONE SLOWED DOWN...
...THEY MIGHT DISCOVER WHAT GOES UNNOTICED. ANOTHER WORLD...
...A WORLD OF STRANGE AND PRECIOUS THINGS... WHERE LOOKING DOESN'T MEAN SEEING.
WHERE, AT SUNSET, A LITTLE NEIGHBORHOOD DISAPPEARS IN THE SHADOW OF THE SKYSCRAPERS...

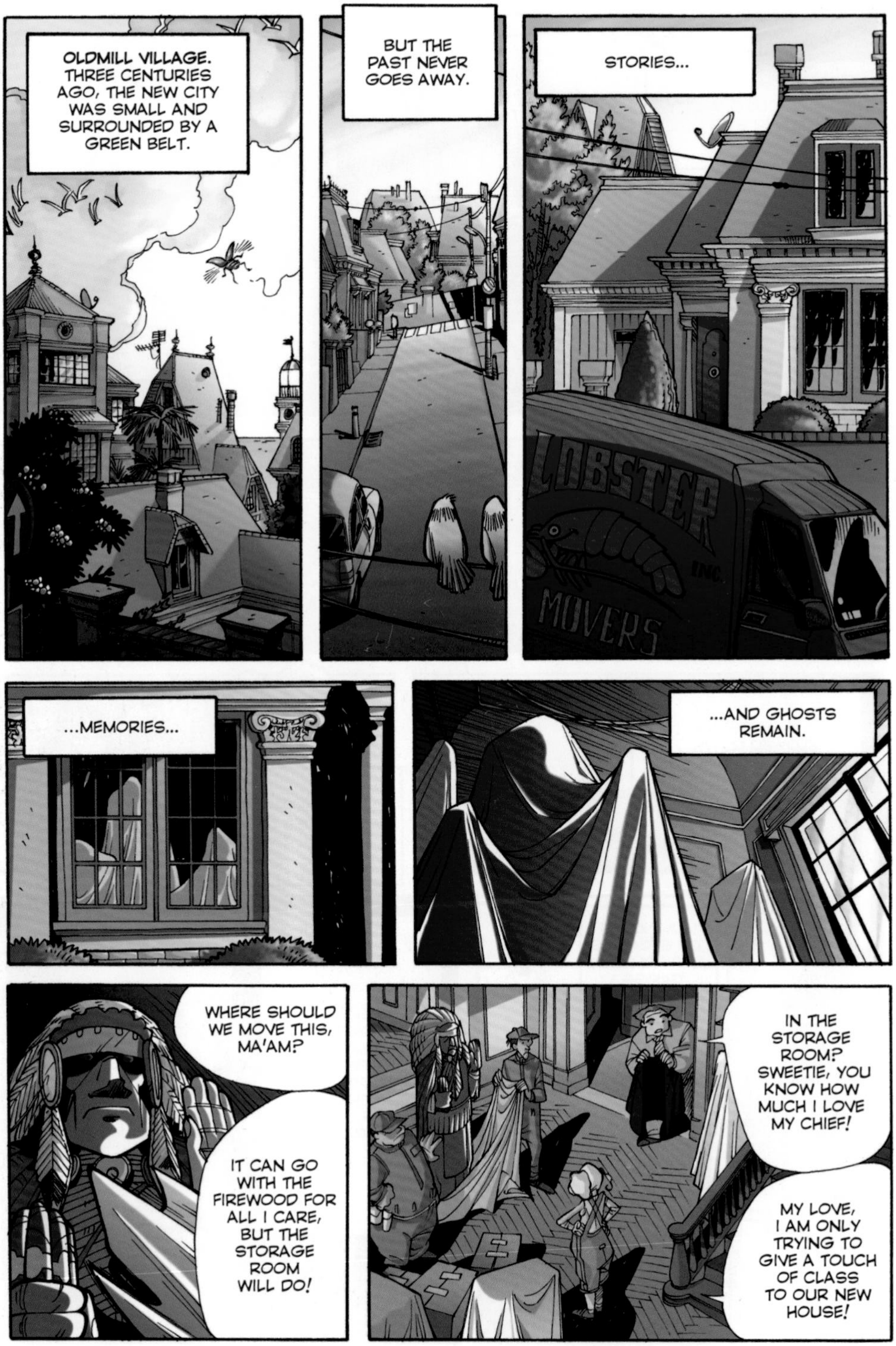
OLDMILL VILLAGE. THREE CENTURIES AGO, THE NEW CITY WAS SMALL AND SURROUNDED BY A GREEN BELT.
BUT THE PAST NEVER GOES AWAY.
STORIES...
LOBSTER
INC.
MOVERS
...MEMORIES...
...AND GHOSTS REMAIN.
WHERE SHOULD WE MOVE THIS, MA'AM?
IT CAN GO WITH THE FIREWOOD FOR ALL I CARE, BUT THE STORAGE ROOM WILL DO!
IN THE STORAGE ROOM? SWEETIE, YOU KNOW HOW MUCH I LOVE MY CHIEF!
MY LOVE, I AM ONLY TRYING TO GIVE A TOUCH OF CLASS TO OUR NEW HOUSE!

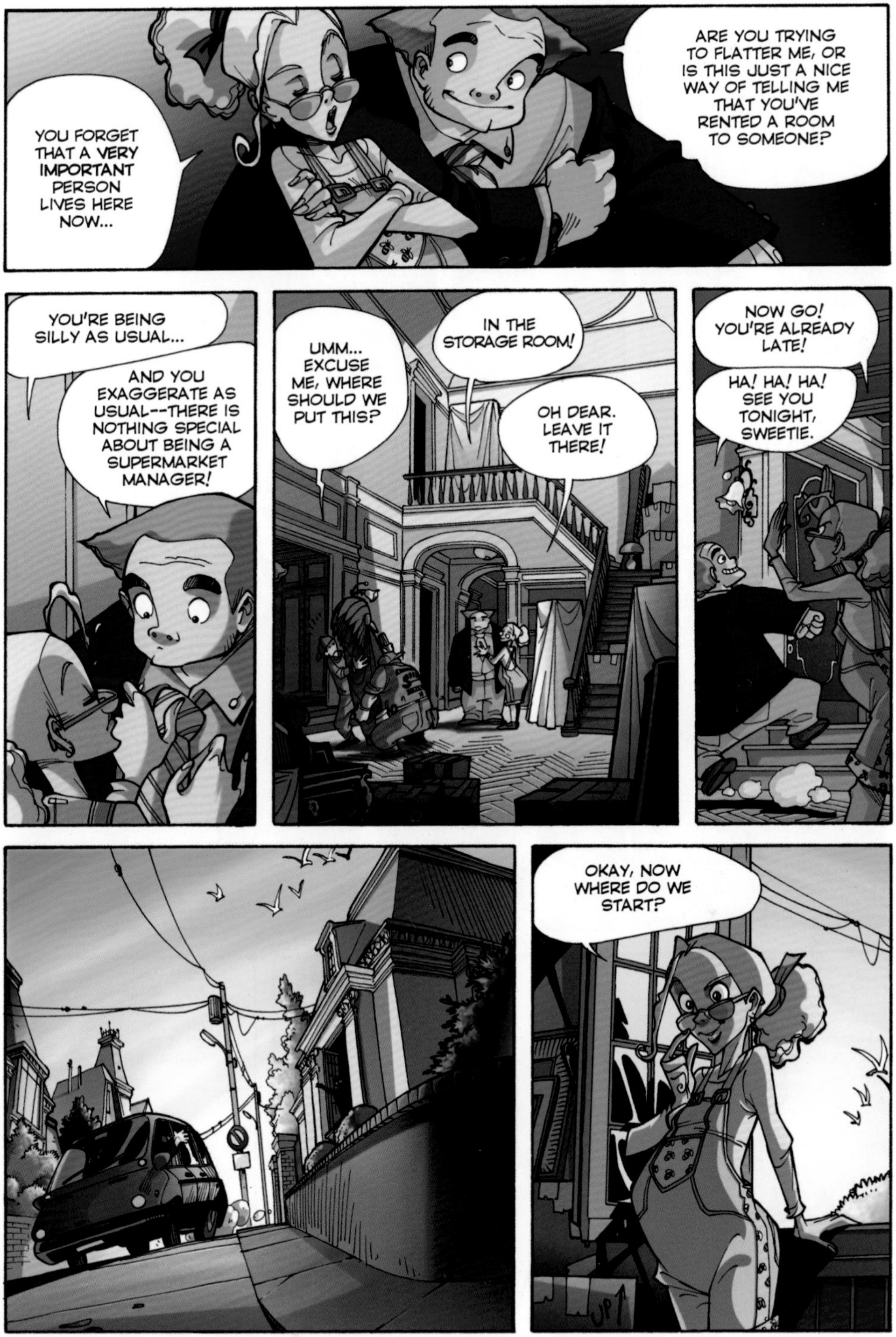
YOU FORGET THAT A VERY IMPORTANT PERSON LIVES HERE NOW...
ARE YOU TRYING TO FLATTER ME, OR IS THIS JUST A NICE WAY OF TELLING ME THAT YOU'VE RENTED A ROOM TO SOMEONE?
YOU'RE BEING SILLY AS USUAL...
AND YOU EXAGGERATE AS USUAL--THERE IS NOTHING SPECIAL ABOUT BEING A SUPERMARKET MANAGER!
UMM... EXCUSE ME, WHERE SHOULD WE PUT THIS?
IN THE STORAGE ROOM!
OH DEAR. LEAVE IT THERE!
NOW GO! YOU'RE ALREADY LATE!
HA! HA! HA! SEE YOU TONIGHT, SWEETIE.
OKAY, NOW WHERE DO WE START?
UP

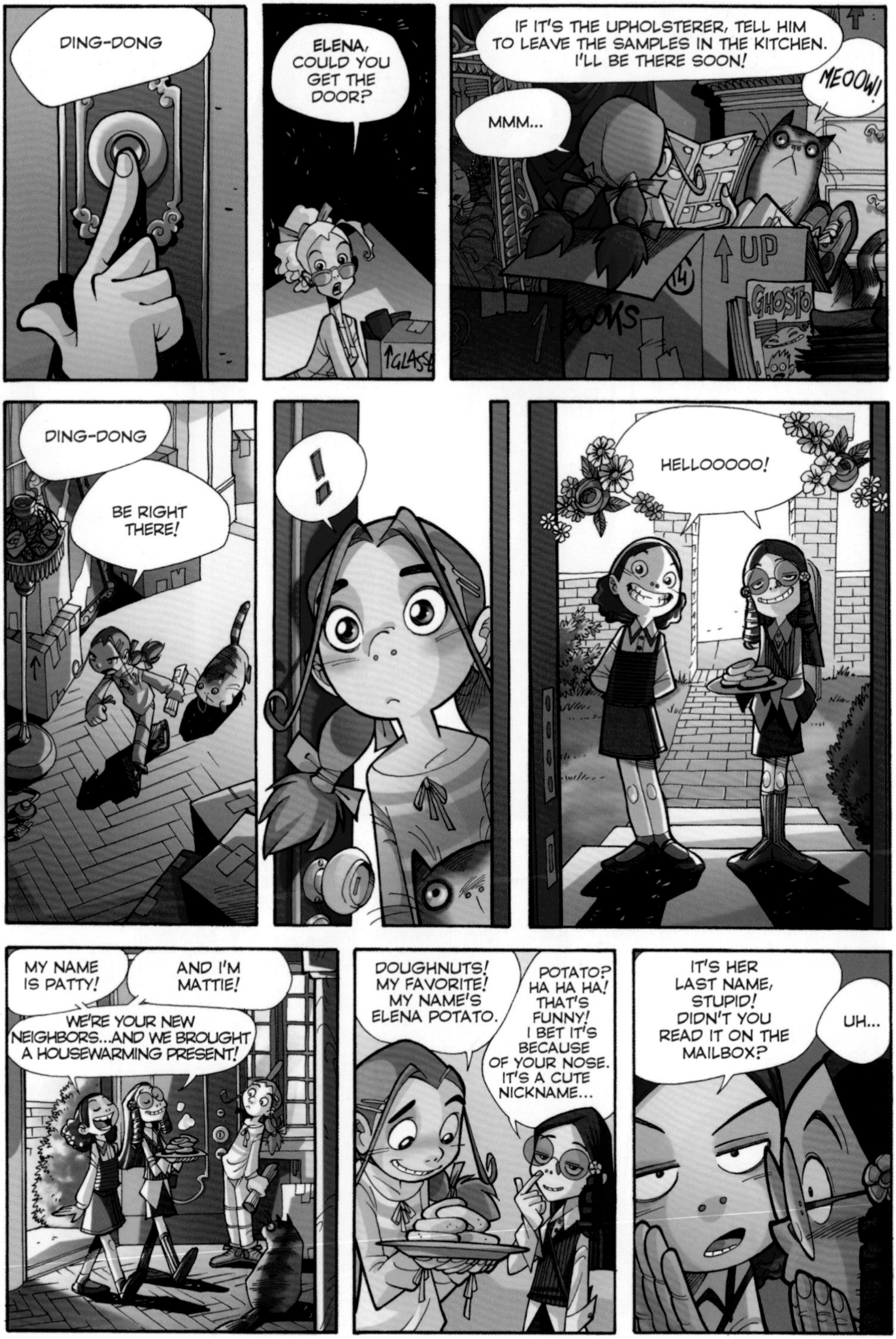
DING-DONG
ELENA, COULD YOU GET THE DOOR?
IF IT'S THE UPHOLSTERER, TELL HIM TO LEAVE THE SAMPLES IN THE KITCHEN. I'LL BE THERE SOON!
MMM...
MEOOW!
UP
BOOKS
GLASS
GHOSTO
DING-DONG
BE RIGHT THERE!
!
HELLOOOOO!
MY NAME IS PATTY!
AND I'M MATTIE!
WE'RE YOUR NEW NEIGHBORS...AND WE BROUGHT A HOUSEWARMING PRESENT!
DOUGHNUTS! MY FAVORITE! MY NAME'S ELENA POTATO.
POTATO? HA HA HA! THAT'S FUNNY! I BET IT'S BECAUSE OF YOUR NOSE. IT'S A CUTE NICKNAME...
IT'S HER LAST NAME, STUPID! DIDN'T YOU READ IT ON THE MAILBOX?
UH...

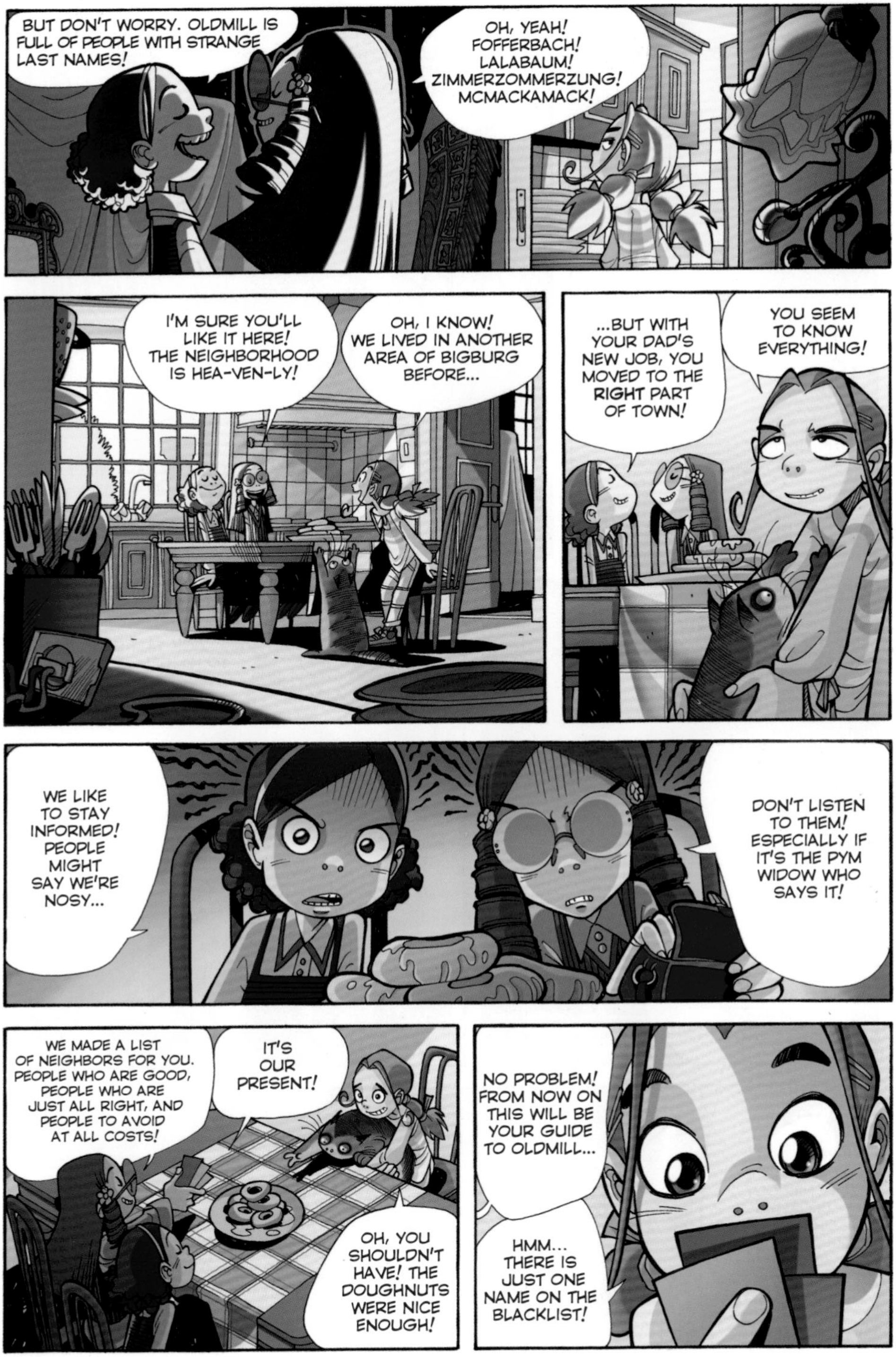
BUT DON'T WORRY. OLDMILL IS FULL OF PEOPLE WITH STRANGE LAST NAMES!
OH, YEAH! FOFFERBACH! LALABAUM! ZIMMERZOMMERZUNG! MCMACKAMACK!
I'M SURE YOU'LL LIKE IT HERE! THE NEIGHBORHOOD IS HEA-VEN-LY!
OH, I KNOW! WE LIVED IN ANOTHER AREA OF BIGBURG BEFORE...
...BUT WITH YOUR DAD'S NEW JOB, YOU MOVED TO THE RIGHT PART OF TOWN!
YOU SEEM TO KNOW EVERYTHING!
WE LIKE TO STAY INFORMED! PEOPLE MIGHT SAY WE'RE NOSY...
DON'T LISTEN TO THEM! ESPECIALLY IF IT'S THE PYM WIDOW WHO SAYS IT!
WE MADE A LIST OF NEIGHBORS FOR YOU. PEOPLE WHO ARE GOOD, PEOPLE WHO ARE JUST ALL RIGHT, AND PEOPLE TO AVOID AT ALL COSTS!
IT'S OUR PRESENT!
OH, YOU SHOULDN'T HAVE! THE DOUGHNUTS WERE NICE ENOUGH!
NO PROBLEM! FROM NOW ON THIS WILL BE YOUR GUIDE TO OLDMILL...
HMM... THERE IS JUST ONE NAME ON THE BLACKLIST!

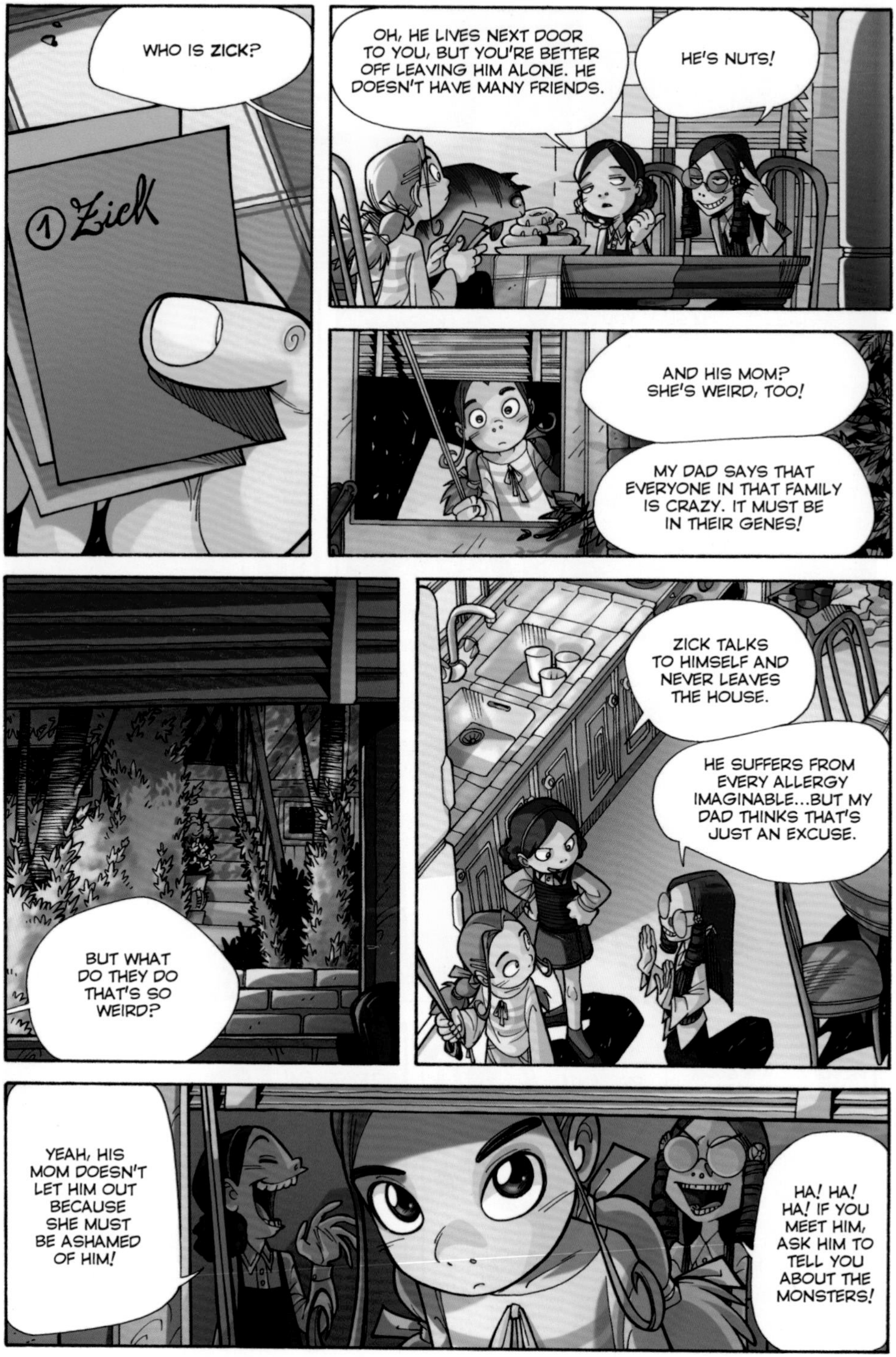
WHO IS ZICK?
1 Zick
OH, HE LIVES NEXT DOOR TO YOU, BUT YOU'RE BETTER OFF LEAVING HIM ALONE. HE DOESN'T HAVE MANY FRIENDS.
HE'S NUTS!
AND HIS MOM? SHE'S WEIRD, TOO!
MY DAD SAYS THAT EVERYONE IN THAT FAMILY IS CRAZY. IT MUST BE IN THEIR GENES!
BUT WHAT DO THEY DO THAT'S SO WEIRD?
ZICK TALKS TO HIMSELF AND NEVER LEAVES THE HOUSE.
HE SUFFERS FROM EVERY ALLERGY IMAGINABLE...BUT MY DAD THINKS THAT'S JUST AN EXCUSE.
YEAH, HIS MOM DOESN'T LET HIM OUT BECAUSE SHE MUST BE ASHAMED OF HIM!
HA! HA! HA! IF YOU MEET HIM, ASK HIM TO TELL YOU ABOUT THE MONSTERS!

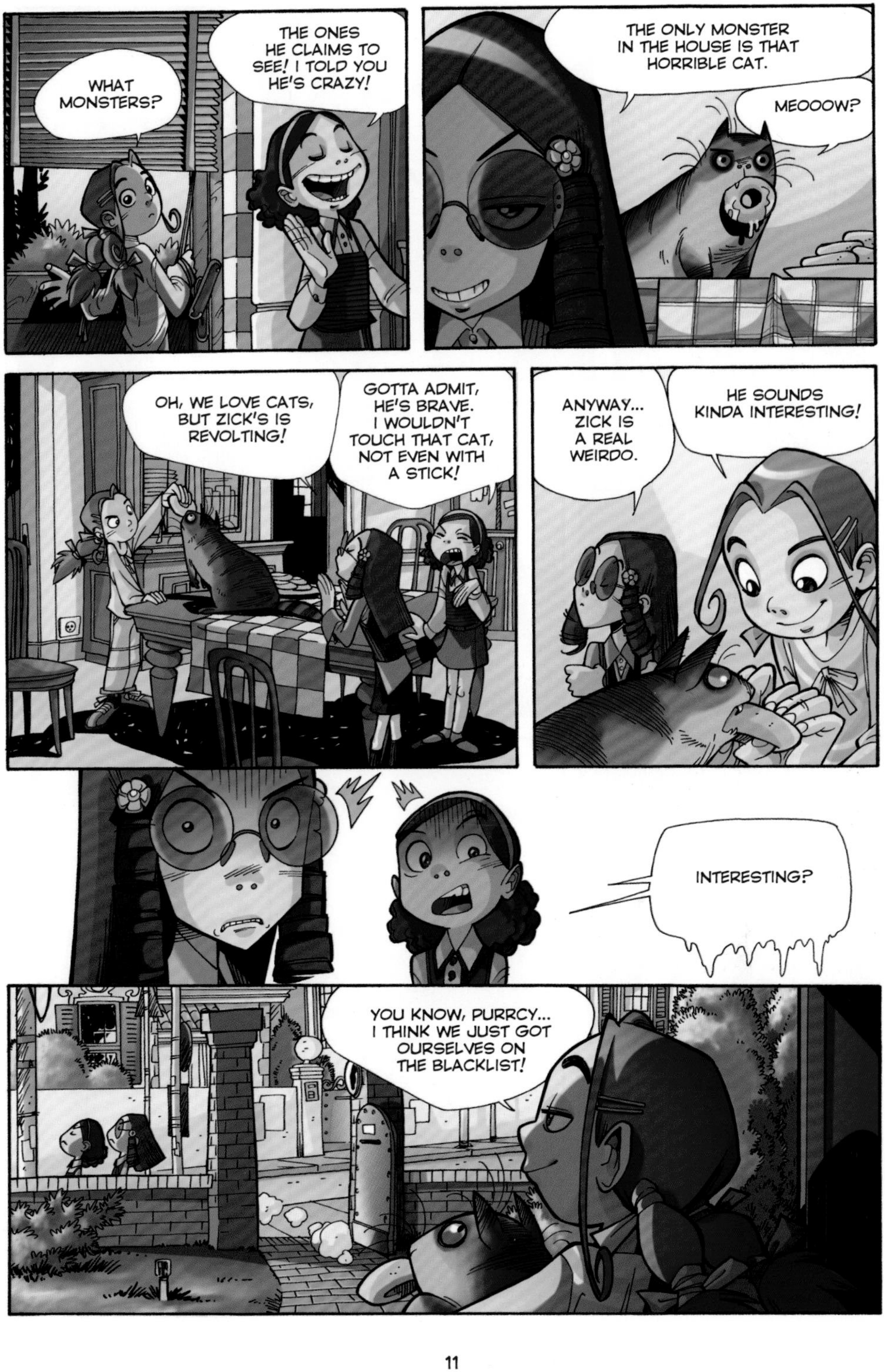
WHAT MONSTERS?
THE ONES HE CLAIMS TO SEE! I TOLD YOU HE'S CRAZY!
THE ONLY MONSTER IN THE HOUSE IS THAT HORRIBLE CAT.
MEOOOW?
OH, WE LOVE CATS, BUT ZICK'S IS REVOLTING!
GOTTA ADMIT, HE'S BRAVE. I WOULDN'T TOUCH THAT CAT, NOT EVEN WITH A STICK!
ANYWAY... ZICK IS A REAL WEIRDO.
HE SOUNDS KINDA INTERESTING!
INTERESTING?
YOU KNOW, PURRCY... I THINK WE JUST GOT OURSELVES ON THE BLACKLIST!

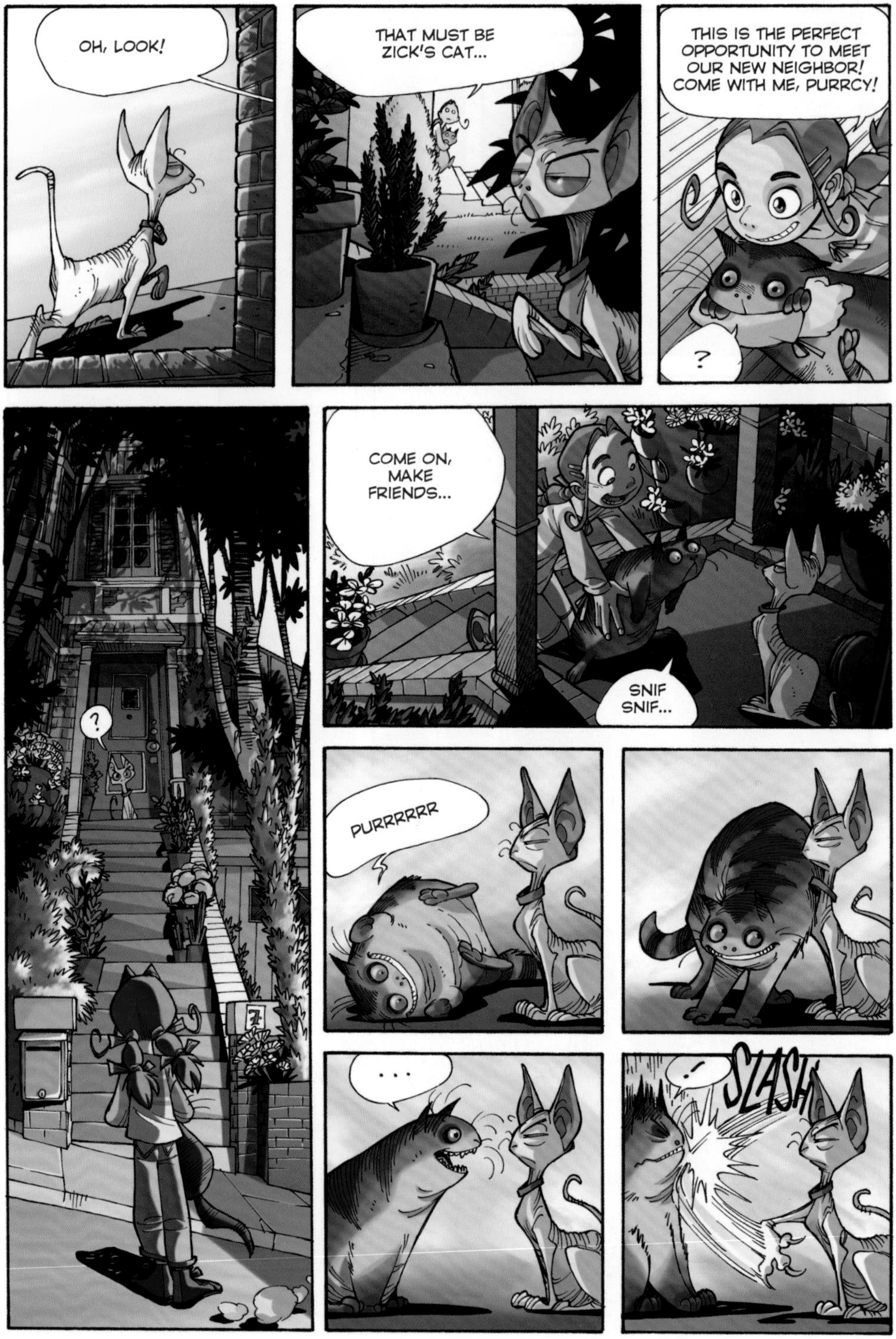
OH, LOOK!
THAT MUST BE ZICK'S CAT...
THIS IS THE PERFECT OPPORTUNITY TO MEET OUR NEW NEIGHBOR! COME WITH ME, PURRCY!
?
?
COME ON, MAKE FRIENDS...
SNIF SNIF...
PURRRRRR
. . .
!
SLASH

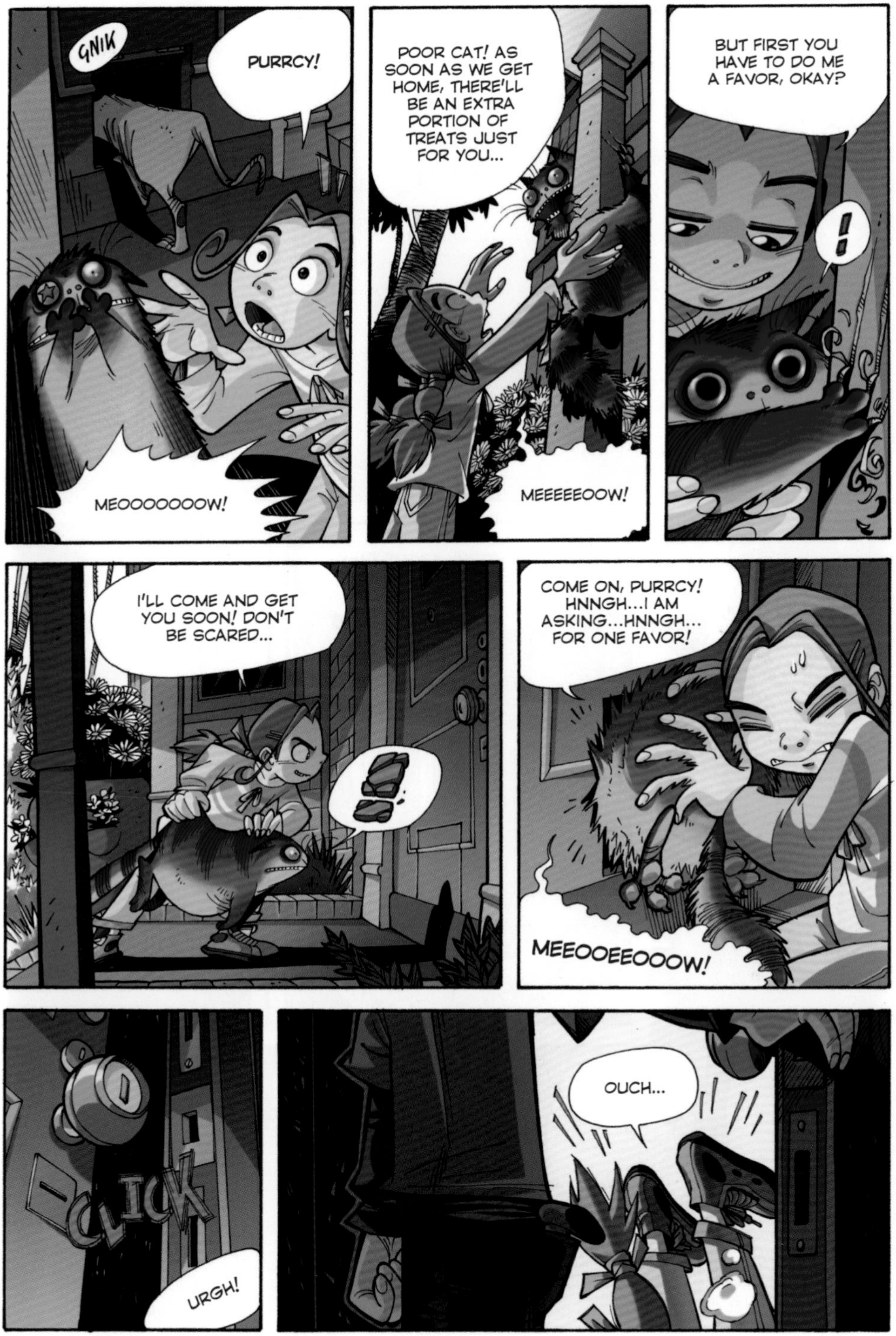
GNIK
PURRCY!
MEOOOOOOOW!
POOR CAT! AS SOON AS WE GET HOME, THERE'LL BE AN EXTRA PORTION OF TREATS JUST FOR YOU...
MEEEEEOOW!
BUT FIRST YOU HAVE TO DO ME A FAVOR, OKAY?
!
I'LL COME AND GET YOU SOON! DON'T BE SCARED...
COME ON, PURRCY! HNNGH...I AM ASKING...HNNGH... FOR ONE FAVOR!
MEEOOEEOOOW!
CLICK
URGH!
OUCH...

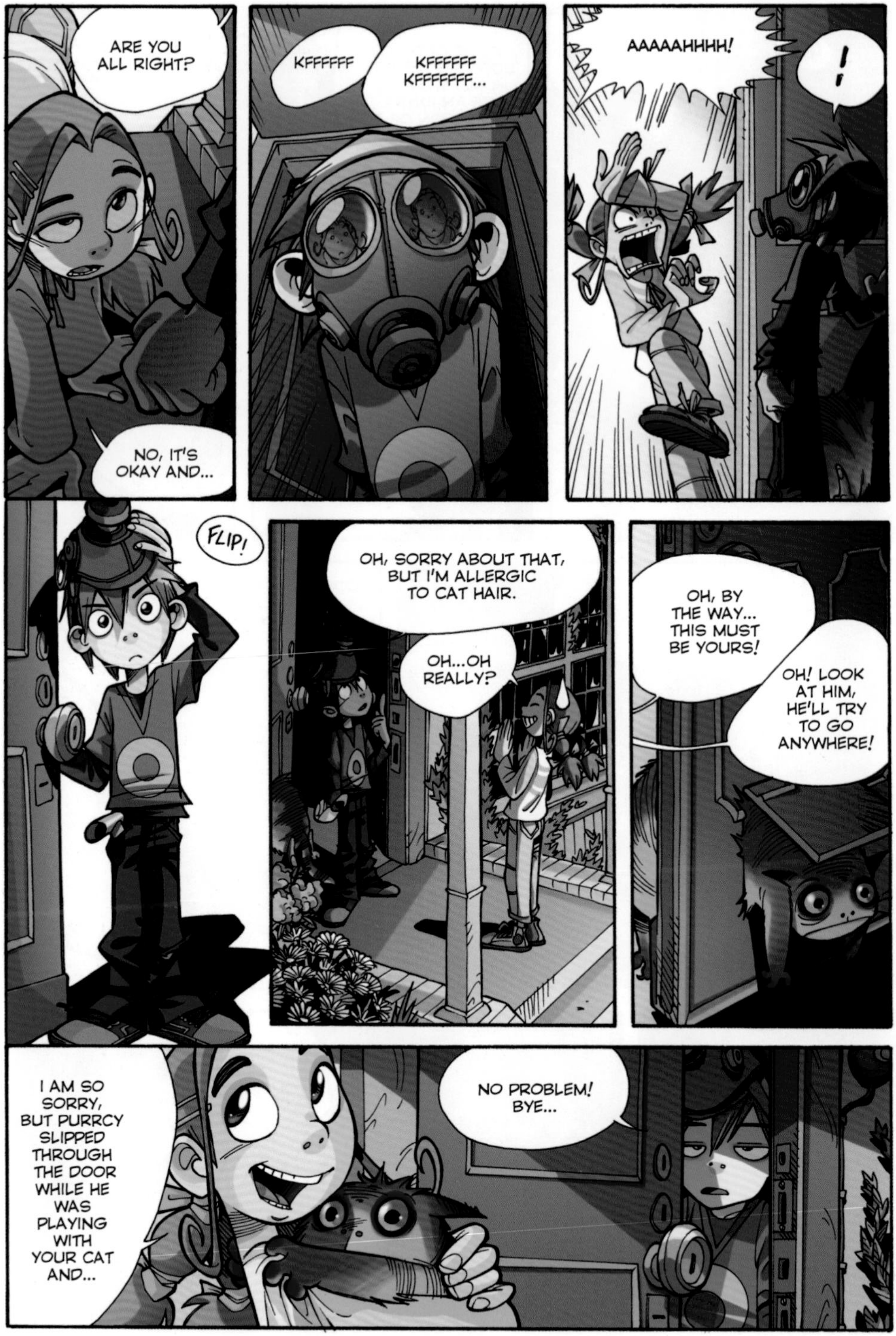
ARE YOU ALL RIGHT?
NO, IT'S OKAY AND...
KFFFFFF
KFFFFFF KFFFFFFF...
AAAAAHHHH!
!
FLIP!
OH, SORRY ABOUT THAT, BUT I'M ALLERGIC TO CAT HAIR.
OH...OH REALLY?
OH, BY THE WAY... THIS MUST BE YOURS!
OH! LOOK AT HIM, HE'LL TRY TO GO ANYWHERE!
I AM SO SORRY, BUT PURRCY SLIPPED THROUGH THE DOOR WHILE HE WAS PLAYING WITH YOUR CAT AND...
NO PROBLEM! BYE...

UM... MY NAME'S ELENA! I'M YOUR NEW NEIGHBOR...

YOUR HAIRLESS CAT IS REALLY NICE! WE SHOULD LET THEM PLAY TOGETHER SOMETIME. THEY SEEM TO GET ALONG GREAT!

MEEEEEEEEEOW!

WHAT A NICE HOME YOU HAVE!

THANKS! BUT NOW, IF YOU DON'T MIND, I SHOULD REALLY SHUT THE DOOR. THE DRAFT BRINGS IN A LOT OF DUST...

...AND I'M ALLERGIC TO DUST! ξCOUGH!ξ ξCOUGH!ξ ξCOUGH!ξ

WAIT, ZICK! I HAVE... I HAVE TO GIVE YOU SOMETHING!

IT'S A...UMM...A FRIENDSHIP DOUGHNUT! I'M GIVING ONE OUT TO EVERYBODY IN THE NEIGHBORHOOD, SO I THOUGHT THAT...

YOU'RE REALLY NICE, ELENA... ξCOUGHξ ξCOUGHξ

...BUT I'M ALLERGIC TO MAPLE SYRUP TOO! ξCOUGH!ξ ξCOUGH!ξ ξCOUGH!ξ

SLAM

HE REALLY IS ALLERGIC TO EVERYTHING!

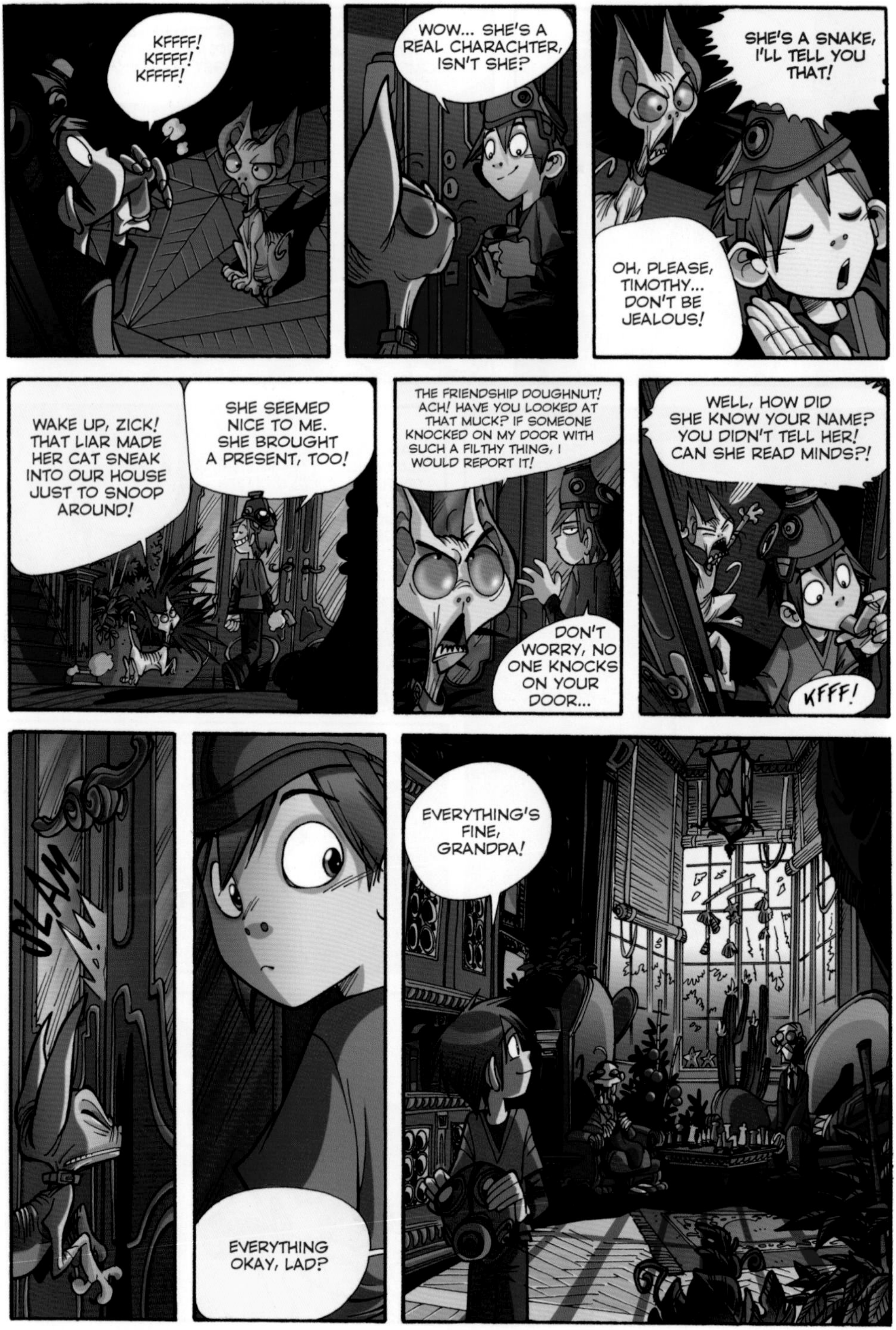
KFFFF! KFFFF! KFFFF!
WOW... SHE'S A REAL CHARACHTER, ISN'T SHE?
SHE'S A SNAKE, I'LL TELL YOU THAT!
OH, PLEASE, TIMOTHY... DON'T BE JEALOUS!
WAKE UP, ZICK! THAT LIAR MADE HER CAT SNEAK INTO OUR HOUSE JUST TO SNOOP AROUND!
SHE SEEMED NICE TO ME. SHE BROUGHT A PRESENT, TOO!
THE FRIENDSHIP DOUGHNUT! ACH! HAVE YOU LOOKED AT THAT MUCK? IF SOMEONE KNOCKED ON MY DOOR WITH SUCH A FILTHY THING, I WOULD REPORT IT!
DON'T WORRY, NO ONE KNOCKS ON YOUR DOOR...
WELL, HOW DID SHE KNOW YOUR NAME? YOU DIDN'T TELL HER! CAN SHE READ MINDS?!
KFFF!
SLAM!
EVERYTHING OKAY, LAD?
EVERYTHING'S FINE, GRANDPA!

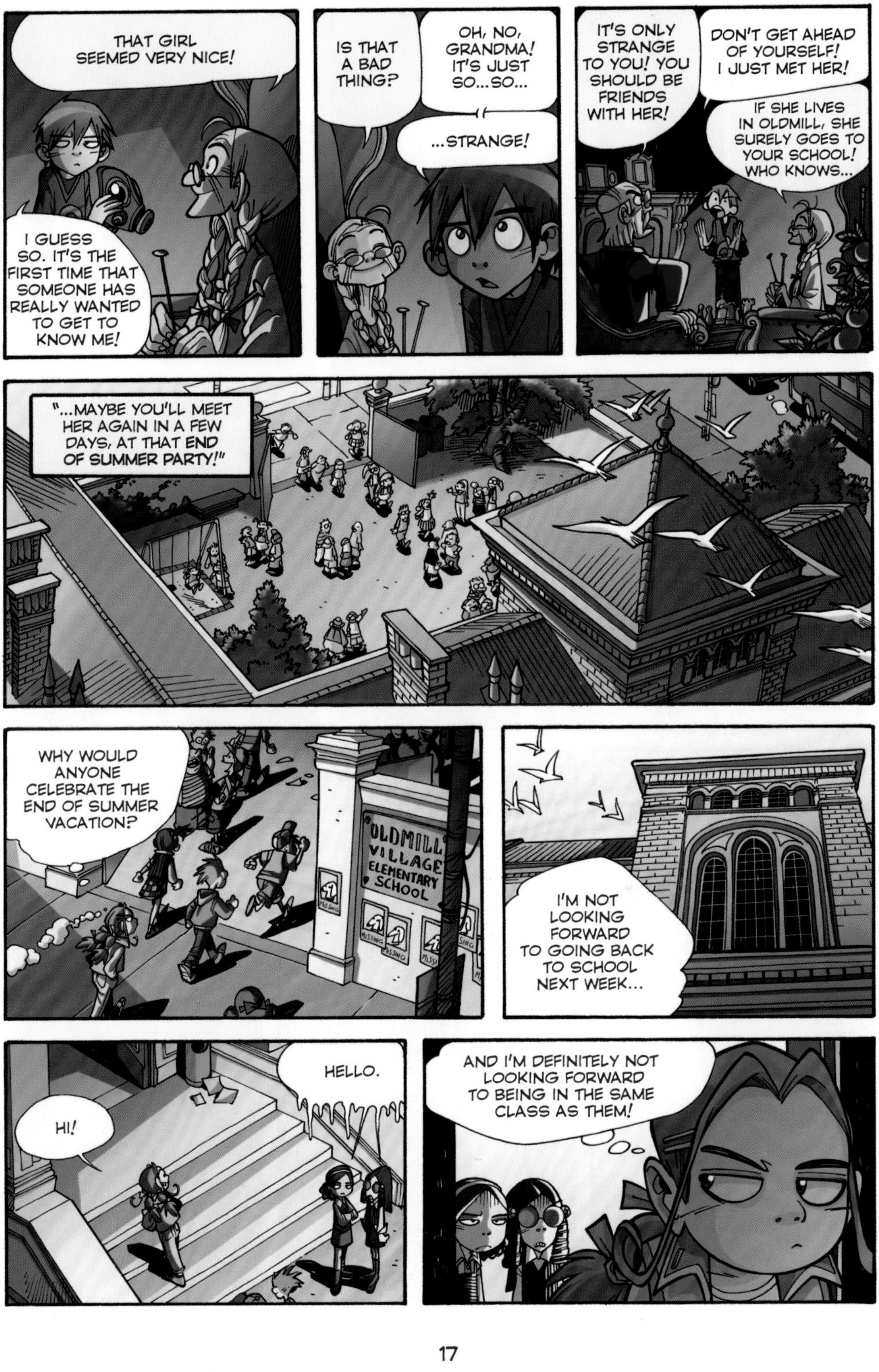
THAT GIRL SEEMED VERY NICE!
I GUESS SO. IT'S THE FIRST TIME THAT SOMEONE HAS REALLY WANTED TO GET TO KNOW ME!
IS THAT A BAD THING?
OH, NO, GRANDMA! IT'S JUST SO... SO...
...STRANGE!
IT'S ONLY STRANGE TO YOU! YOU SHOULD BE FRIENDS WITH HER!
DON'T GET AHEAD OF YOURSELF! I JUST MET HER!
IF SHE LIVES IN OLDMILL, SHE SURELY GOES TO YOUR SCHOOL! WHO KNOWS...
"...MAYBE YOU'LL MEET HER AGAIN IN A FEW DAYS, AT THAT END OF SUMMER PARTY!"
WHY WOULD ANYONE CELEBRATE THE END OF SUMMER VACATION?
OLDMILL VILLAGE ELEMENTARY SCHOOL
I'M NOT LOOKING FORWARD TO GOING BACK TO SCHOOL NEXT WEEK...
HELLO.
HI!
AND I'M DEFINITELY NOT LOOKING FORWARD TO BEING IN THE SAME CLASS AS THEM!

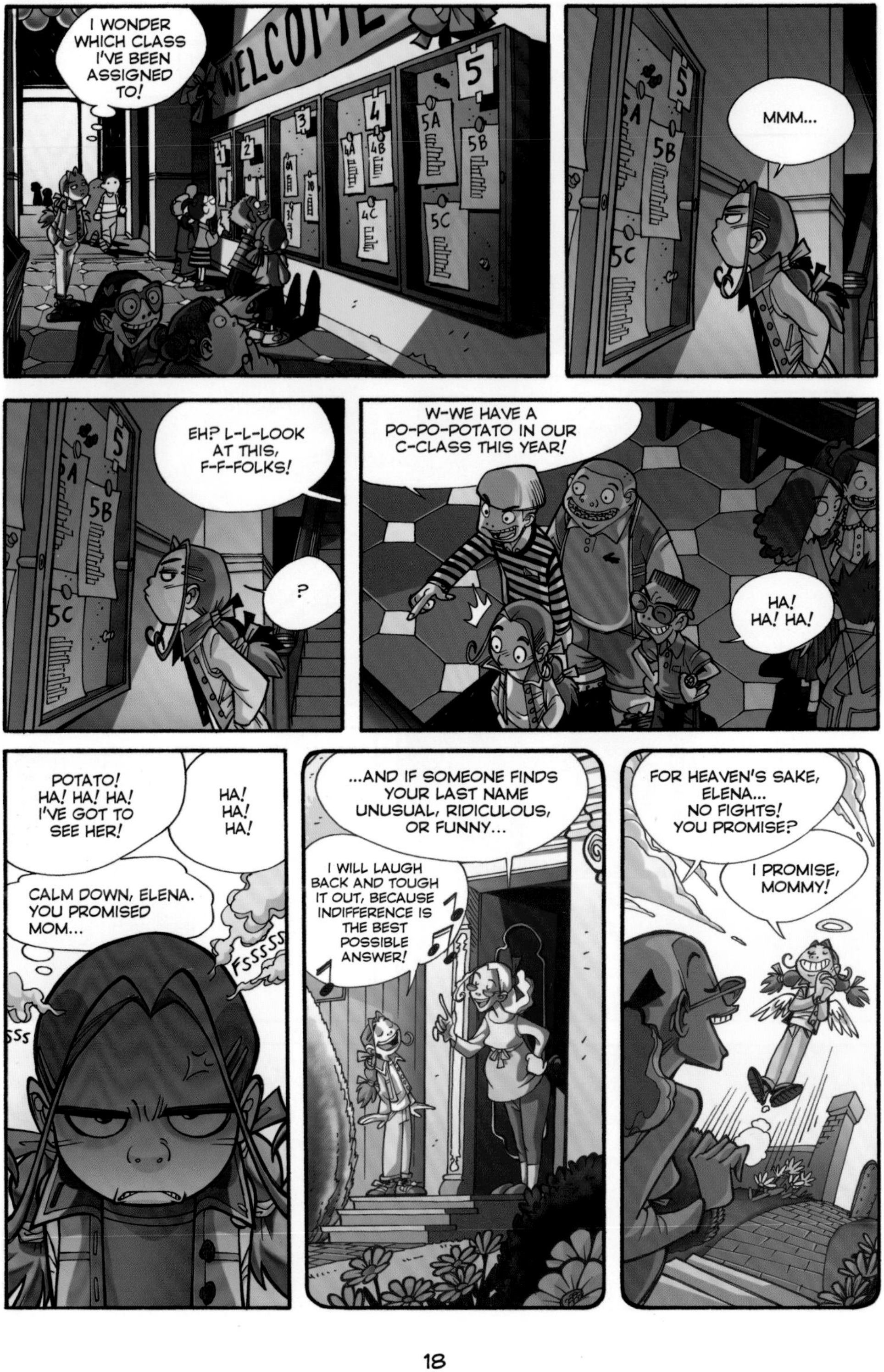
I WONDER WHICH CLASS I'VE BEEN ASSIGNED TO!
WELCOME
1
2
3
4
5
5A
5B
5C
4A
4B
4C
MMM...
EH? L-L-LOOK AT THIS, F-F-FOLKS!
?
W-WE HAVE A PO-PO-POTATO IN OUR C-CLASS THIS YEAR!
HA! HA! HA!
POTATO! HA! HA! HA! I'VE GOT TO SEE HER!
HA! HA! HA!
CALM DOWN, ELENA. YOU PROMISED MOM...
FSSSSS
SSS
...AND IF SOMEONE FINDS YOUR LAST NAME UNUSUAL, RIDICULOUS, OR FUNNY...
I WILL LAUGH BACK AND TOUGH IT OUT, BECAUSE INDIFFERENCE IS THE BEST POSSIBLE ANSWER!
FOR HEAVEN'S SAKE, ELENA... NO FIGHTS! YOU PROMISE?
I PROMISE, MOMMY!

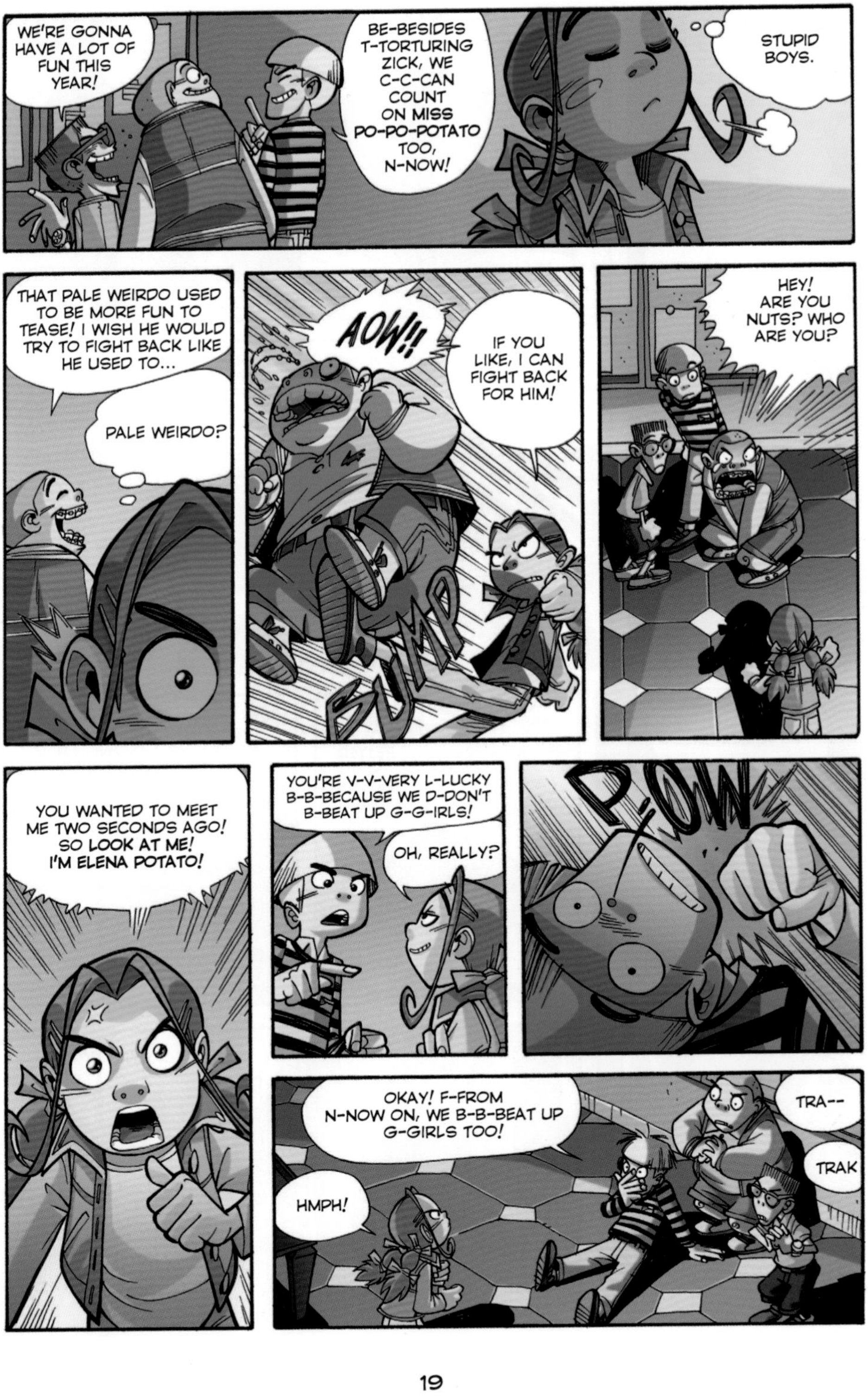
WE'RE GONNA HAVE A LOT OF FUN THIS YEAR!
BE-BESIDES T-TORTURING ZICK, WE C-C-CAN COUNT ON MISS PO-PO-POTATO TOO, N-NOW!
STUPID BOYS.
THAT PALE WEIRDO USED TO BE MORE FUN TO TEASE! I WISH HE WOULD TRY TO FIGHT BACK LIKE HE USED TO...
PALE WEIRDO?
AOW!!
IF YOU LIKE, I CAN FIGHT BACK FOR HIM!
BUMP
HEY! ARE YOU NUTS? WHO ARE YOU?
YOU WANTED TO MEET ME TWO SECONDS AGO! SO LOOK AT ME! I'M ELENA POTATO!
YOU'RE V-V-VERY L-LUCKY B-B-BECAUSE WE D-DON'T B-BEAT UP G-G-IRLS!
OH, REALLY?
POW
OKAY! F-FROM N-NOW ON, WE B-B-BEAT UP G-GIRLS TOO!
TRA--
TRAK
HMPH!

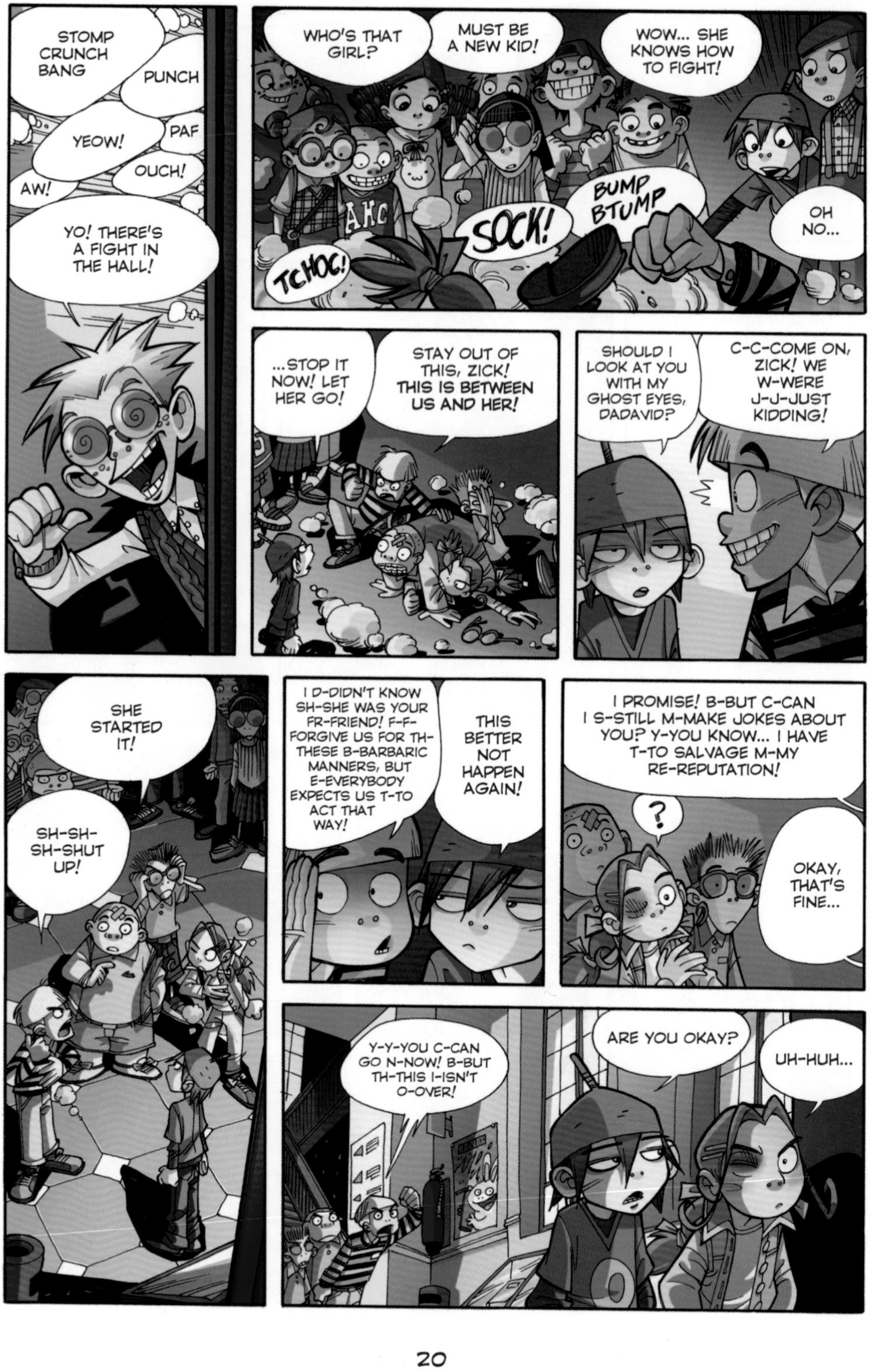
STOMP CRUNCH BANG
PUNCH
YEOW!
PAF
OUCH!
AW!
YO! THERE'S A FIGHT IN THE HALL!
WHO'S THAT GIRL?
MUST BE A NEW KID!
WOW... SHE KNOWS HOW TO FIGHT!
BUMP BTUMP
SOCK!
TCHOC!
OH NO...
...STOP IT NOW! LET HER GO!
STAY OUT OF THIS, ZICK! THIS IS BETWEEN US AND HER!
SHOULD I LOOK AT YOU WITH MY GHOST EYES, DADAVID?
C-C-COME ON, ZICK! WE W-WERE J-J-JUST KIDDING!
SHE STARTED IT!
SH-SH-SH-SHUT UP!
I D-DIDN'T KNOW SH-SHE WAS YOUR FR-FRIEND! F-F-FORGIVE US FOR TH-THESE B-BARBARIC MANNERS, BUT E-EVERYBODY EXPECTS US T-TO ACT THAT WAY!
THIS BETTER NOT HAPPEN AGAIN!
I PROMISE! B-BUT C-CAN I S-STILL M-MAKE JOKES ABOUT YOU? Y-YOU KNOW... I HAVE T-TO SALVAGE M-MY RE-REPUTATION!
?
OKAY, THAT'S FINE...
Y-Y-YOU C-CAN GO N-NOW! B-BUT TH-THIS I-ISN'T O-OVER!
ARE YOU OKAY?
UH-HUH...

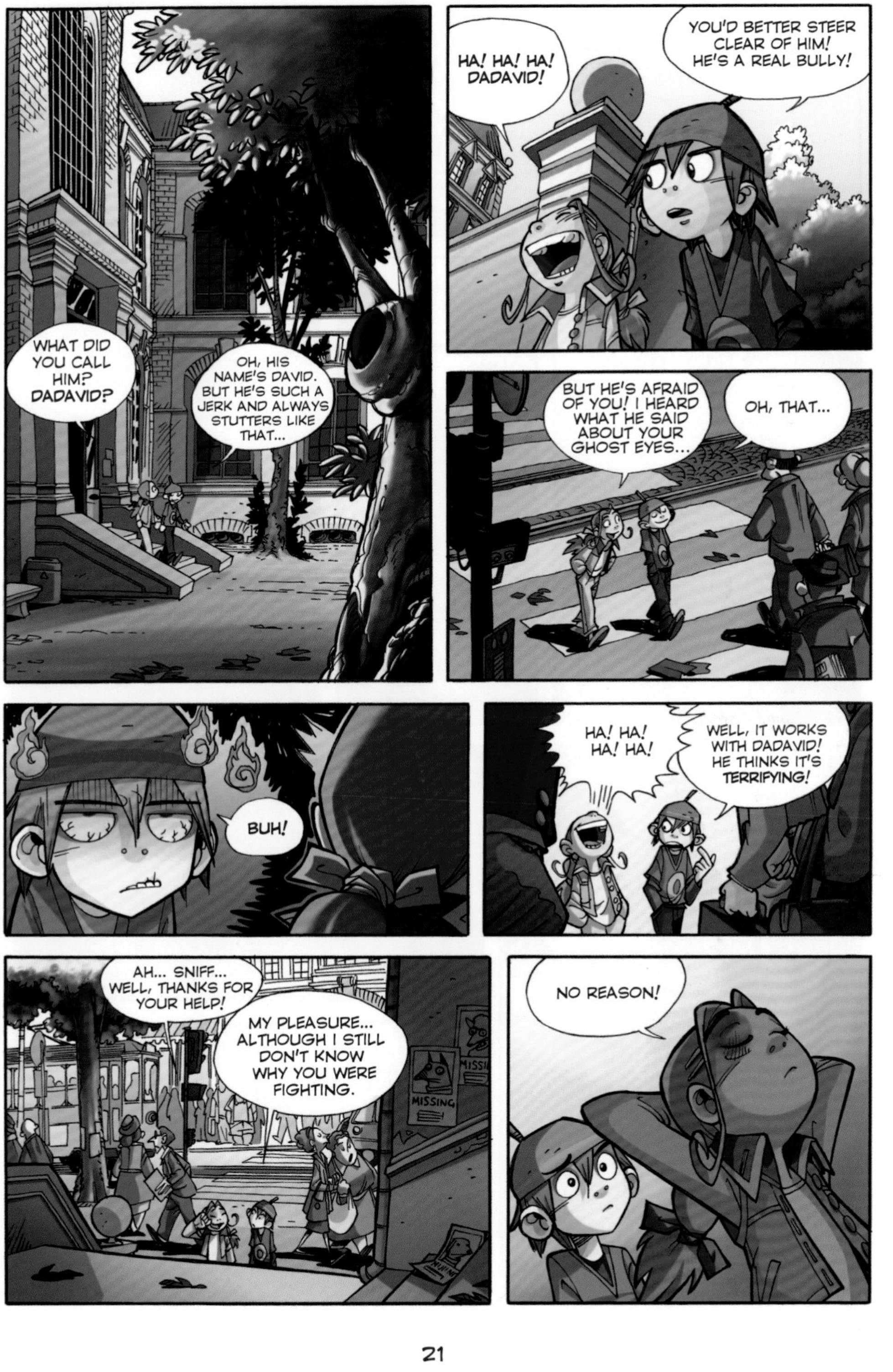
WHAT DID YOU CALL HIM? DADAVID?
OH, HIS NAME'S DAVID. BUT HE'S SUCH A JERK AND ALWAYS STUTTERS LIKE THAT...
HA! HA! HA! DADAVID!
YOU'D BETTER STEER CLEAR OF HIM! HE'S A REAL BULLY!
BUT HE'S AFRAID OF YOU! I HEARD WHAT HE SAID ABOUT YOUR GHOST EYES...
OH, THAT...
BUH!
HA! HA! HA! HA!
WELL, IT WORKS WITH DADAVID! HE THINKS IT'S TERRIFYING!
AH... SNIFF... WELL, THANKS FOR YOUR HELP!
MY PLEASURE... ALTHOUGH I STILL DON'T KNOW WHY YOU WERE FIGHTING.
MISSING
MISSING
NO REASON!

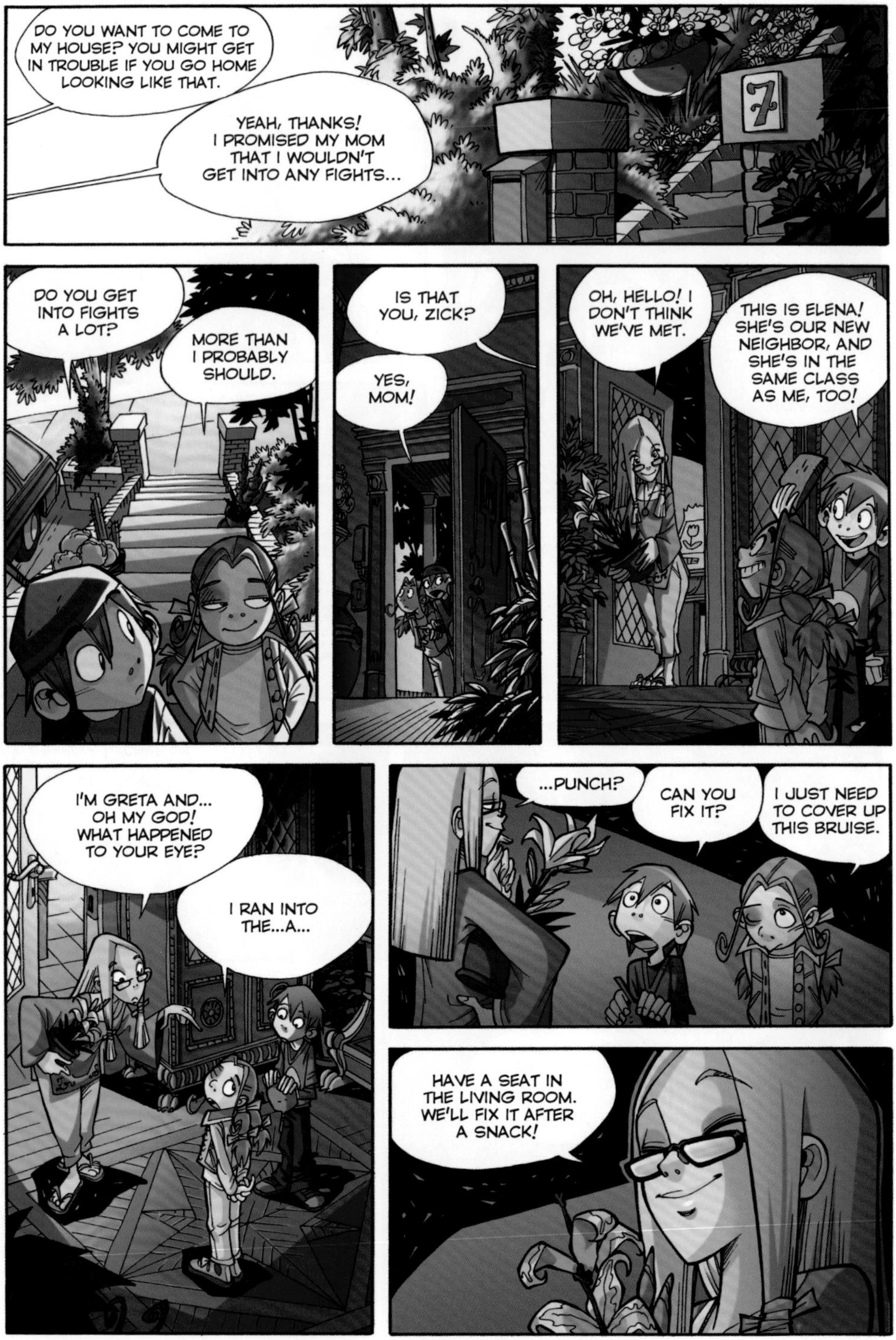
DO YOU WANT TO COME TO MY HOUSE? YOU MIGHT GET IN TROUBLE IF YOU GO HOME LOOKING LIKE THAT.
YEAH, THANKS! I PROMISED MY MOM THAT I WOULDN'T GET INTO ANY FIGHTS...
7
DO YOU GET INTO FIGHTS A LOT?
MORE THAN I PROBABLY SHOULD.
IS THAT YOU, ZICK?
YES, MOM!
OH, HELLO! I DON'T THINK WE'VE MET.
THIS IS ELENA! SHE'S OUR NEW NEIGHBOR, AND SHE'S IN THE SAME CLASS AS ME, TOO!
I'M GRETA AND... OH MY GOD! WHAT HAPPENED TO YOUR EYE?
I RAN INTO THE...A...
...PUNCH?
CAN YOU FIX IT?
I JUST NEED TO COVER UP THIS BRUISE.
HAVE A SEAT IN THE LIVING ROOM. WE'LL FIX IT AFTER A SNACK!

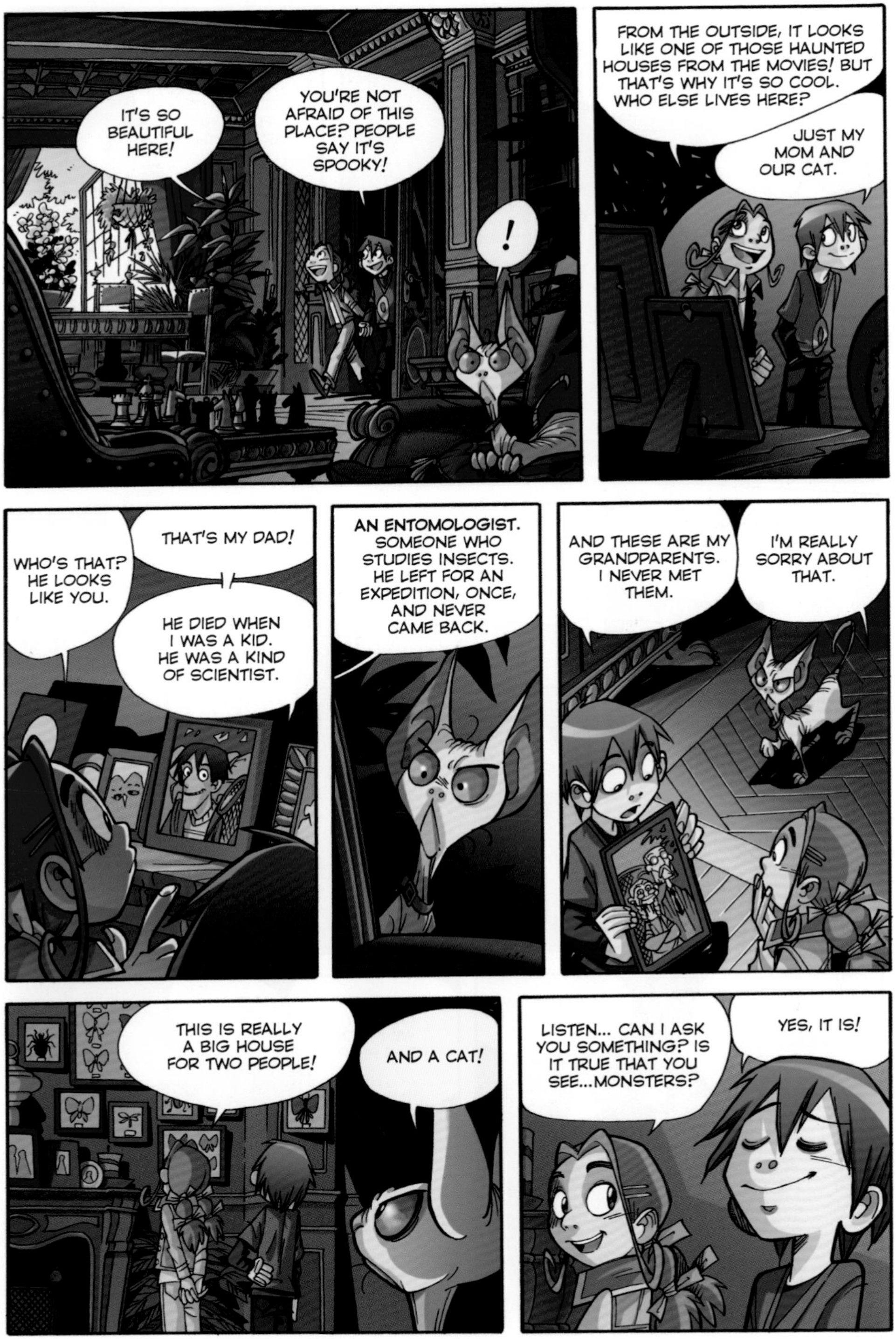
IT'S SO BEAUTIFUL HERE!
YOU'RE NOT AFRAID OF THIS PLACE? PEOPLE SAY IT'S SPOOKY!
!
FROM THE OUTSIDE, IT LOOKS LIKE ONE OF THOSE HAUNTED HOUSES FROM THE MOVIES! BUT THAT'S WHY IT'S SO COOL. WHO ELSE LIVES HERE?
JUST MY MOM AND OUR CAT.
WHO'S THAT? HE LOOKS LIKE YOU.
THAT'S MY DAD!
HE DIED WHEN I WAS A KID. HE WAS A KIND OF SCIENTIST.
AN ENTOMOLOGIST. SOMEONE WHO STUDIES INSECTS. HE LEFT FOR AN EXPEDITION, ONCE, AND NEVER CAME BACK.
AND THESE ARE MY GRANDPARENTS. I NEVER MET THEM.
I'M REALLY SORRY ABOUT THAT.
THIS IS REALLY A BIG HOUSE FOR TWO PEOPLE!
AND A CAT!
LISTEN... CAN I ASK YOU SOMETHING? IS IT TRUE THAT YOU SEE...MONSTERS?
YES, IT IS!

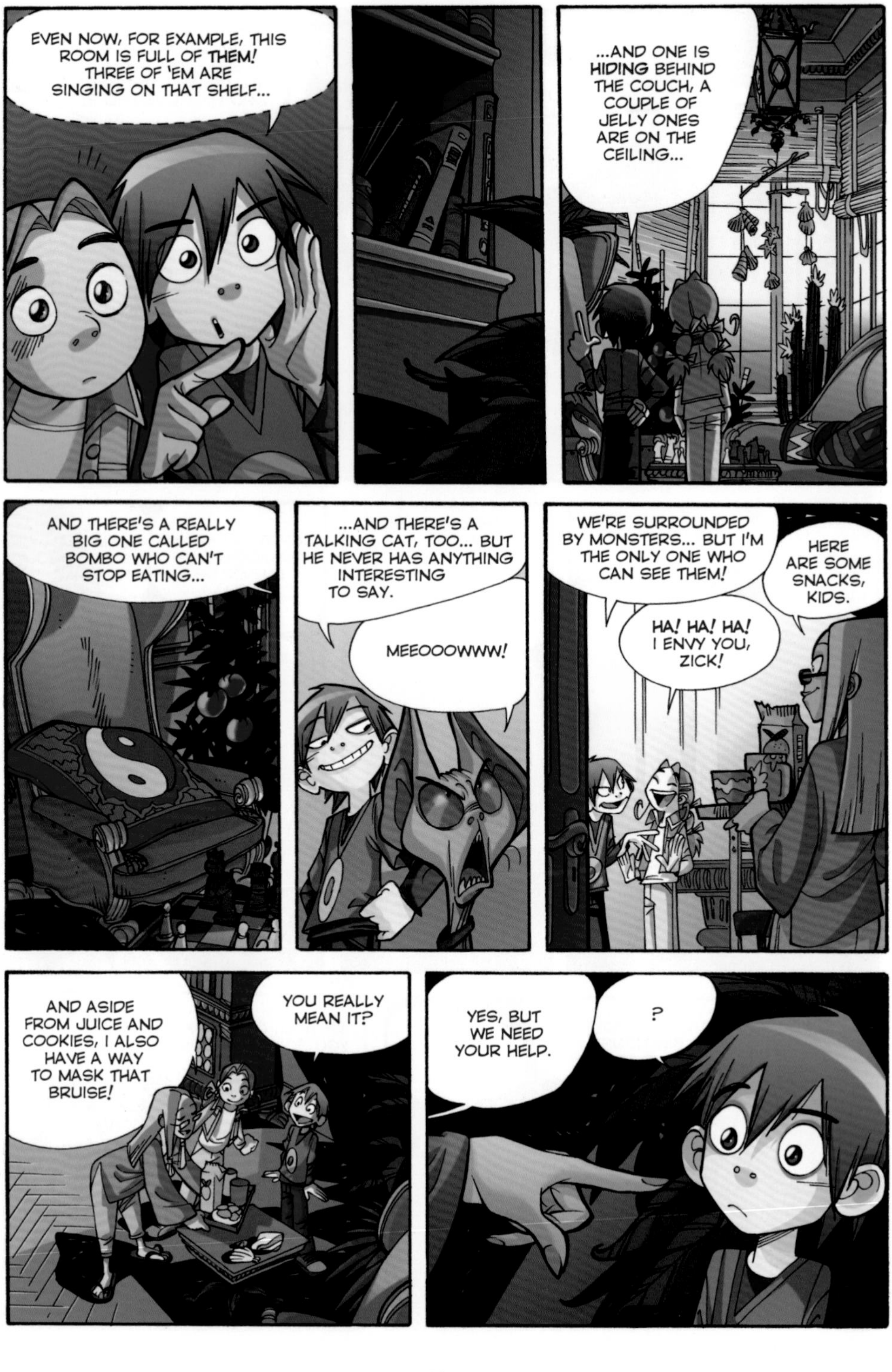
EVEN NOW, FOR EXAMPLE, THIS ROOM IS FULL OF THEM! THREE OF 'EM ARE SINGING ON THAT SHELF...
...AND ONE IS HIDING BEHIND THE COUCH, A COUPLE OF JELLY ONES ARE ON THE CEILING...
AND THERE'S A REALLY BIG ONE CALLED BOMBO WHO CAN'T STOP EATING...
...AND THERE'S A TALKING CAT, TOO... BUT HE NEVER HAS ANYTHING INTERESTING TO SAY.
MEEOOOWWW!
WE'RE SURROUNDED BY MONSTERS... BUT I'M THE ONLY ONE WHO CAN SEE THEM!
HA! HA! HA! I ENVY YOU, ZICK!
HERE ARE SOME SNACKS, KIDS.
AND ASIDE FROM JUICE AND COOKIES, I ALSO HAVE A WAY TO MASK THAT BRUISE!
YOU REALLY MEAN IT?
YES, BUT WE NEED YOUR HELP.
?

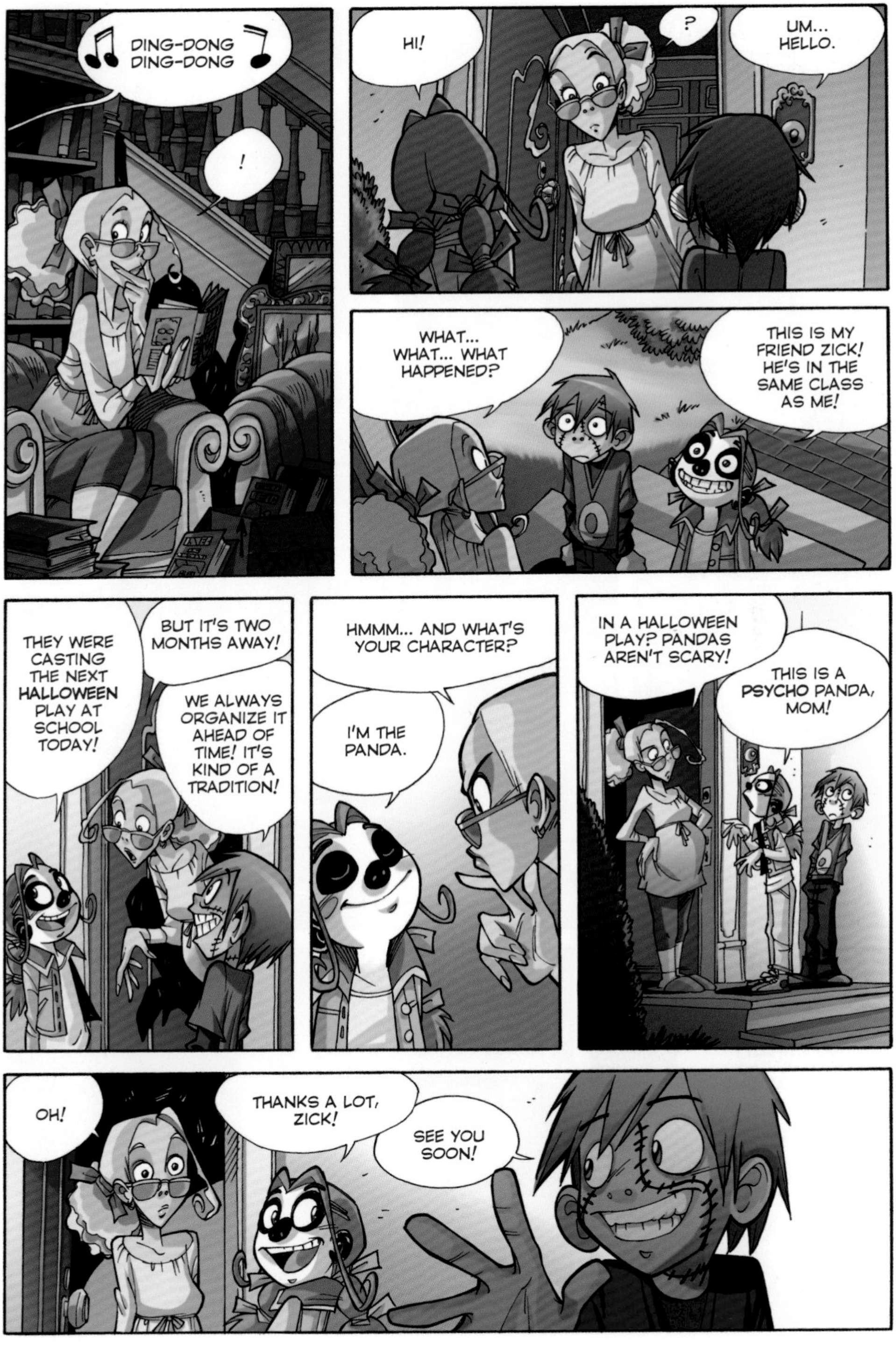
DING-DONG DING-DONG
!
HI!
?
UM... HELLO.
WHAT... WHAT... WHAT HAPPENED?
THIS IS MY FRIEND ZICK! HE'S IN THE SAME CLASS AS ME!
THEY WERE CASTING THE NEXT HALLOWEEN PLAY AT SCHOOL TODAY!
BUT IT'S TWO MONTHS AWAY!
WE ALWAYS ORGANIZE IT AHEAD OF TIME! IT'S KIND OF A TRADITION!
HMMM... AND WHAT'S YOUR CHARACTER?
I'M THE PANDA.
IN A HALLOWEEN PLAY? PANDAS AREN'T SCARY!
THIS IS A PSYCHO PANDA, MOM!
OH!
THANKS A LOT, ZICK!
SEE YOU SOON!

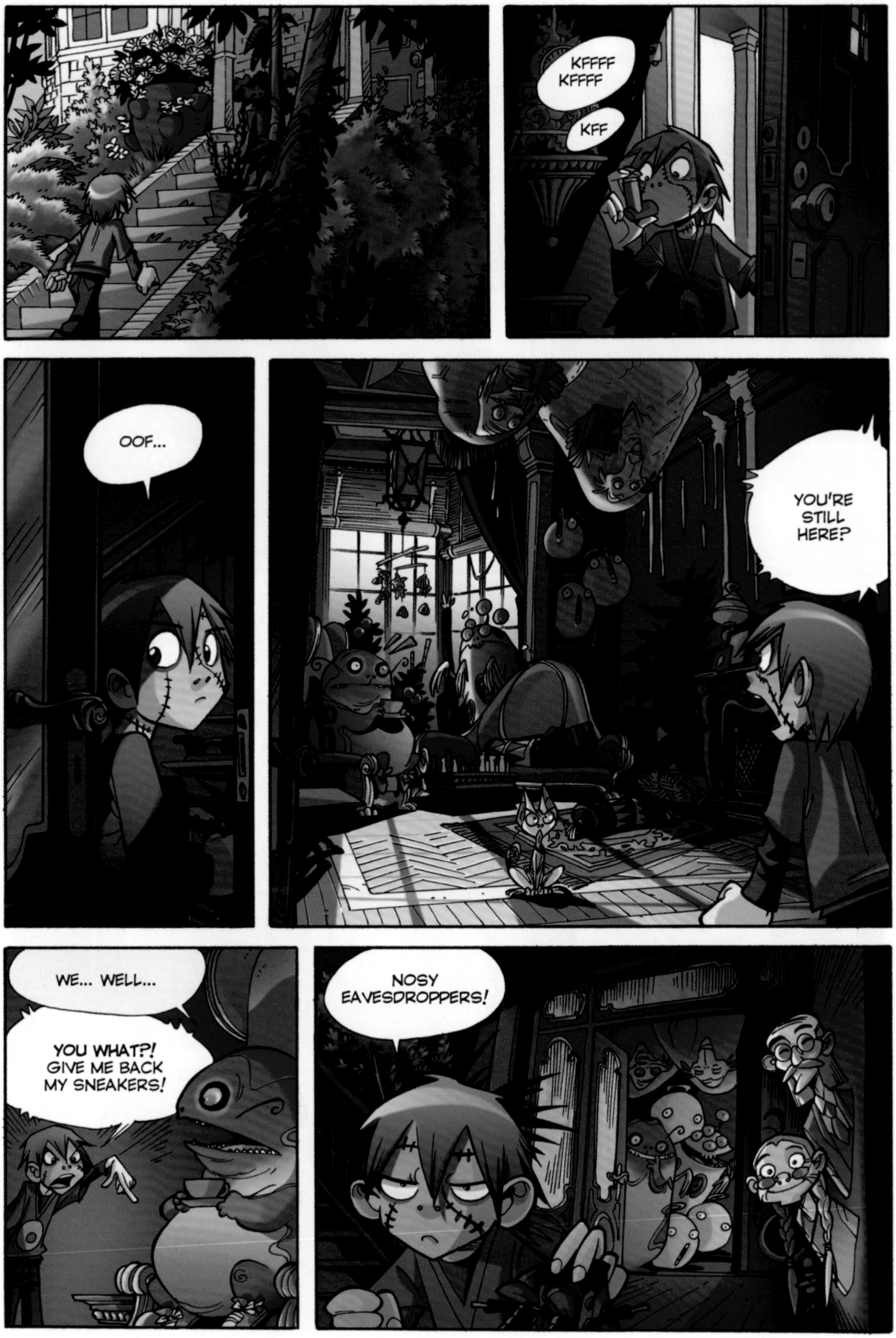
KFFFF
KFFFF
KFF
OOF...
YOU'RE STILL HERE?
WE... WELL...
YOU WHAT?! GIVE ME BACK MY SNEAKERS!
NOSY EAVESDROPPERS!

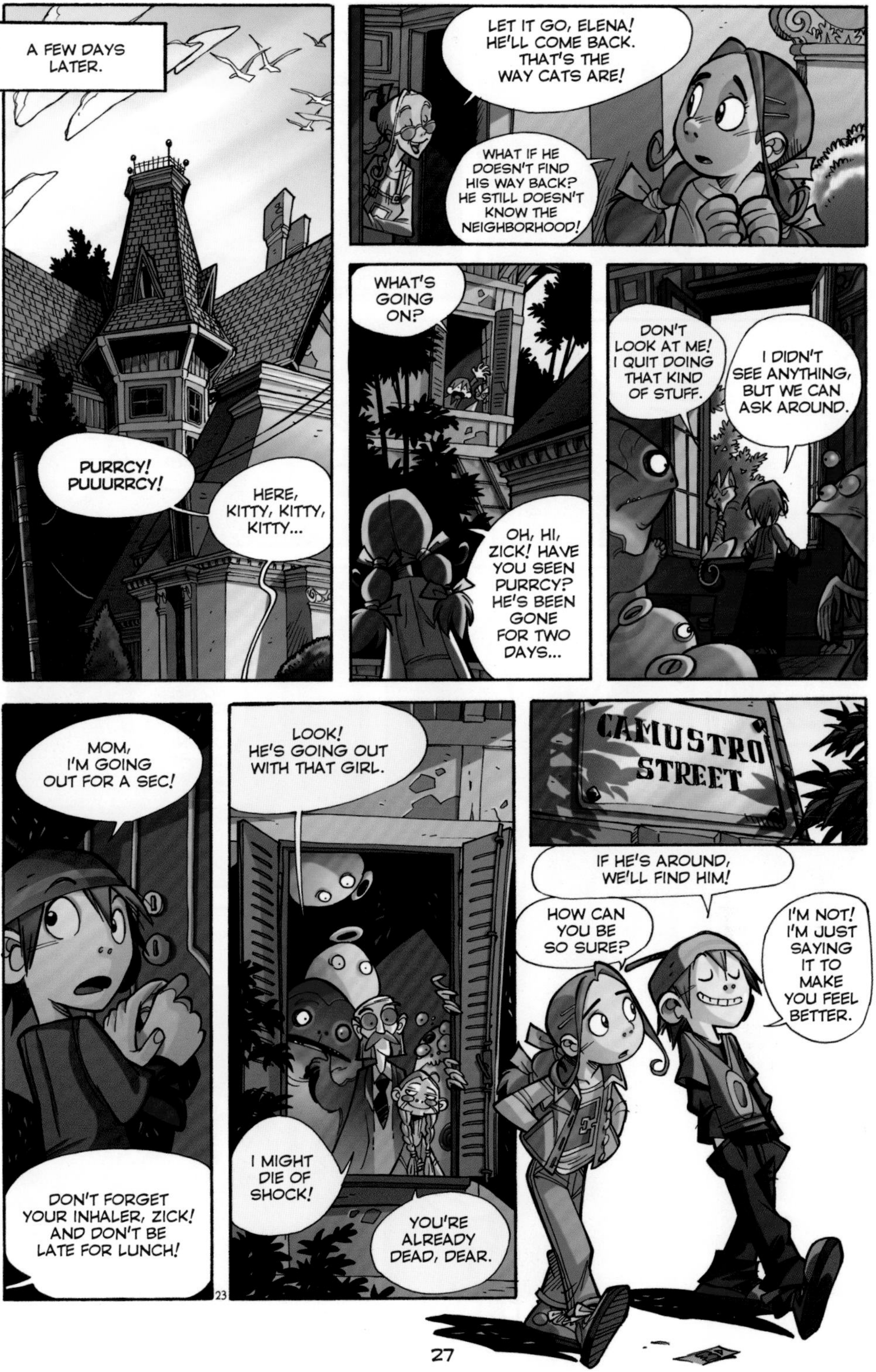
A FEW DAYS LATER.
PURRCY! PUUURRCY!
HERE, KITTY, KITTY, KITTY...
LET IT GO, ELENA! HE'LL COME BACK. THAT'S THE WAY CATS ARE!
WHAT IF HE DOESN'T FIND HIS WAY BACK? HE STILL DOESN'T KNOW THE NEIGHBORHOOD!
WHAT'S GOING ON?
OH, HI, ZICK! HAVE YOU SEEN PURRCY? HE'S BEEN GONE FOR TWO DAYS...
DON'T LOOK AT ME! I QUIT DOING THAT KIND OF STUFF.
I DIDN'T SEE ANYTHING, BUT WE CAN ASK AROUND.
MOM, I'M GOING OUT FOR A SEC!
DON'T FORGET YOUR INHALER, ZICK! AND DON'T BE LATE FOR LUNCH!
23
LOOK! HE'S GOING OUT WITH THAT GIRL.
I MIGHT DIE OF SHOCK!
YOU'RE ALREADY DEAD, DEAR.
CAMUSTRO STREET
IF HE'S AROUND, WE'LL FIND HIM!
HOW CAN YOU BE SO SURE?
I'M NOT! I'M JUST SAYING IT TO MAKE YOU FEEL BETTER.

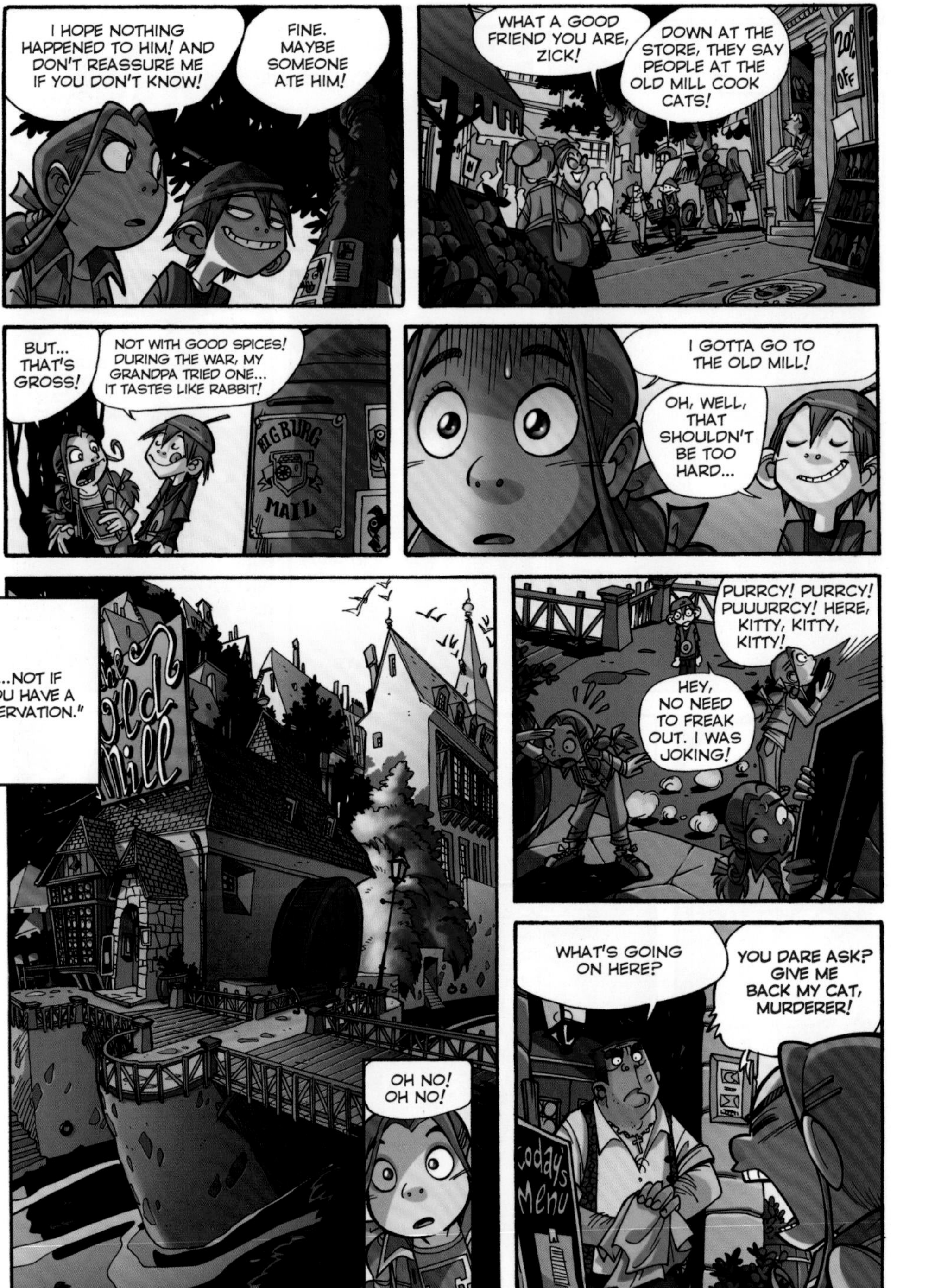
I HOPE NOTHING HAPPENED TO HIM! AND DON'T REASSURE ME IF YOU DON'T KNOW!
FINE. MAYBE SOMEONE ATE HIM!
WHAT A GOOD FRIEND YOU ARE, ZICK!
DOWN AT THE STORE, THEY SAY PEOPLE AT THE OLD MILL COOK CATS!
20% OFF
BUT... THAT'S GROSS!
NOT WITH GOOD SPICES! DURING THE WAR, MY GRANDPA TRIED ONE... IT TASTES LIKE RABBIT!
BIGBURG MAIL
I GOTTA GO TO THE OLD MILL!
OH, WELL, THAT SHOULDN'T BE TOO HARD...
"...NOT IF YOU HAVE A RESERVATION."
The Old Mill
OH NO! OH NO!
PURRCY! PURRCY! PUUURRCY! HERE, KITTY, KITTY, KITTY!
HEY, NO NEED TO FREAK OUT. I WAS JOKING!
WHAT'S GOING ON HERE?
YOU DARE ASK? GIVE ME BACK MY CAT, MURDERER!
Today's Menu

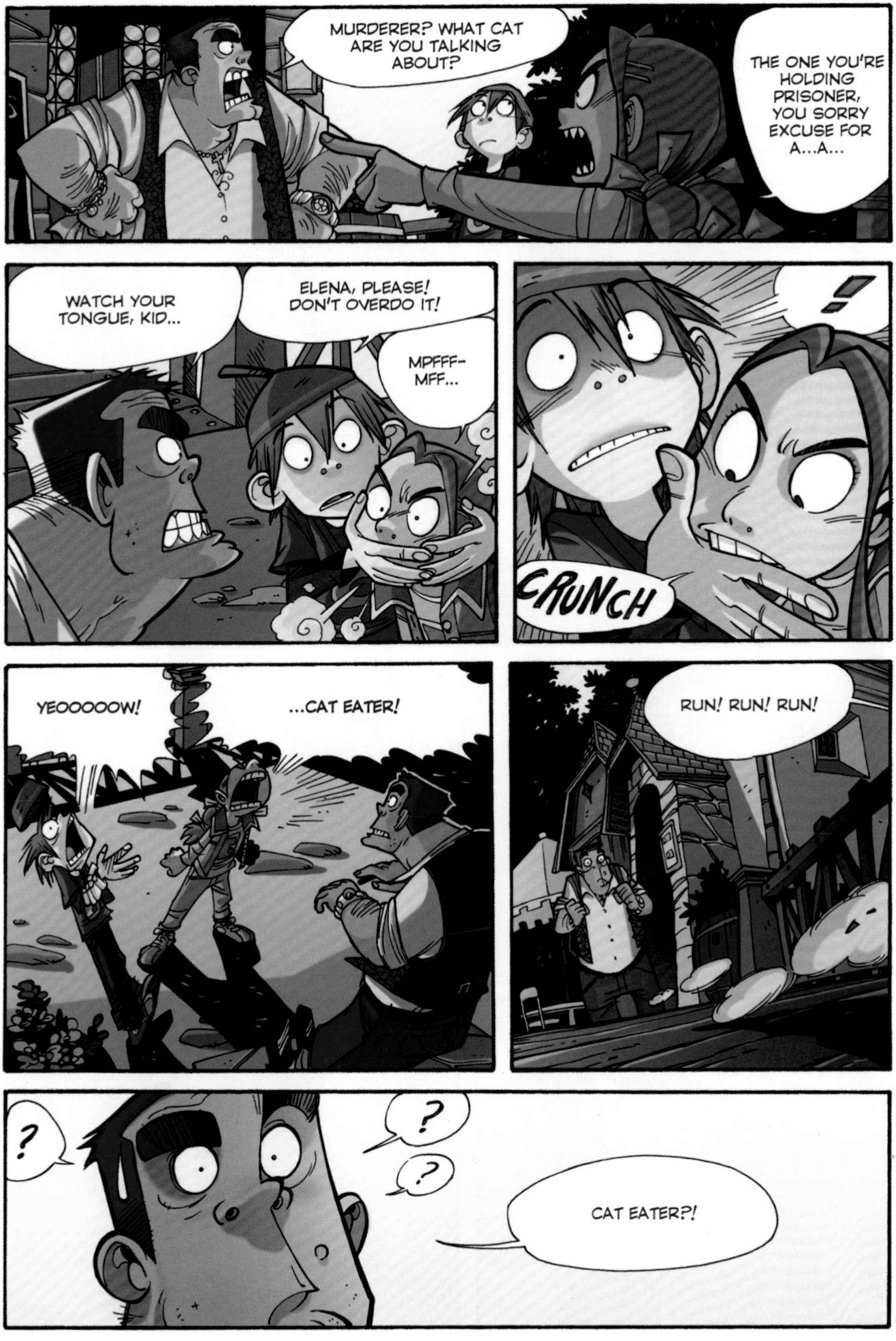
MURDERER? WHAT CAT ARE YOU TALKING ABOUT?
THE ONE YOU'RE HOLDING PRISONER, YOU SORRY EXCUSE FOR A...A...
WATCH YOUR TONGUE, KID...
ELENA, PLEASE! DON'T OVERDO IT!
MPFFF-MFF...
!
CRUNCH
YEOOOOOW!
...CAT EATER!
RUN! RUN! RUN!
?
?
?
CAT EATER?!

HERE YOU GO! A VANILLA AND BANANA DOUBLE MILKSHAKE! THE HOUSE SPECIALTY!

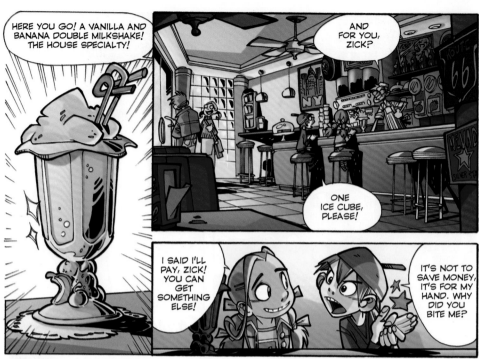

AND FOR YOU, ZICK?

ONE ICE CUBE, PLEASE!

I SAID I'LL PAY, ZICK! YOU CAN GET SOMETHING ELSE!

IT'S NOT TO SAVE MONEY, IT'S FOR MY HAND. WHY DID YOU BITE ME?

I...DON'T KNOW WHAT GOT INTO ME. THE THOUGHT OF PURRCY OUT THERE ALL ALONE...

OH, CATS ALWAYS MANAGE...

...BUT IF HE DOESN'T COME BACK, I HAVE GREAT BULLDOG PUPPIES TO GIVE AWAY. ARE YOU INTERESTED?

PFFT...

I WANT PURRCY...

BUT A BULLDOG IS LIKE A CAT--IT JUST BARKS AND LOOKS LIKE A DOG!

I'LL TAKE THEM, IF YOU'RE OFFERING. THEY CAN JOIN ME ON MY MAIL ROUTE!

YOU'RE A REAL PAL, FRED!

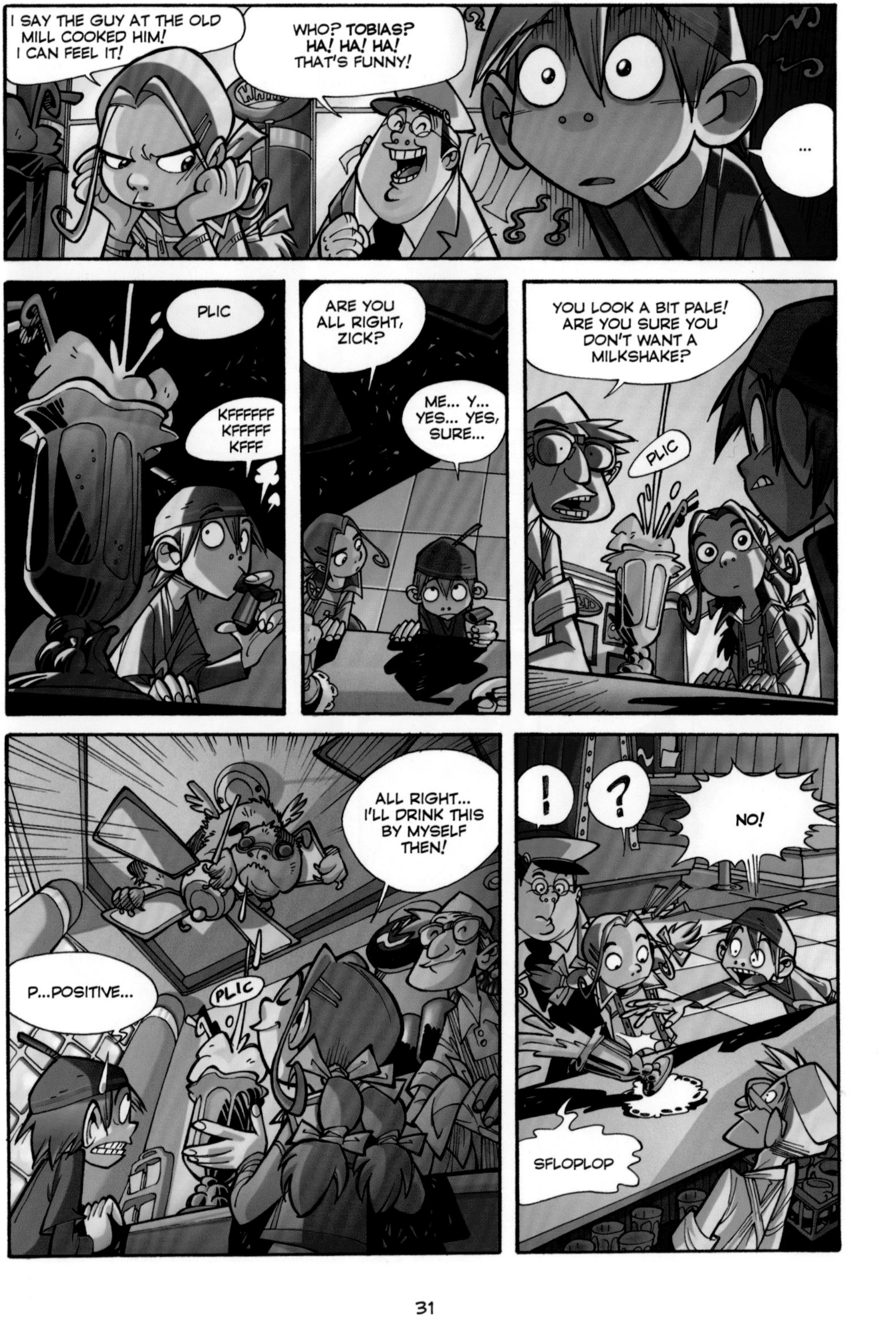
I SAY THE GUY AT THE OLD MILL COOKED HIM! I CAN FEEL IT!
WHO? TOBIAS? HA! HA! HA! THAT'S FUNNY!
...
PLIC
KFFFFFF KFFFFF KFFF
ARE YOU ALL RIGHT, ZICK?
ME... Y... YES... YES, SURE...
YOU LOOK A BIT PALE! ARE YOU SURE YOU DON'T WANT A MILKSHAKE?
PLIC
ALL RIGHT... I'LL DRINK THIS BY MYSELF THEN!
P...POSITIVE...
PLIC
!
?
NO!
SFLOPLOP

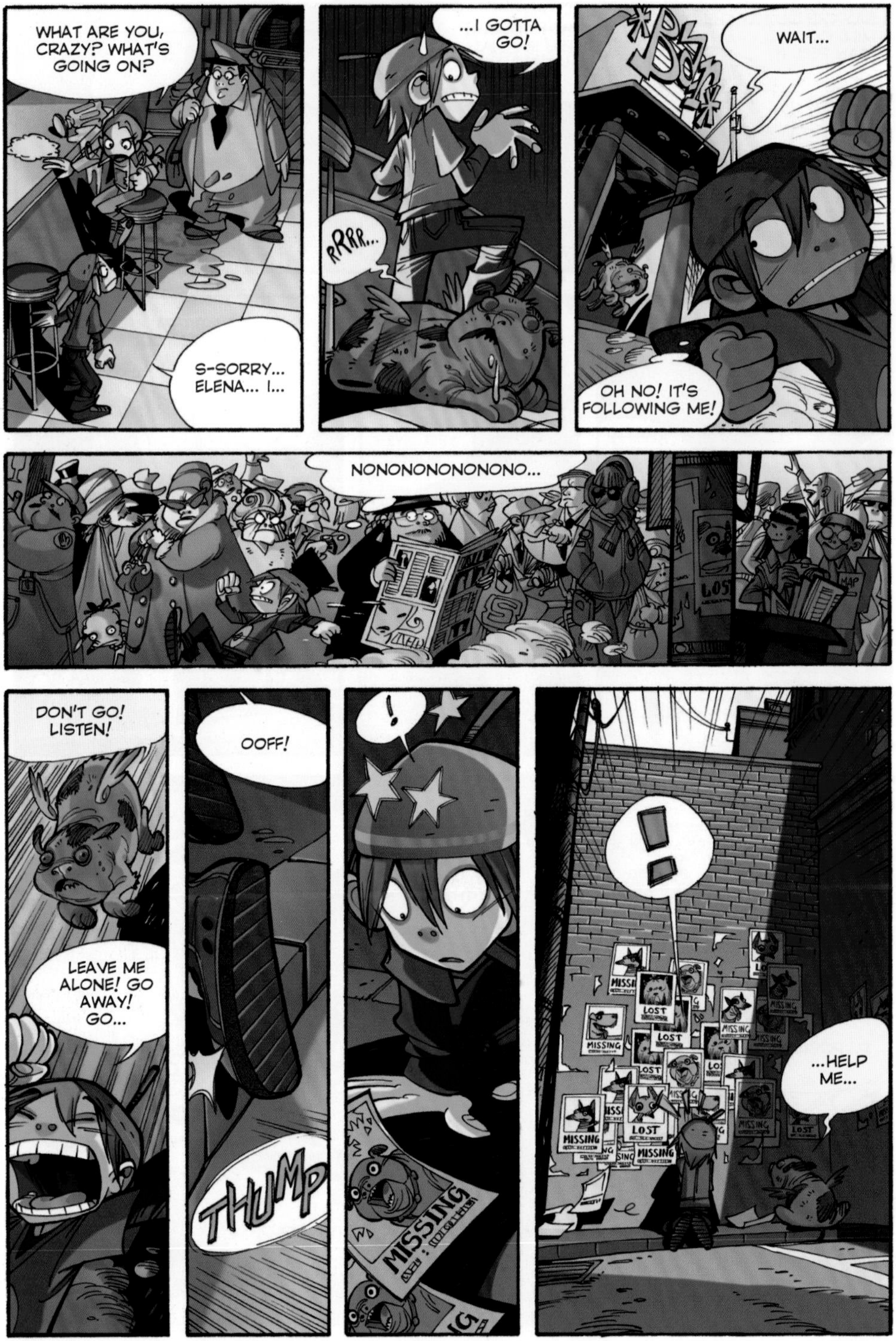
WHAT ARE YOU, CRAZY? WHAT'S GOING ON?
S-SORRY... ELENA... I...
...I GOTTA GO!
RRRR...
WAIT...
OH NO! IT'S FOLLOWING ME!
NONONONONONONO...
LOST
MAP
DON'T GO! LISTEN!
LEAVE ME ALONE! GO AWAY! GO...
OOFF!
THUMP
!
MISSING
!
MISSING
LOST
...HELP ME...

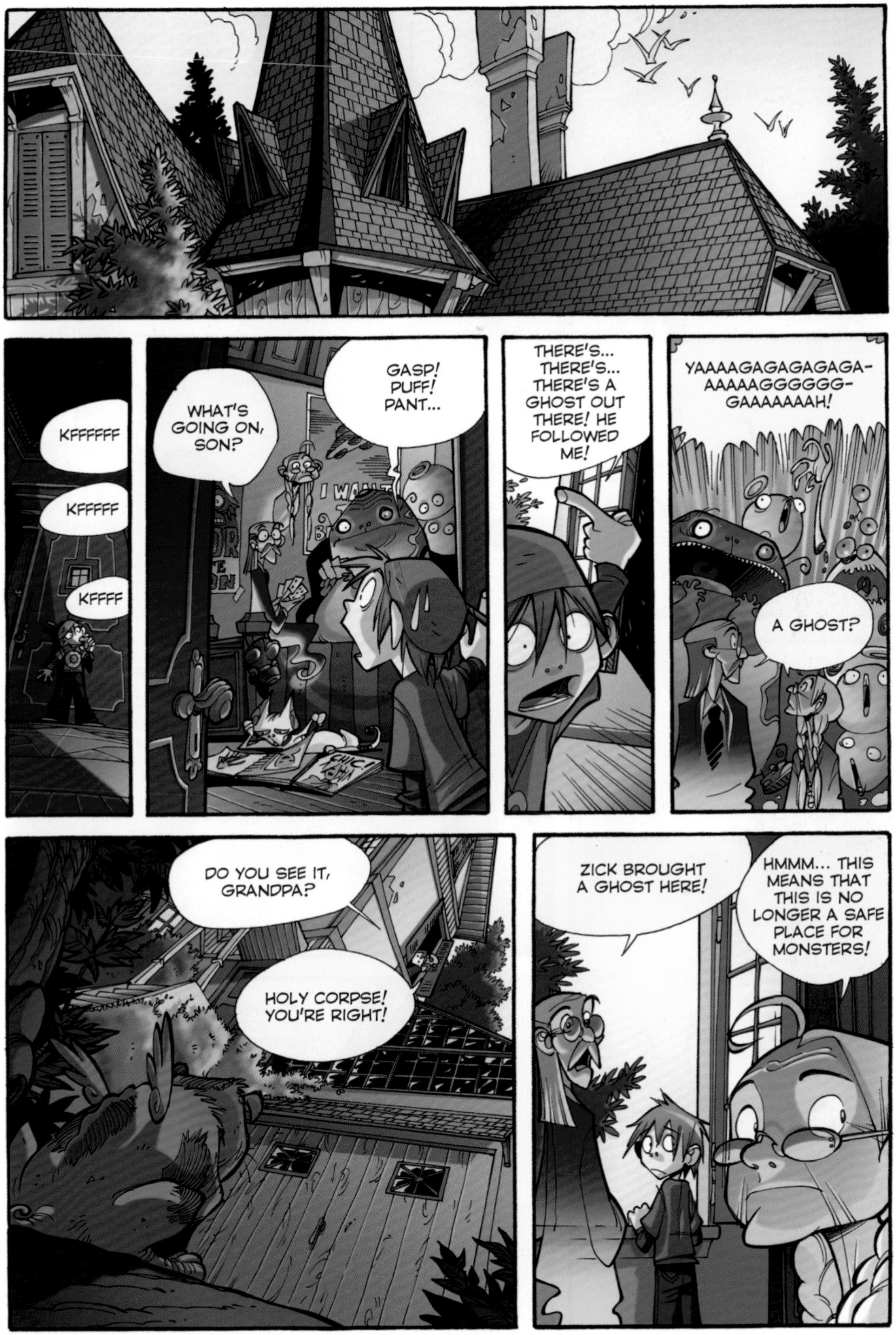
KFFFFFF
KFFFFF
KFFFF
WHAT'S GOING ON, SON?
GASP! PUFF! PANT...
THERE'S... THERE'S... THERE'S A GHOST OUT THERE! HE FOLLOWED ME!
YAAAAGAGAGAGAGA-AAAAAGGGGGG-GAAAAAAAH!
A GHOST?
DO YOU SEE IT, GRANDPA?
HOLY CORPSE! YOU'RE RIGHT!
ZICK BROUGHT A GHOST HERE!
HMMM... THIS MEANS THAT THIS IS NO LONGER A SAFE PLACE FOR MONSTERS!

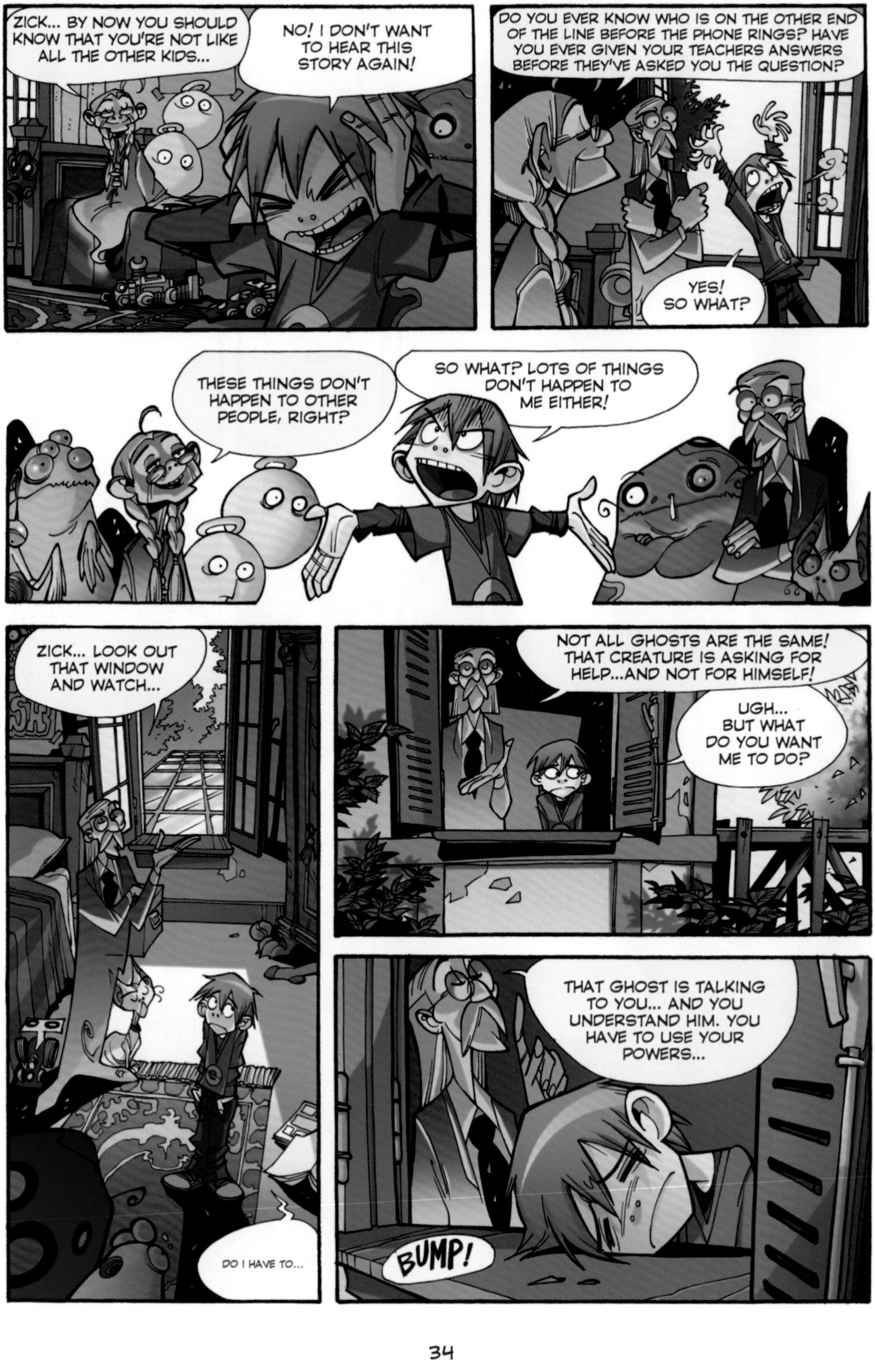

ZICK... BY NOW YOU SHOULD KNOW THAT YOU'RE NOT LIKE ALL THE OTHER KIDS...
NO! I DON'T WANT TO HEAR THIS STORY AGAIN!
DO YOU EVER KNOW WHO IS ON THE OTHER END OF THE LINE BEFORE THE PHONE RINGS? HAVE YOU EVER GIVEN YOUR TEACHERS ANSWERS BEFORE THEY'VE ASKED YOU THE QUESTION?
YES! SO WHAT?
THESE THINGS DON'T HAPPEN TO OTHER PEOPLE, RIGHT?
SO WHAT? LOTS OF THINGS DON'T HAPPEN TO ME EITHER!
ZICK... LOOK OUT THAT WINDOW AND WATCH...
DO I HAVE TO...
NOT ALL GHOSTS ARE THE SAME! THAT CREATURE IS ASKING FOR HELP...AND NOT FOR HIMSELF!
UGH... BUT WHAT DO YOU WANT ME TO DO?
THAT GHOST IS TALKING TO YOU... AND YOU UNDERSTAND HIM. YOU HAVE TO USE YOUR POWERS...
BUMP!

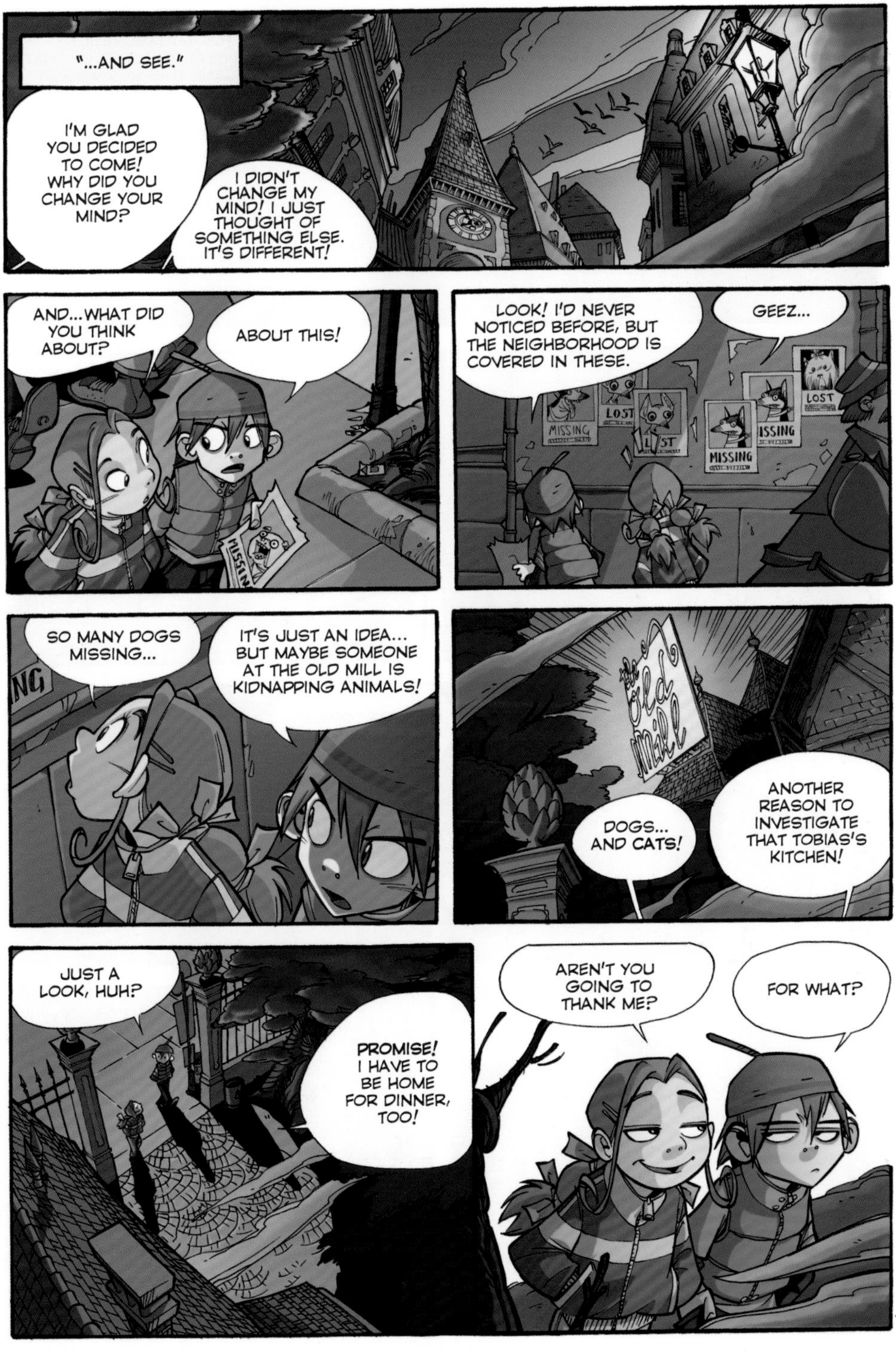
"...AND SEE."
I'M GLAD YOU DECIDED TO COME! WHY DID YOU CHANGE YOUR MIND?
I DIDN'T CHANGE MY MIND! I JUST THOUGHT OF SOMETHING ELSE. IT'S DIFFERENT!
AND...WHAT DID YOU THINK ABOUT?
ABOUT THIS!
MISSING
LOOK! I'D NEVER NOTICED BEFORE, BUT THE NEIGHBORHOOD IS COVERED IN THESE.
GEEZ...
MISSING
LOST
LOST
MISSING
MISSING
LOST
SO MANY DOGS MISSING...
IT'S JUST AN IDEA... BUT MAYBE SOMEONE AT THE OLD MILL IS KIDNAPPING ANIMALS!
the old mill
DOGS... AND CATS!
ANOTHER REASON TO INVESTIGATE THAT TOBIAS'S KITCHEN!
JUST A LOOK, HUH?
PROMISE! I HAVE TO BE HOME FOR DINNER, TOO!
AREN'T YOU GOING TO THANK ME?
FOR WHAT?

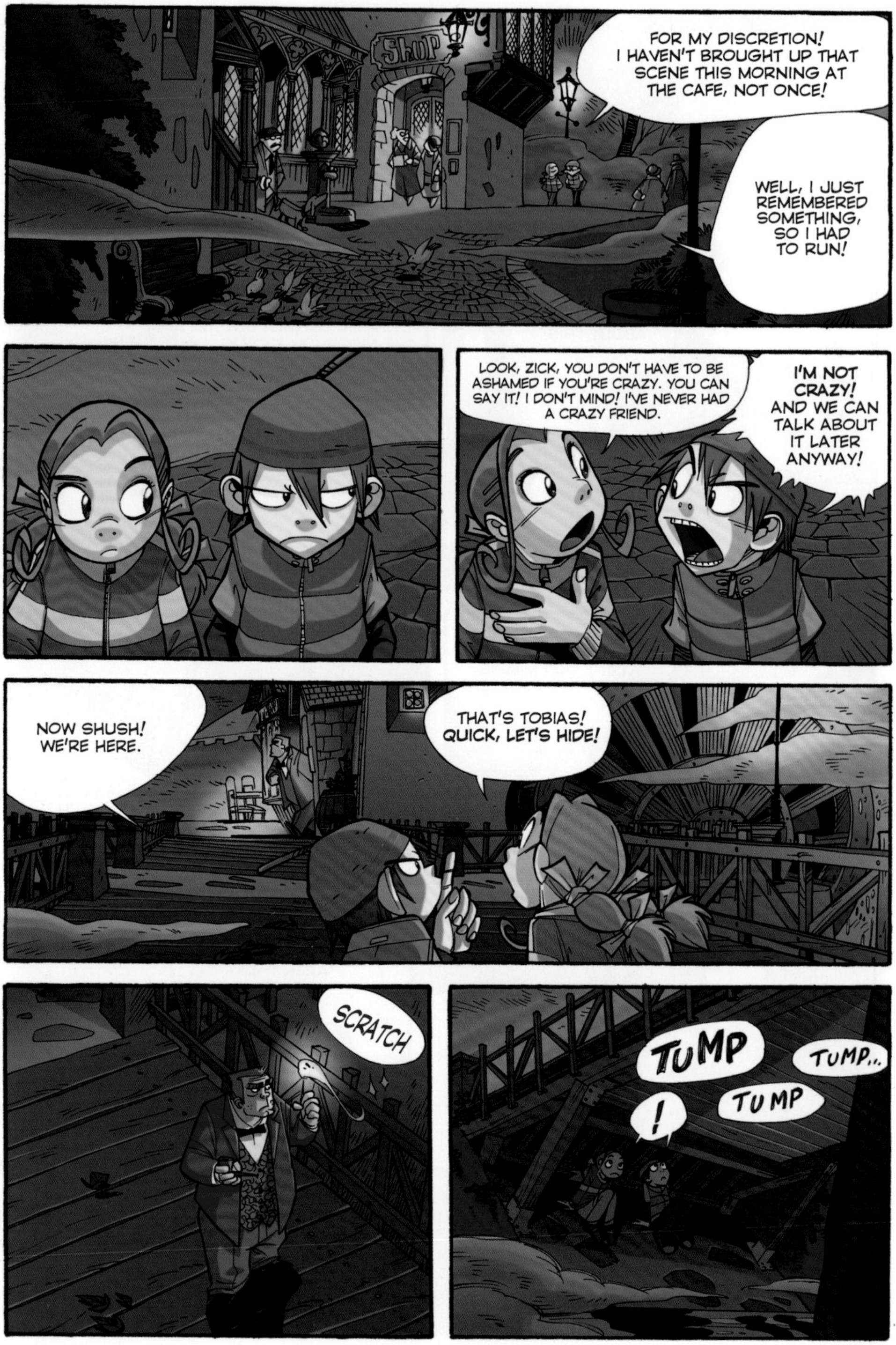
FOR MY DISCRETION! I HAVEN'T BROUGHT UP THAT SCENE THIS MORNING AT THE CAFE, NOT ONCE!
WELL, I JUST REMEMBERED SOMETHING, SO I HAD TO RUN!
LOOK, ZICK, YOU DON'T HAVE TO BE ASHAMED IF YOU'RE CRAZY. YOU CAN SAY IT! I DON'T MIND! I'VE NEVER HAD A CRAZY FRIEND.
I'M NOT CRAZY! AND WE CAN TALK ABOUT IT LATER ANYWAY!
NOW SHUSH! WE'RE HERE.
THAT'S TOBIAS! QUICK, LET'S HIDE!
SCRATCH
TUMP
TUMP...
!
TUMP

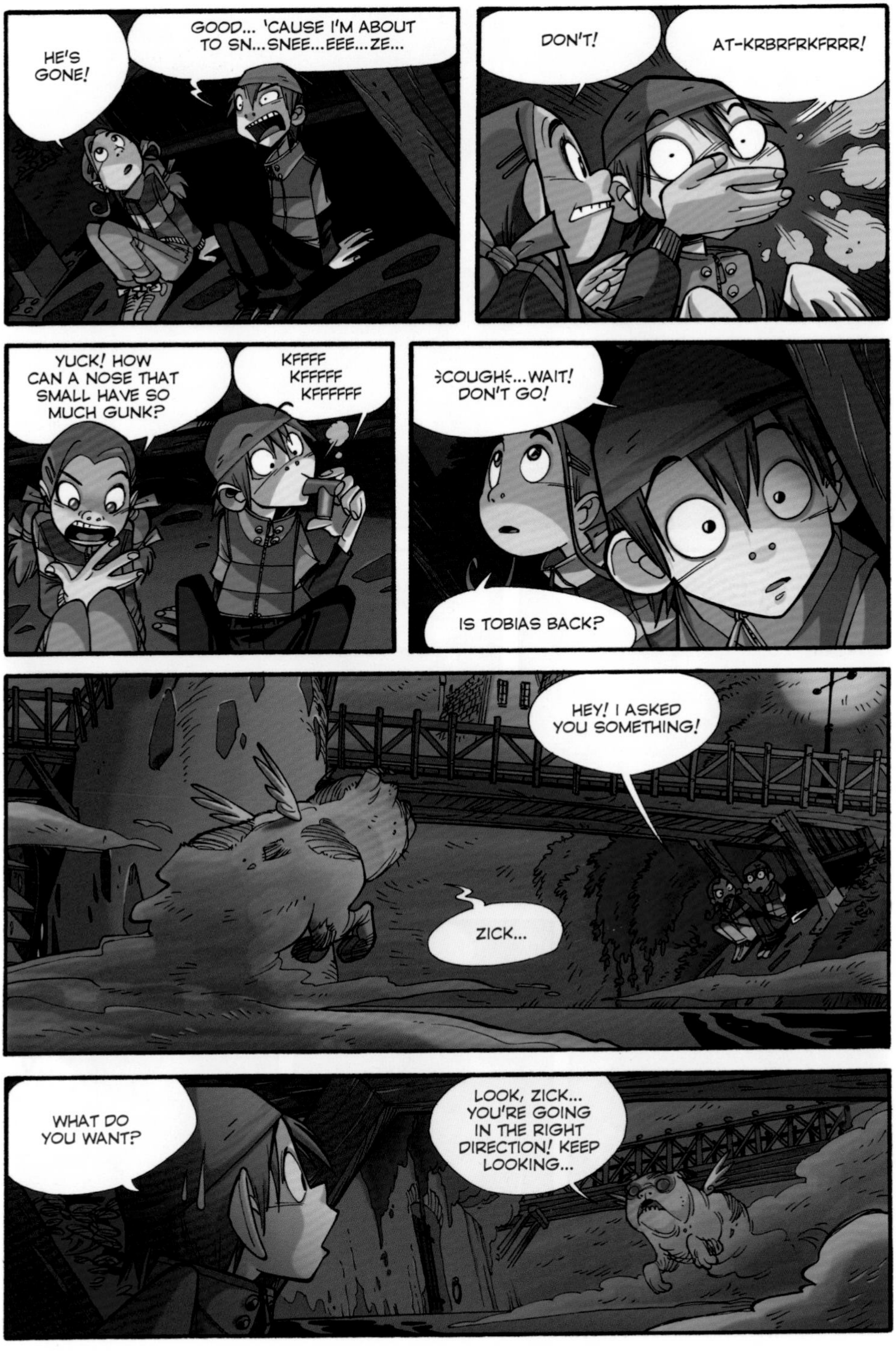
HE'S GONE!
GOOD... 'CAUSE I'M ABOUT TO SN...SNEE...EEE...ZE...
DON'T!
AT-KRBRFRKFRRR!
YUCK! HOW CAN A NOSE THAT SMALL HAVE SO MUCH GUNK?
KFFFF KFFFFF KFFFFFF
COUGH...WAIT! DON'T GO!
IS TOBIAS BACK?
HEY! I ASKED YOU SOMETHING!
ZICK...
WHAT DO YOU WANT?
LOOK, ZICK... YOU'RE GOING IN THE RIGHT DIRECTION! KEEP LOOKING...

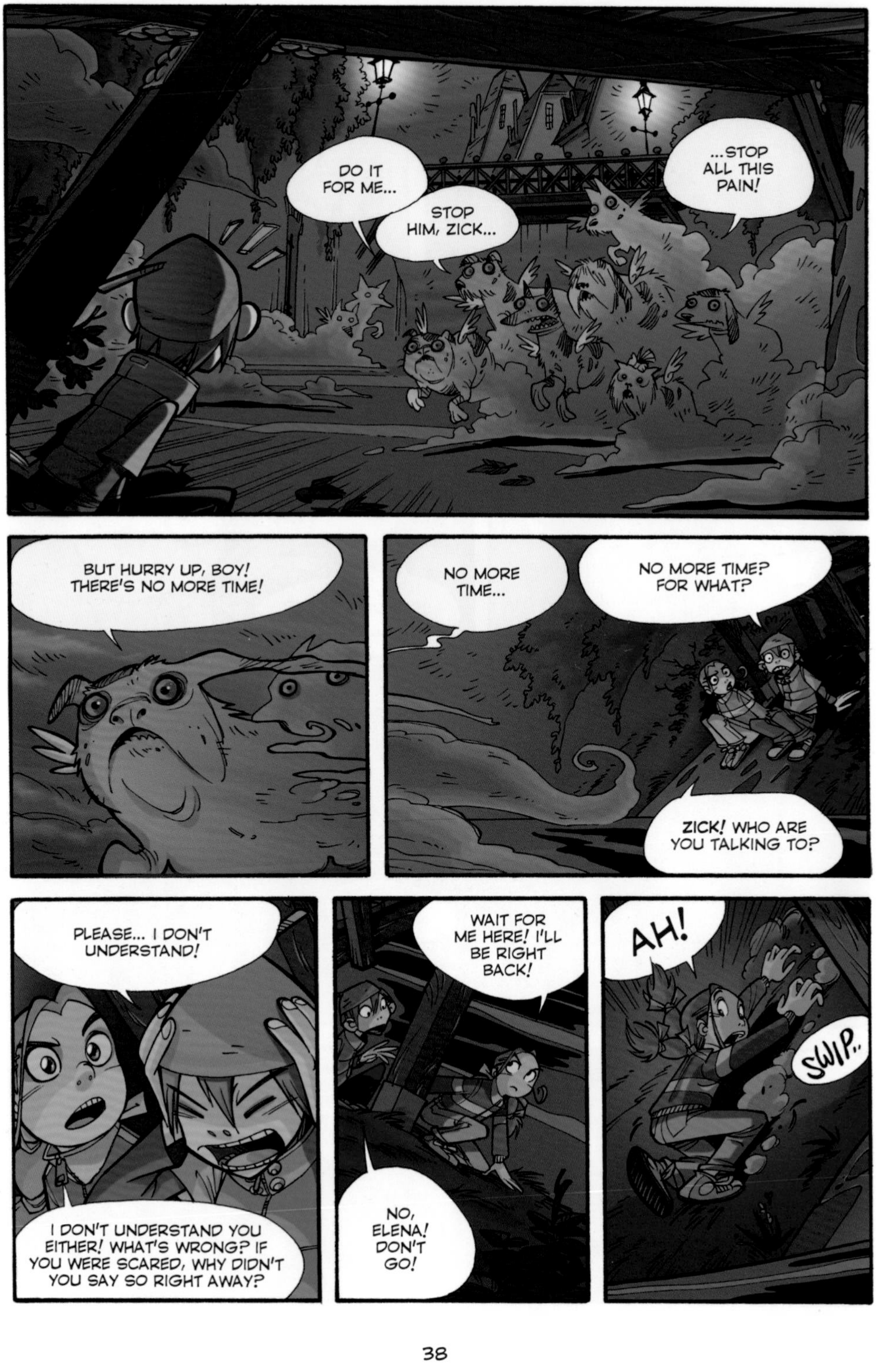
DO IT FOR ME...
STOP HIM, ZICK...
...STOP ALL THIS PAIN!
BUT HURRY UP, BOY! THERE'S NO MORE TIME!
NO MORE TIME...
NO MORE TIME? FOR WHAT?
ZICK! WHO ARE YOU TALKING TO?
PLEASE... I DON'T UNDERSTAND!
I DON'T UNDERSTAND YOU EITHER! WHAT'S WRONG? IF YOU WERE SCARED, WHY DIDN'T YOU SAY SO RIGHT AWAY?
WAIT FOR ME HERE! I'LL BE RIGHT BACK!
NO, ELENA! DON'T GO!
AH!
SWIP..

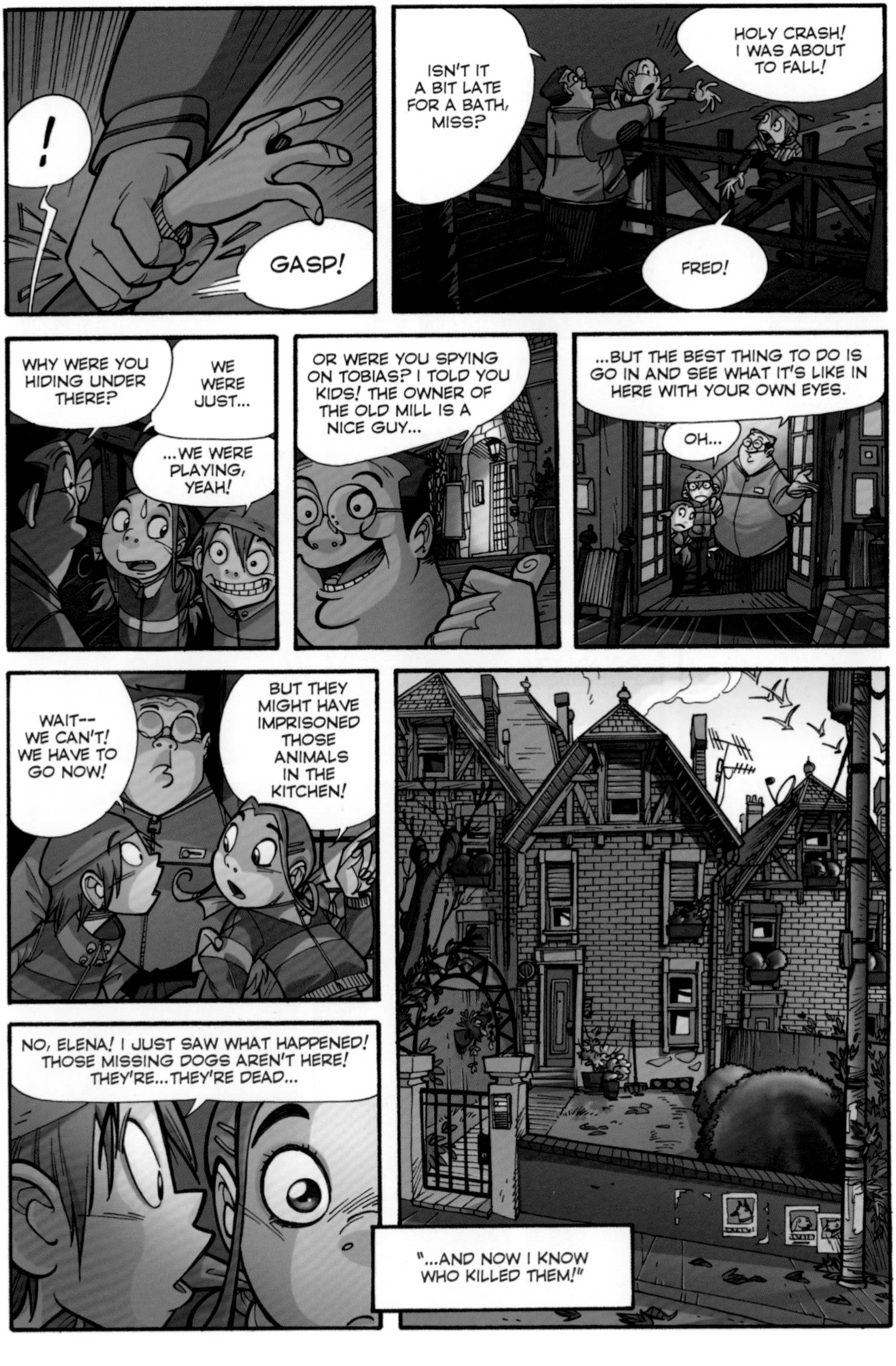
!
GASP!
ISN'T IT A BIT LATE FOR A BATH, MISS?
HOLY CRASH! I WAS ABOUT TO FALL!
FRED!
WHY WERE YOU HIDING UNDER THERE?
WE WERE JUST...
...WE WERE PLAYING, YEAH!
OR WERE YOU SPYING ON TOBIAS? I TOLD YOU KIDS! THE OWNER OF THE OLD MILL IS A NICE GUY...
...BUT THE BEST THING TO DO IS GO IN AND SEE WHAT IT'S LIKE IN HERE WITH YOUR OWN EYES.
OH...
WAIT-- WE CAN'T! WE HAVE TO GO NOW!
BUT THEY MIGHT HAVE IMPRISONED THOSE ANIMALS IN THE KITCHEN!
NO, ELENA! I JUST SAW WHAT HAPPENED! THOSE MISSING DOGS AREN'T HERE! THEY'RE...THEY'RE DEAD...
"...AND NOW I KNOW WHO KILLED THEM!"

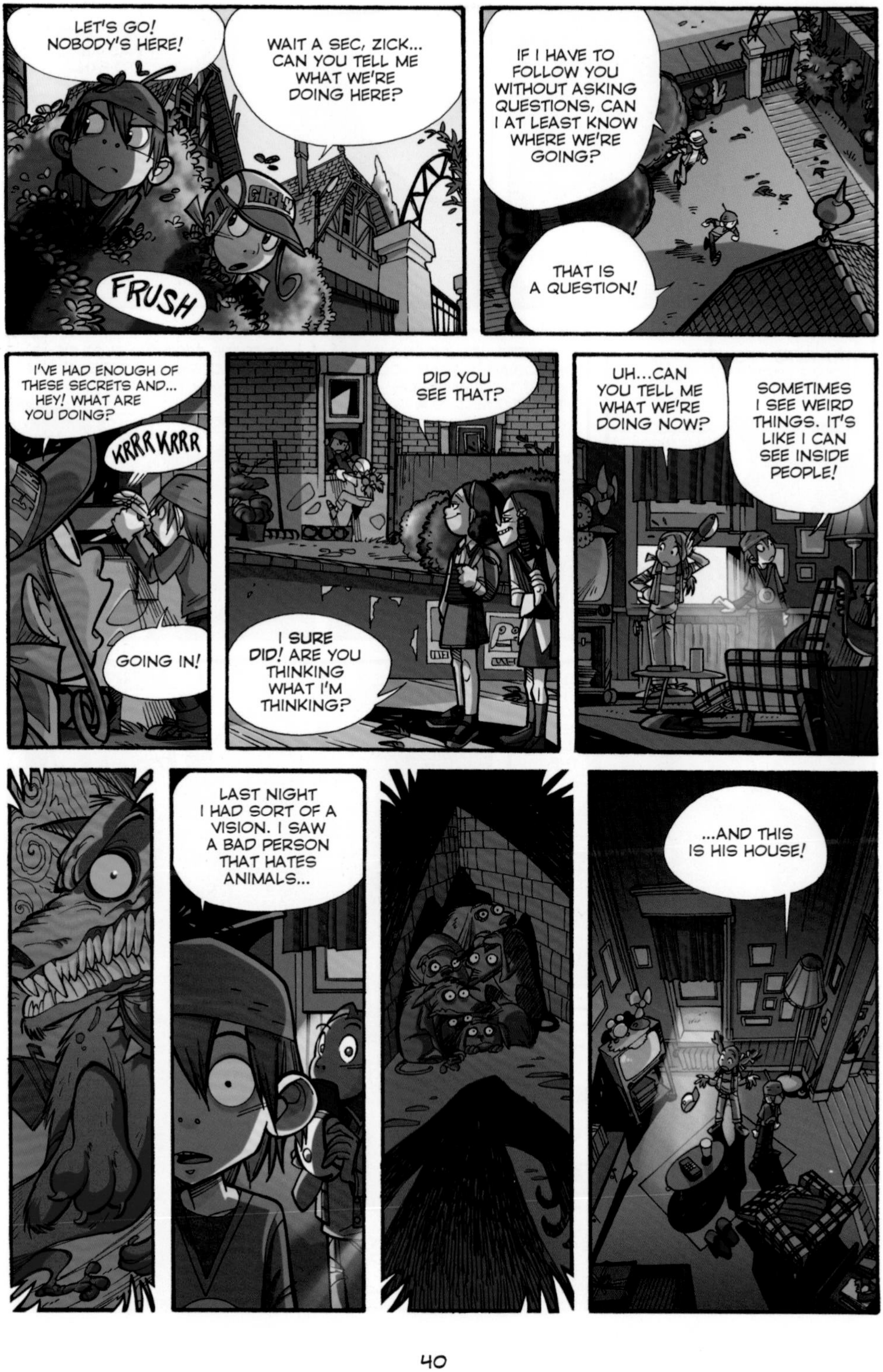

LET'S GO! NOBODY'S HERE!
WAIT A SEC, ZICK... CAN YOU TELL ME WHAT WE'RE DOING HERE?
FRUSH
IF I HAVE TO FOLLOW YOU WITHOUT ASKING QUESTIONS, CAN I AT LEAST KNOW WHERE WE'RE GOING?
THAT IS A QUESTION!
I'VE HAD ENOUGH OF THESE SECRETS AND... HEY! WHAT ARE YOU DOING?
KRRR KRRR
GOING IN!
DID YOU SEE THAT?
I SURE DID! ARE YOU THINKING WHAT I'M THINKING?
UH...CAN YOU TELL ME WHAT WE'RE DOING NOW?
SOMETIMES I SEE WEIRD THINGS. IT'S LIKE I CAN SEE INSIDE PEOPLE!
LAST NIGHT I HAD SORT OF A VISION. I SAW A BAD PERSON THAT HATES ANIMALS...
...AND THIS IS HIS HOUSE!

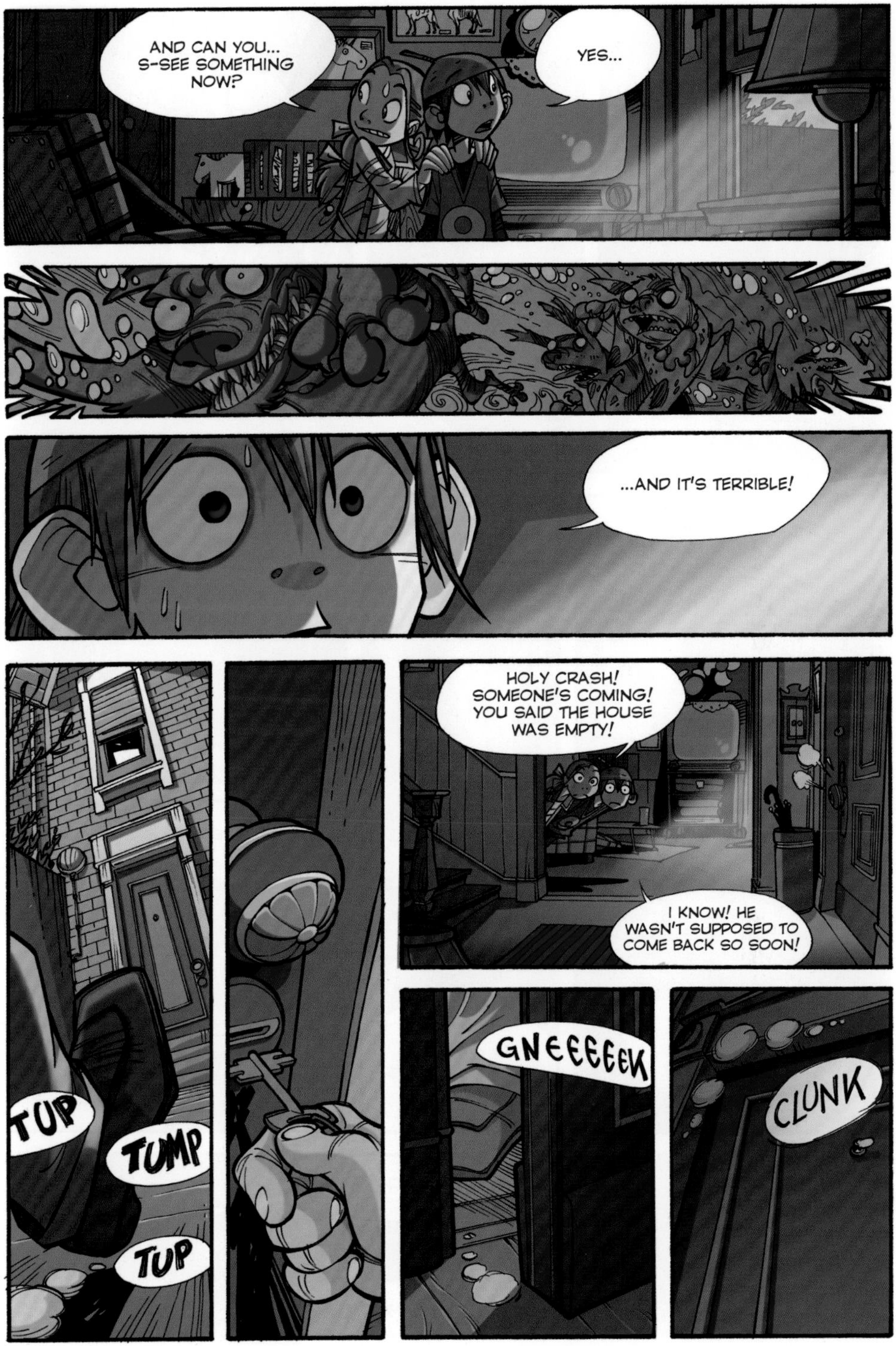
AND CAN YOU... S-SEE SOMETHING NOW?
YES...
...AND IT'S TERRIBLE!
TUP
TUMP
TUP
HOLY CRASH! SOMEONE'S COMING! YOU SAID THE HOUSE WAS EMPTY!
I KNOW! HE WASN'T SUPPOSED TO COME BACK SO SOON!
GNEEEEEK
CLUNK

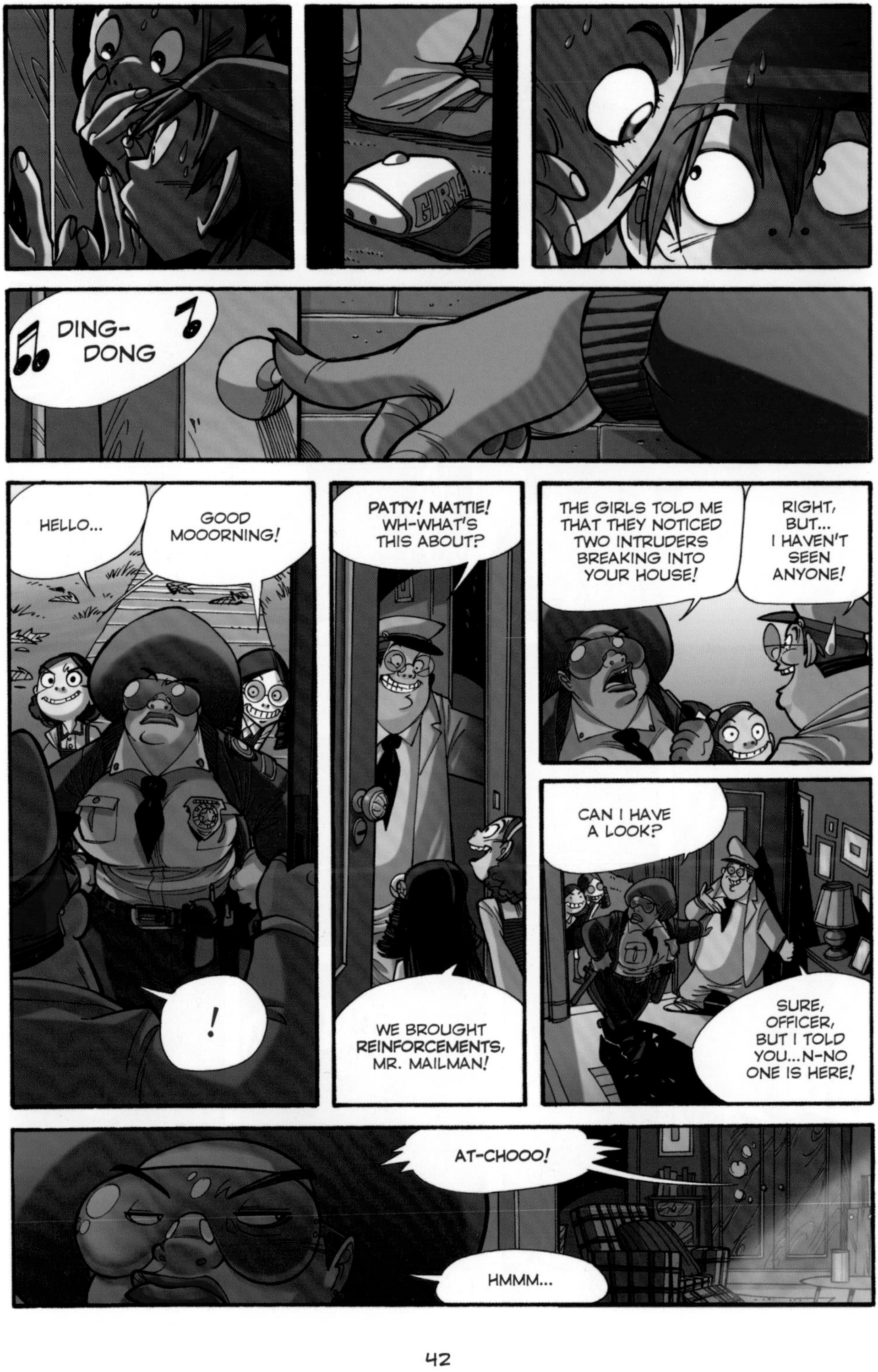
DING-DONG
HELLO...
GOOD MOOORNING!
!
PATTY! MATTIE! WH-WHAT'S THIS ABOUT?
WE BROUGHT REINFORCEMENTS, MR. MAILMAN!
THE GIRLS TOLD ME THAT THEY NOTICED TWO INTRUDERS BREAKING INTO YOUR HOUSE!
RIGHT, BUT... I HAVEN'T SEEN ANYONE!
CAN I HAVE A LOOK?
SURE, OFFICER, BUT I TOLD YOU...N-NO ONE IS HERE!
AT-CHOOO!
HMMM...

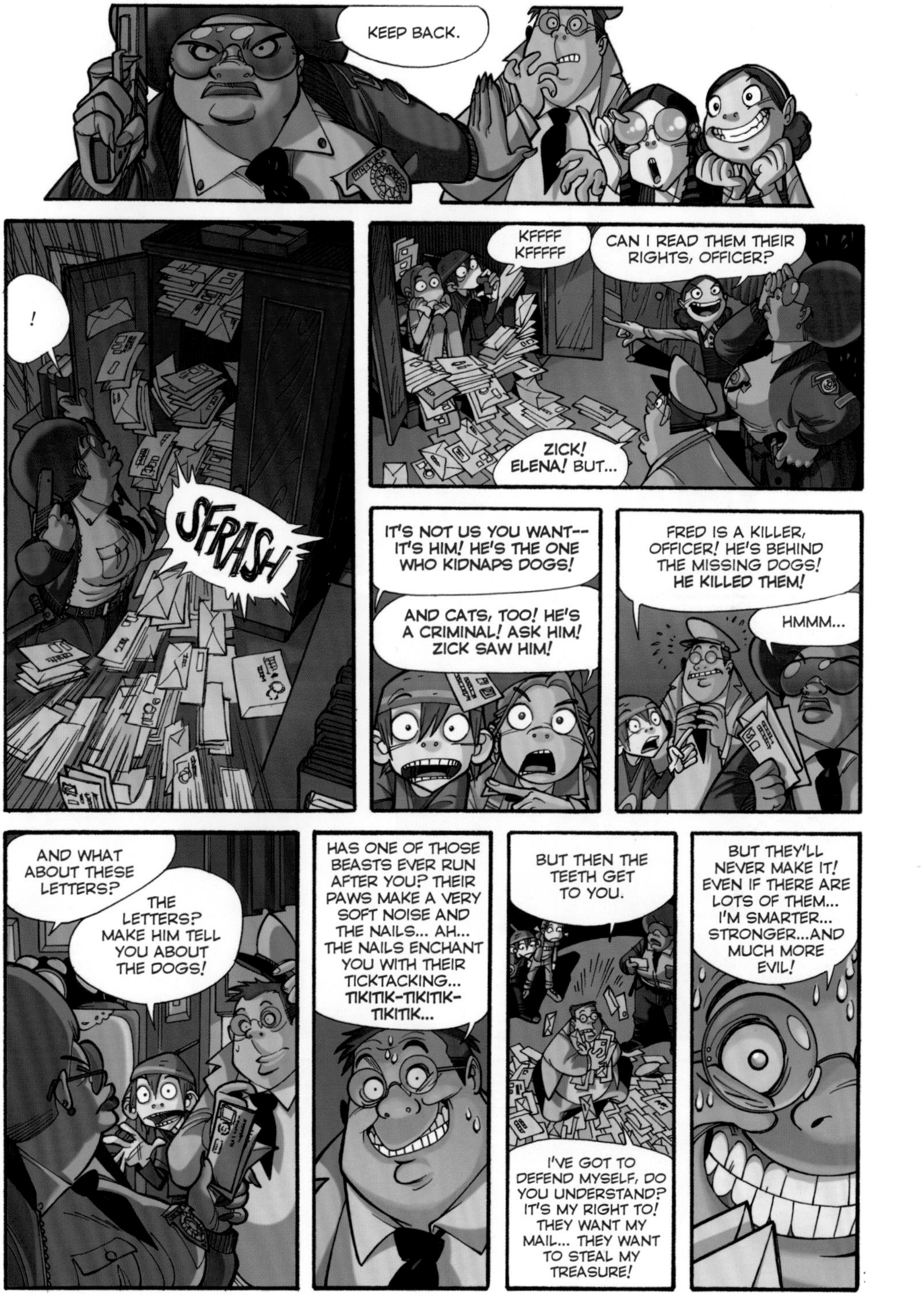

KEEP BACK.
!
SFRASH
KFFFF KFFFFF
CAN I READ THEM THEIR RIGHTS, OFFICER?
ZICK! ELENA! BUT...
IT'S NOT US YOU WANT-- IT'S HIM! HE'S THE ONE WHO KIDNAPS DOGS!
AND CATS, TOO! HE'S A CRIMINAL! ASK HIM! ZICK SAW HIM!
FRED IS A KILLER, OFFICER! HE'S BEHIND THE MISSING DOGS! HE KILLED THEM!
HMMM...
AND WHAT ABOUT THESE LETTERS?
THE LETTERS? MAKE HIM TELL YOU ABOUT THE DOGS!
HAS ONE OF THOSE BEASTS EVER RUN AFTER YOU? THEIR PAWS MAKE A VERY SOFT NOISE AND THE NAILS... AH... THE NAILS ENCHANT YOU WITH THEIR TICKTACKING... TIKITIK-TIKITIK-TIKITIK...
BUT THEN THE TEETH GET TO YOU.
I'VE GOT TO DEFEND MYSELF, DO YOU UNDERSTAND? IT'S MY RIGHT TO! THEY WANT MY MAIL... THEY WANT TO STEAL MY TREASURE!
BUT THEY'LL NEVER MAKE IT! EVEN IF THERE ARE LOTS OF THEM... I'M SMARTER... STRONGER...AND MUCH MORE EVIL!

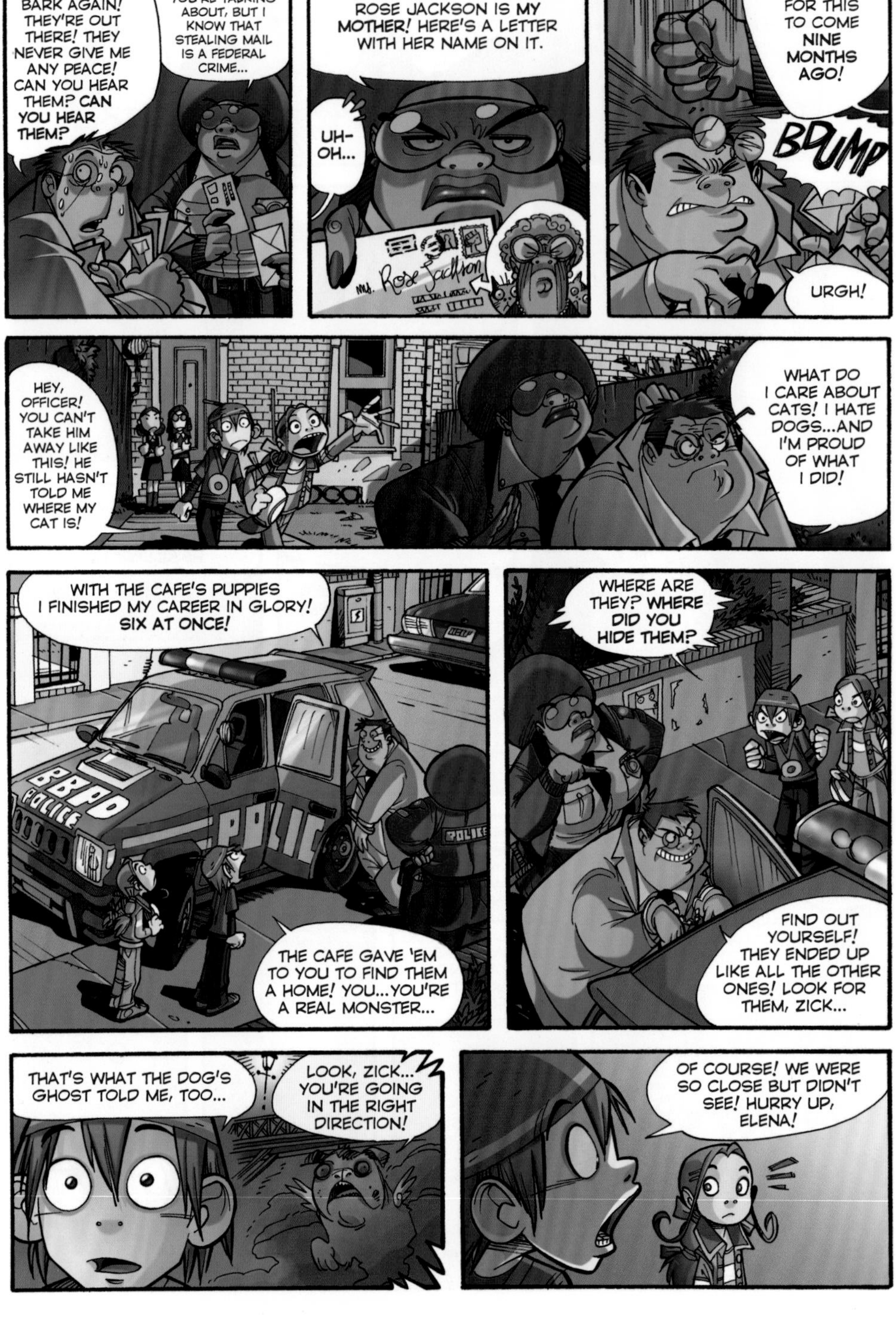
LISTEN, THEY'RE STARTING TO BARK AGAIN! THEY'RE OUT THERE! THEY NEVER GIVE ME ANY PEACE! CAN YOU HEAR THEM? CAN YOU HEAR THEM?
MAN, I DON'T KNOW WHAT YOU'RE TALKING ABOUT, BUT I KNOW THAT STEALING MAIL IS A FEDERAL CRIME...
...AND I ALSO KNOW THAT ROSE JACKSON IS MY MOTHER! HERE'S A LETTER WITH HER NAME ON IT.
UH-OH...
Rose Jackson
SHE WAITED FOR THIS TO COME NINE MONTHS AGO!
BDUMP
URGH!
HEY, OFFICER! YOU CAN'T TAKE HIM AWAY LIKE THIS! HE STILL HASN'T TOLD ME WHERE MY CAT IS!
WHAT DO I CARE ABOUT CATS! I HATE DOGS...AND I'M PROUD OF WHAT I DID!
WITH THE CAFE'S PUPPIES I FINISHED MY CAREER IN GLORY! SIX AT ONCE!
BBPD
POLICE
POLIC
THE CAFE GAVE 'EM TO YOU TO FIND THEM A HOME! YOU...YOU'RE A REAL MONSTER...
WHERE ARE THEY? WHERE DID YOU HIDE THEM?
FIND OUT YOURSELF! THEY ENDED UP LIKE ALL THE OTHER ONES! LOOK FOR THEM, ZICK...
THAT'S WHAT THE DOG'S GHOST TOLD ME, TOO...
LOOK, ZICK... YOU'RE GOING IN THE RIGHT DIRECTION!
OF COURSE! WE WERE SO CLOSE BUT DIDN'T SEE! HURRY UP, ELENA!

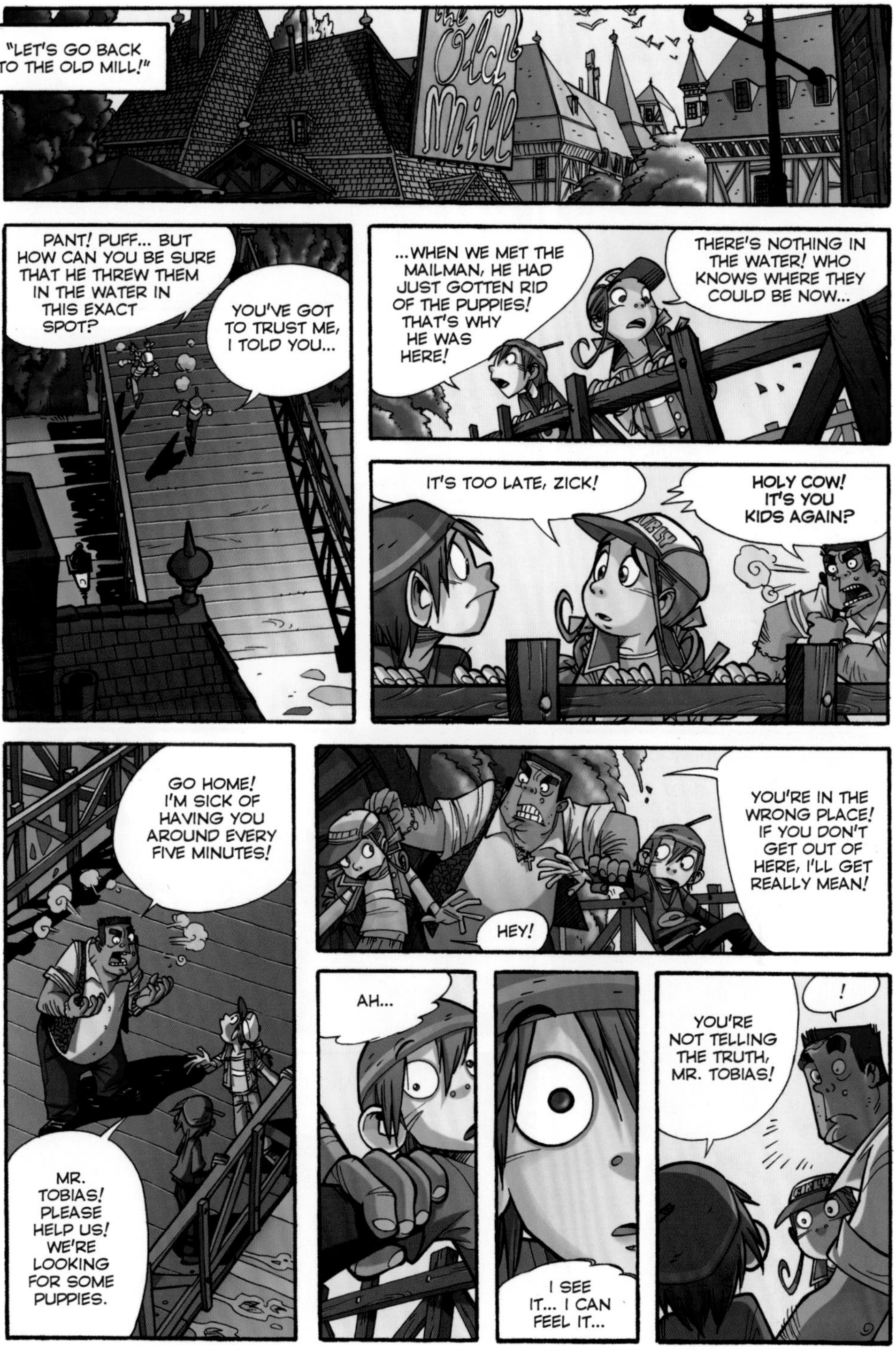
"LET'S GO BACK TO THE OLD MILL!"
The Old Mill
PANT! PUFF... BUT HOW CAN YOU BE SURE THAT HE THREW THEM IN THE WATER IN THIS EXACT SPOT?
YOU'VE GOT TO TRUST ME, I TOLD YOU...
...WHEN WE MET THE MAILMAN, HE HAD JUST GOTTEN RID OF THE PUPPIES! THAT'S WHY HE WAS HERE!
THERE'S NOTHING IN THE WATER! WHO KNOWS WHERE THEY COULD BE NOW...
IT'S TOO LATE, ZICK!
HOLY COW! IT'S YOU KIDS AGAIN?
GO HOME! I'M SICK OF HAVING YOU AROUND EVERY FIVE MINUTES!
MR. TOBIAS! PLEASE HELP US! WE'RE LOOKING FOR SOME PUPPIES.
YOU'RE IN THE WRONG PLACE! IF YOU DON'T GET OUT OF HERE, I'LL GET REALLY MEAN!
HEY!
AH...
I SEE IT... I CAN FEEL IT...
!
YOU'RE NOT TELLING THE TRUTH, MR. TOBIAS!

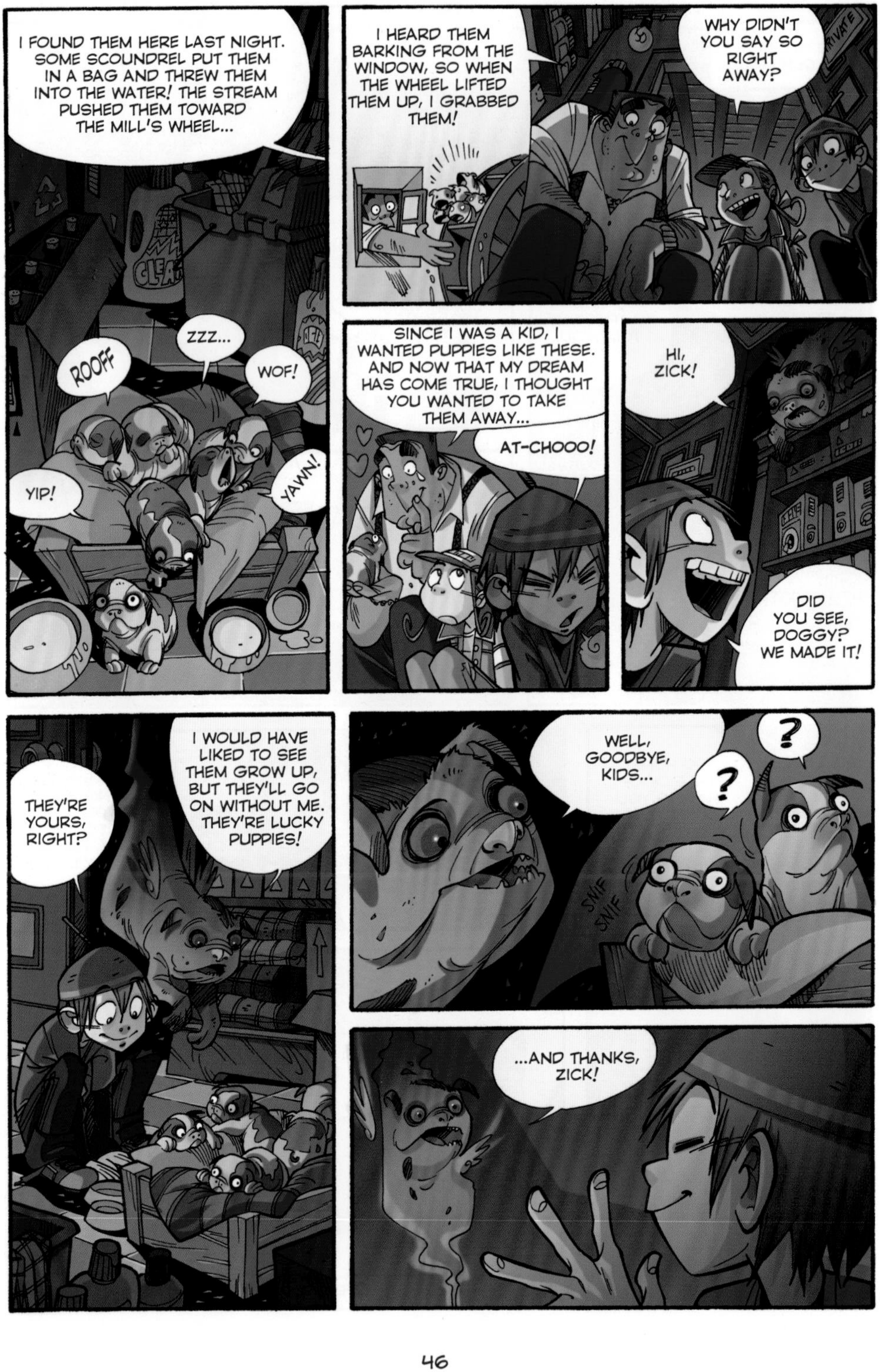
I FOUND THEM HERE LAST NIGHT. SOME SCOUNDREL PUT THEM IN A BAG AND THREW THEM INTO THE WATER! THE STREAM PUSHED THEM TOWARD THE MILL'S WHEEL...
ROOFF
ZZZ...
WOF!
YIP!
YAWN!
I HEARD THEM BARKING FROM THE WINDOW, SO WHEN THE WHEEL LIFTED THEM UP, I GRABBED THEM!
WHY DIDN'T YOU SAY SO RIGHT AWAY?
SINCE I WAS A KID, I WANTED PUPPIES LIKE THESE. AND NOW THAT MY DREAM HAS COME TRUE, I THOUGHT YOU WANTED TO TAKE THEM AWAY...
AT-CHOOO!
HI, ZICK!
DID YOU SEE, DOGGY? WE MADE IT!
THEY'RE YOURS, RIGHT?
I WOULD HAVE LIKED TO SEE THEM GROW UP, BUT THEY'LL GO ON WITHOUT ME. THEY'RE LUCKY PUPPIES!
WELL, GOODBYE, KIDS...
?
?
SNIF SNIF
...AND THANKS, ZICK!

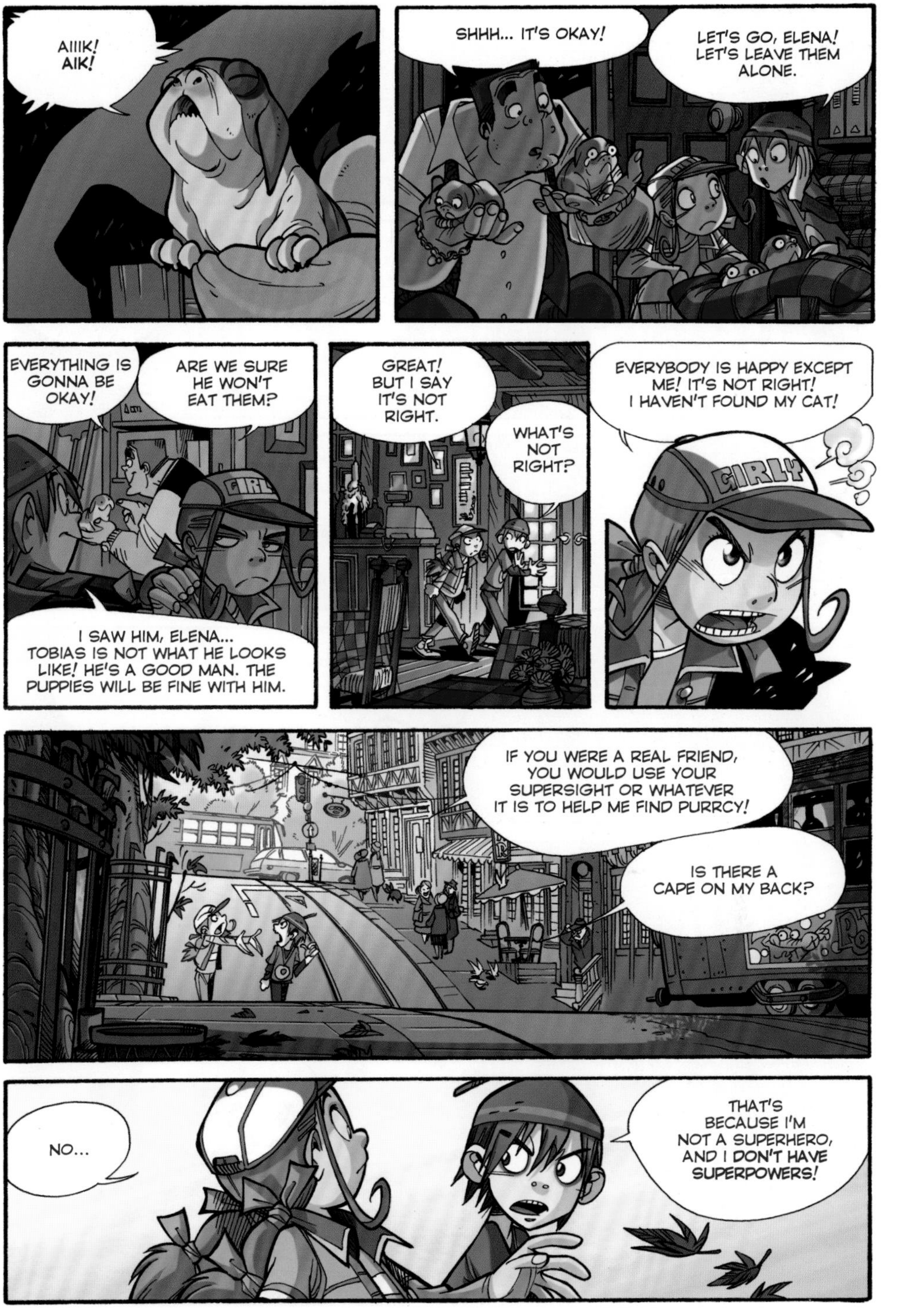
AIIIK! AIK!
SHHH... IT'S OKAY!
LET'S GO, ELENA! LET'S LEAVE THEM ALONE.
EVERYTHING IS GONNA BE OKAY!
ARE WE SURE HE WON'T EAT THEM?
I SAW HIM, ELENA... TOBIAS IS NOT WHAT HE LOOKS LIKE! HE'S A GOOD MAN. THE PUPPIES WILL BE FINE WITH HIM.
GREAT! BUT I SAY IT'S NOT RIGHT.
WHAT'S NOT RIGHT?
EVERYBODY IS HAPPY EXCEPT ME! IT'S NOT RIGHT! I HAVEN'T FOUND MY CAT!
GIRLY
IF YOU WERE A REAL FRIEND, YOU WOULD USE YOUR SUPERSIGHT OR WHATEVER IT IS TO HELP ME FIND PURRCY!
IS THERE A CAPE ON MY BACK?
NO...
THAT'S BECAUSE I'M NOT A SUPERHERO, AND I DON'T HAVE SUPERPOWERS!

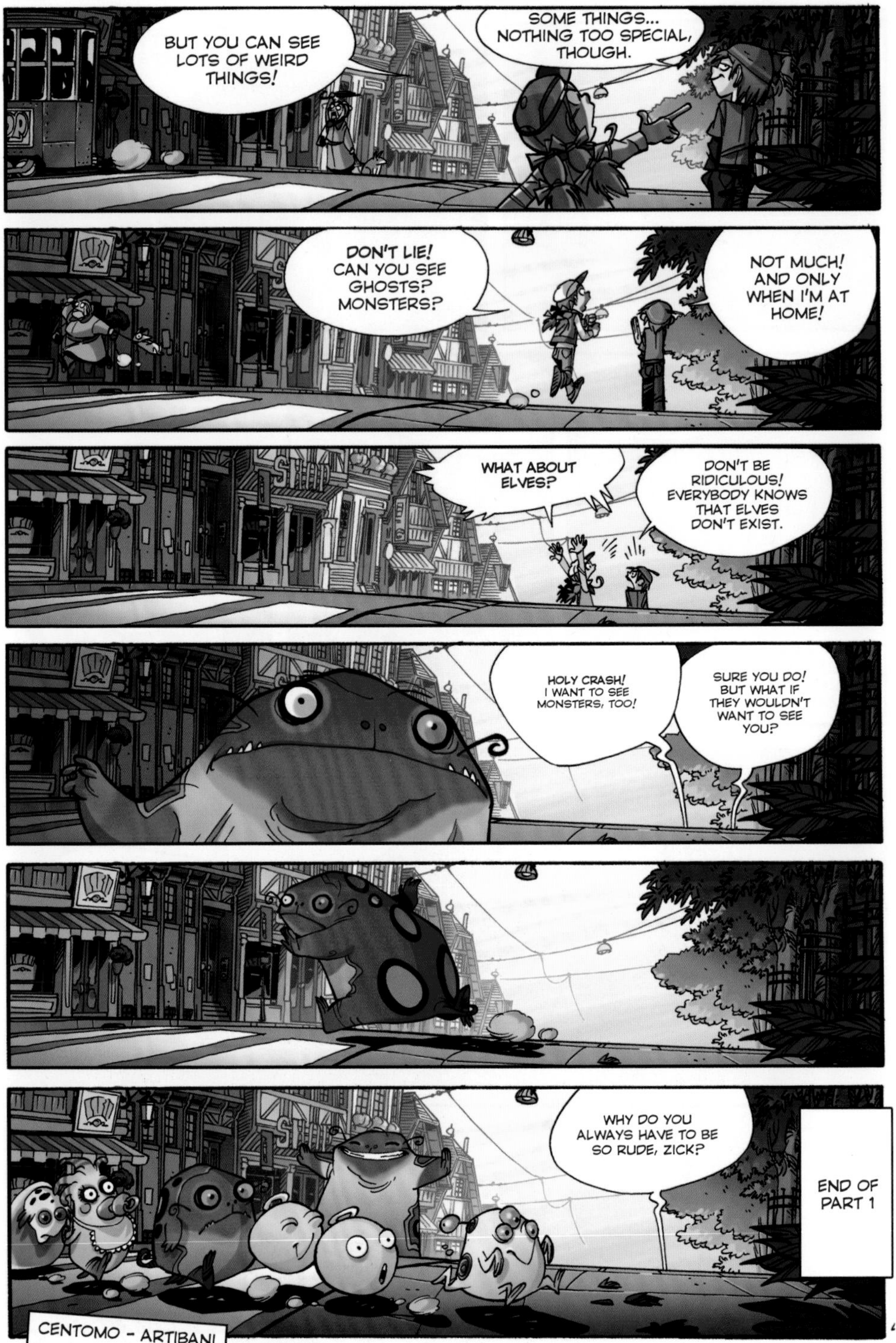

BUT YOU CAN SEE LOTS OF WEIRD THINGS!
SOME THINGS... NOTHING TOO SPECIAL, THOUGH.
DON'T LIE! CAN YOU SEE GHOSTS? MONSTERS?
NOT MUCH! AND ONLY WHEN I'M AT HOME!
WHAT ABOUT ELVES?
DON'T BE RIDICULOUS! EVERYBODY KNOWS THAT ELVES DON'T EXIST.
HOLY CRASH! I WANT TO SEE MONSTERS, TOO!
SURE YOU DO! BUT WHAT IF THEY WOULDN'T WANT TO SEE YOU?
WHY DO YOU ALWAYS HAVE TO BE SO RUDE, ZICK?
END OF PART 1

CENTOMO - ARTIBANI

BARBUCCI - CANEPA

Art by Paolo Campinoti,
Christina Giorgilli, and
Barbara Bargiggia

PART 2

THE PYRAMID OF THE INVULNERABLE

Plot: Katja Centomo
Script: Francesco Artibani
Illustrations: Giovanni Rigano
and Alessandro Barbucci
Colors: Pamela Brughera
and Paola Volonté
Colors Supervision: Barbara Canepa

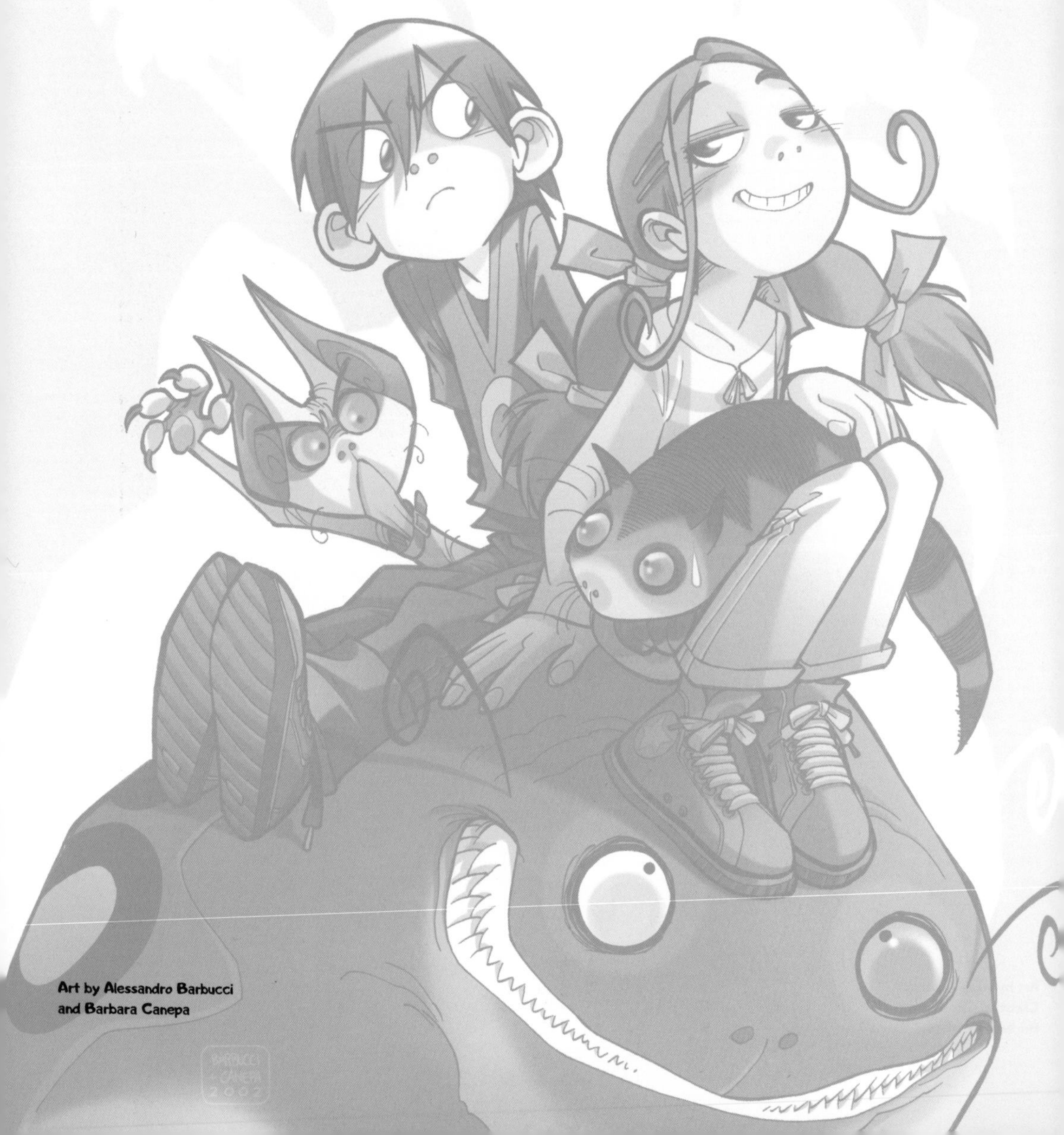

Art by Alessandro Barbucci
and Barbara Canepa

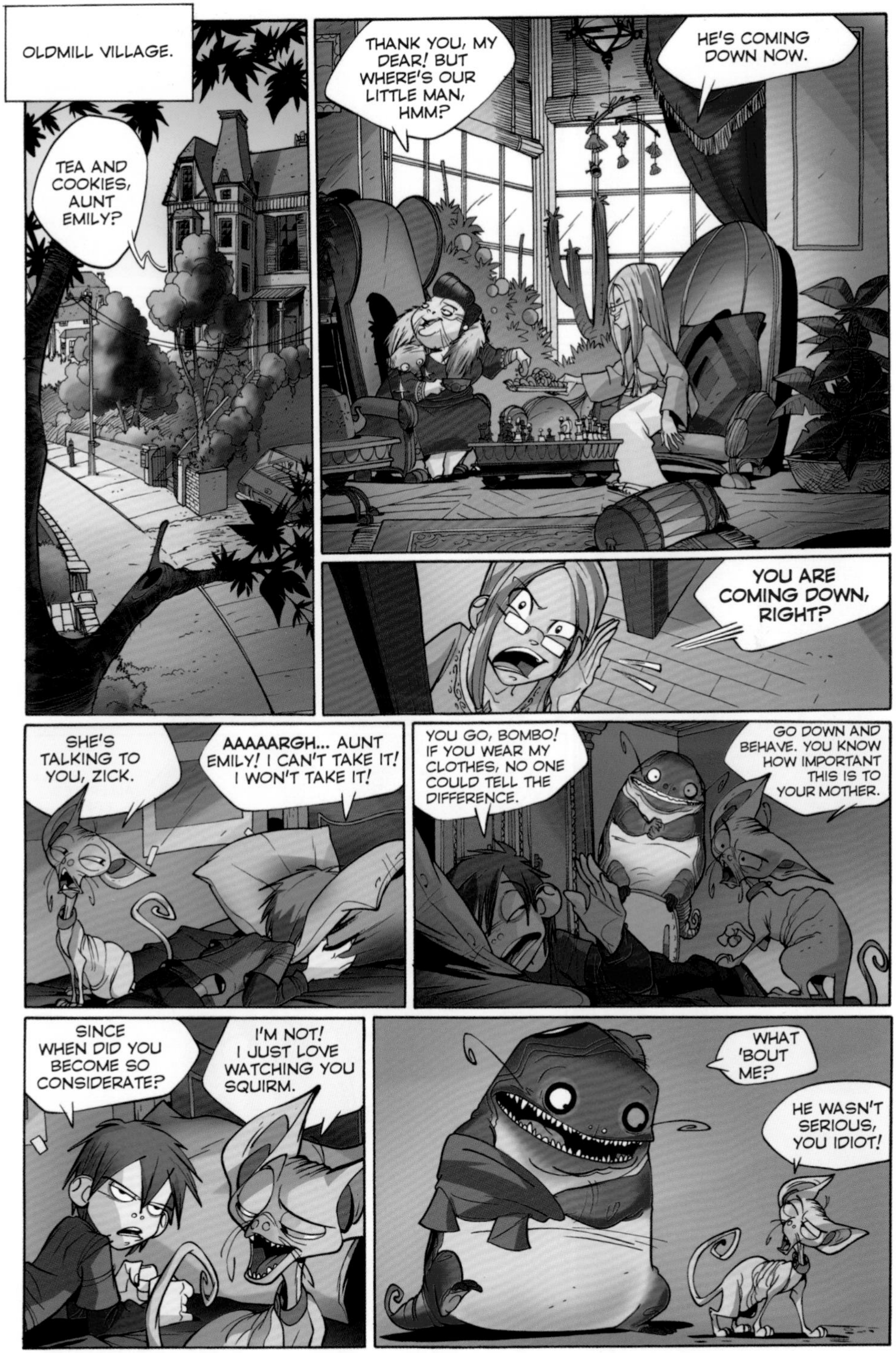

OLDMILL VILLAGE.
TEA AND COOKIES, AUNT EMILY?
THANK YOU, MY DEAR! BUT WHERE'S OUR LITTLE MAN, HMM?
HE'S COMING DOWN NOW.
YOU ARE COMING DOWN, RIGHT?
SHE'S TALKING TO YOU, ZICK.
AAAAARGH... AUNT EMILY! I CAN'T TAKE IT! I WON'T TAKE IT!
YOU GO, BOMBO! IF YOU WEAR MY CLOTHES, NO ONE COULD TELL THE DIFFERENCE.
GO DOWN AND BEHAVE. YOU KNOW HOW IMPORTANT THIS IS TO YOUR MOTHER.
SINCE WHEN DID YOU BECOME SO CONSIDERATE?
I'M NOT! I JUST LOVE WATCHING YOU SQUIRM.
WHAT 'BOUT ME?
HE WASN'T SERIOUS, YOU IDIOT!

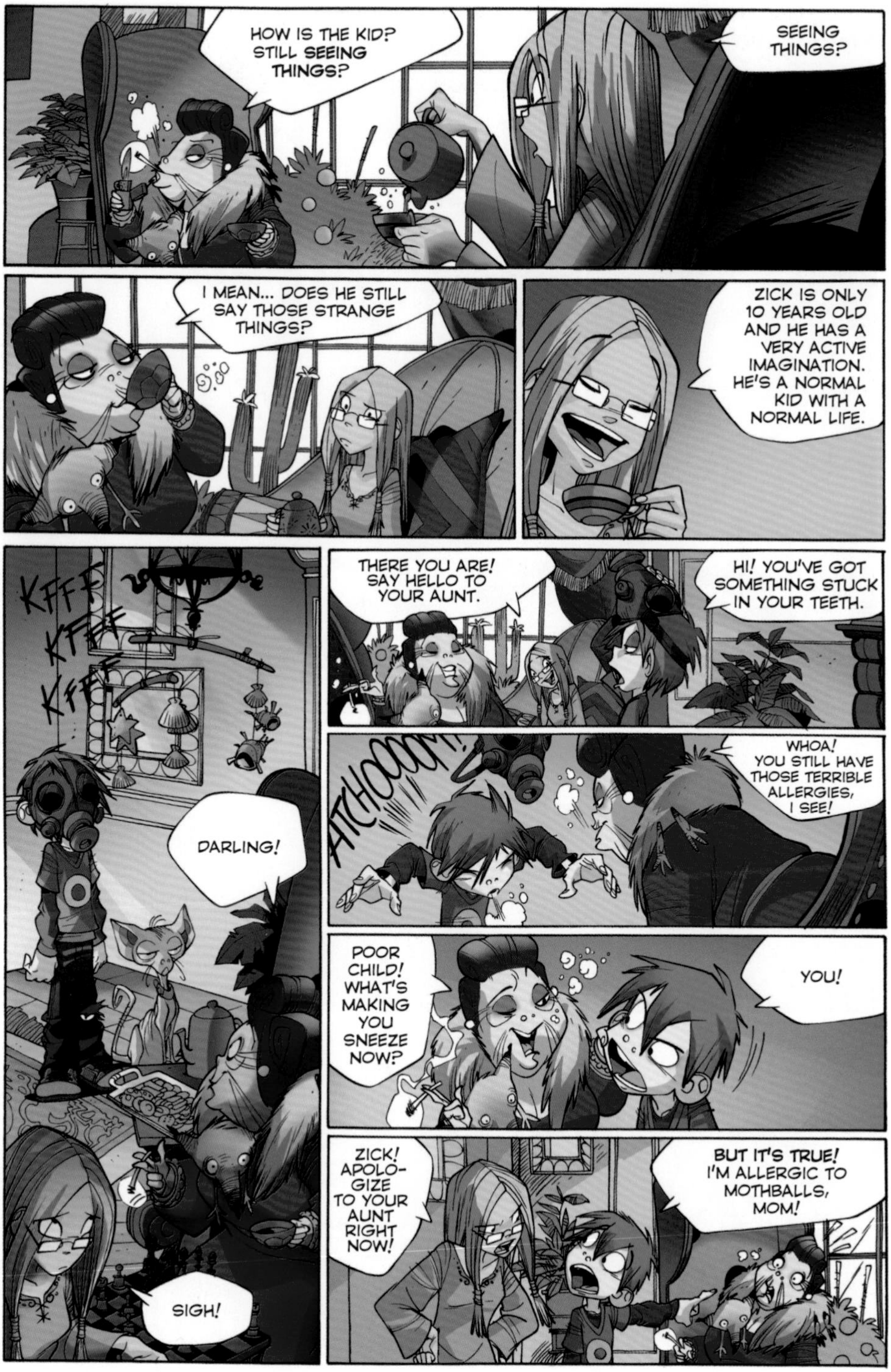
HOW IS THE KID? STILL SEEING THINGS?
SEEING THINGS?
I MEAN... DOES HE STILL SAY THOSE STRANGE THINGS?
ZICK IS ONLY 10 YEARS OLD AND HE HAS A VERY ACTIVE IMAGINATION. HE'S A NORMAL KID WITH A NORMAL LIFE.
KFFF KFFF KFFF
DARLING!
SIGH!
THERE YOU ARE! SAY HELLO TO YOUR AUNT.
HI! YOU'VE GOT SOMETHING STUCK IN YOUR TEETH.
ATCHOOOO!!
WHOA! YOU STILL HAVE THOSE TERRIBLE ALLERGIES, I SEE!
POOR CHILD! WHAT'S MAKING YOU SNEEZE NOW?
YOU!
ZICK! APOLO-GIZE TO YOUR AUNT RIGHT NOW!
BUT IT'S TRUE! I'M ALLERGIC TO MOTHBALLS, MOM!

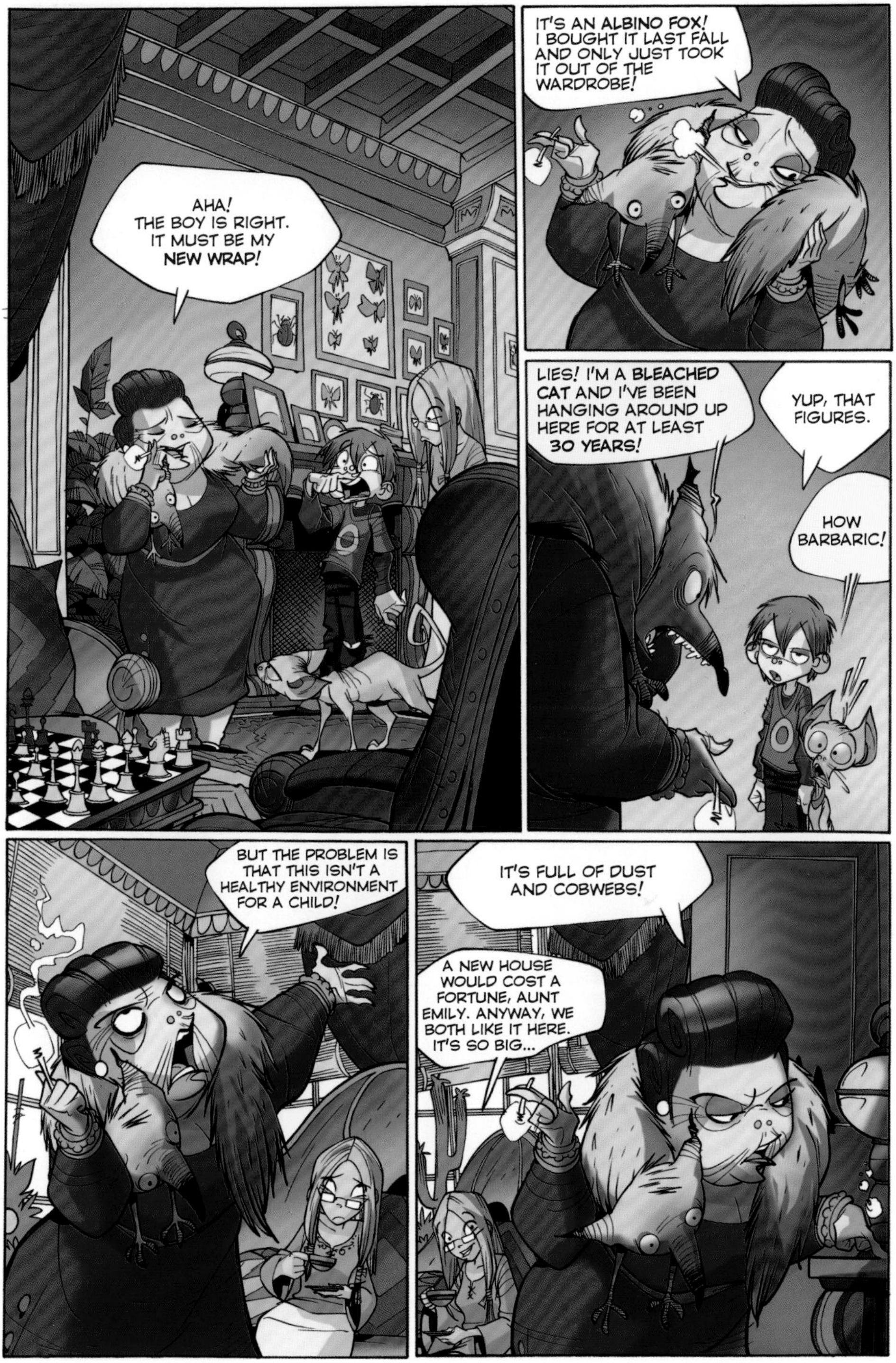
AHA! THE BOY IS RIGHT. IT MUST BE MY **NEW WRAP!**
IT'S AN **ALBINO FOX!** I BOUGHT IT LAST FALL AND ONLY JUST TOOK IT OUT OF THE WARDROBE!
LIES! I'M A **BLEACHED CAT** AND I'VE BEEN HANGING AROUND UP HERE FOR AT LEAST **30 YEARS!**
YUP, THAT FIGURES.
HOW BARBARIC!
BUT THE PROBLEM IS THAT THIS ISN'T A HEALTHY ENVIRONMENT FOR A CHILD!
IT'S FULL OF DUST AND COBWEBS!
A NEW HOUSE WOULD COST A FORTUNE, AUNT EMILY. ANYWAY, WE BOTH LIKE IT HERE. IT'S SO BIG...

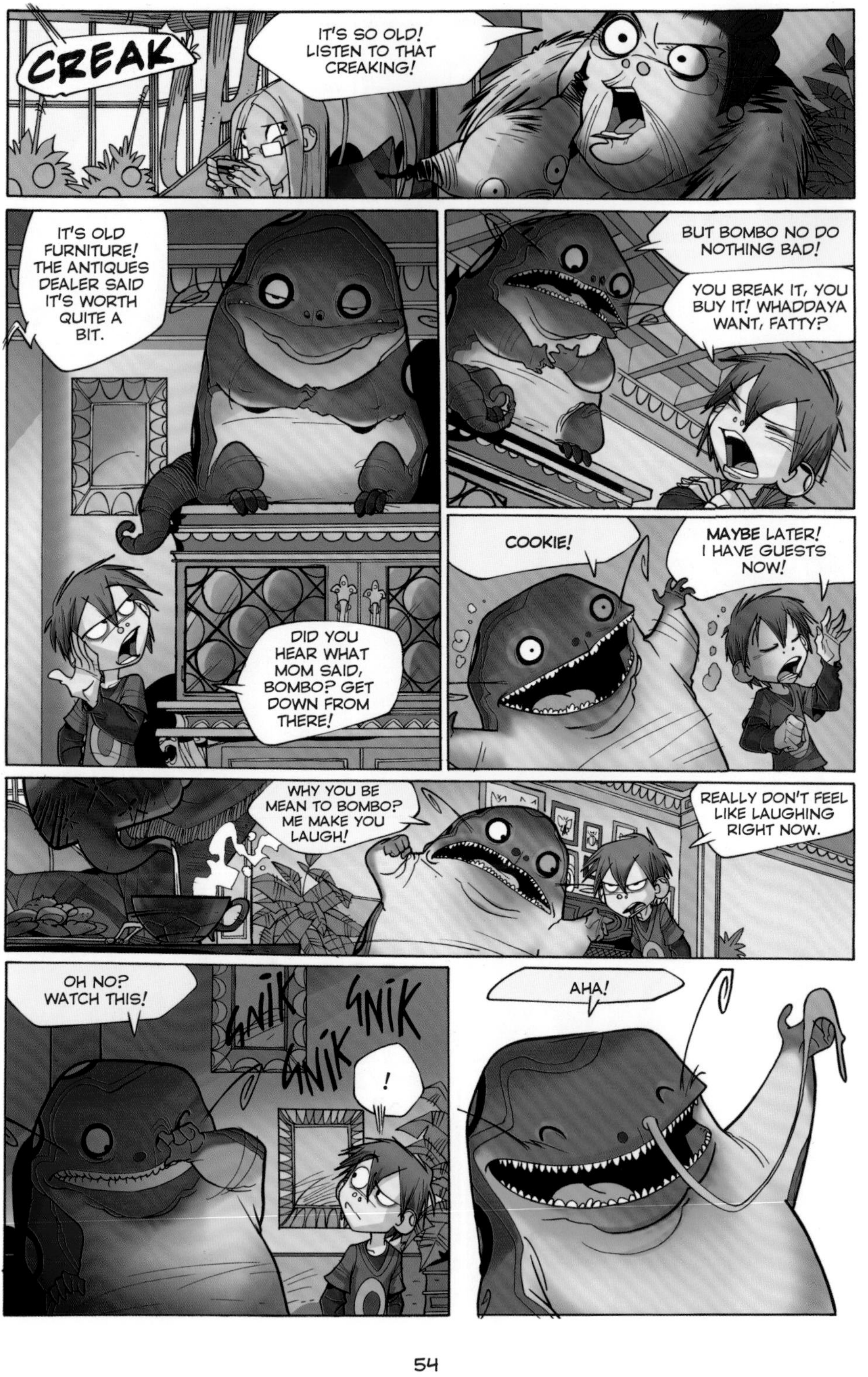
CREAK
IT'S SO OLD! LISTEN TO THAT CREAKING!
IT'S OLD FURNITURE! THE ANTIQUES DEALER SAID IT'S WORTH QUITE A BIT.
DID YOU HEAR WHAT MOM SAID, BOMBO? GET DOWN FROM THERE!
BUT BOMBO NO DO NOTHING BAD!
YOU BREAK IT, YOU BUY IT! WHADDAYA WANT, FATTY?
COOKIE!
MAYBE LATER! I HAVE GUESTS NOW!
WHY YOU BE MEAN TO BOMBO? ME MAKE YOU LAUGH!
REALLY DON'T FEEL LIKE LAUGHING RIGHT NOW.
OH NO? WATCH THIS!
SNIK SNIK SNIK
!
AHA!

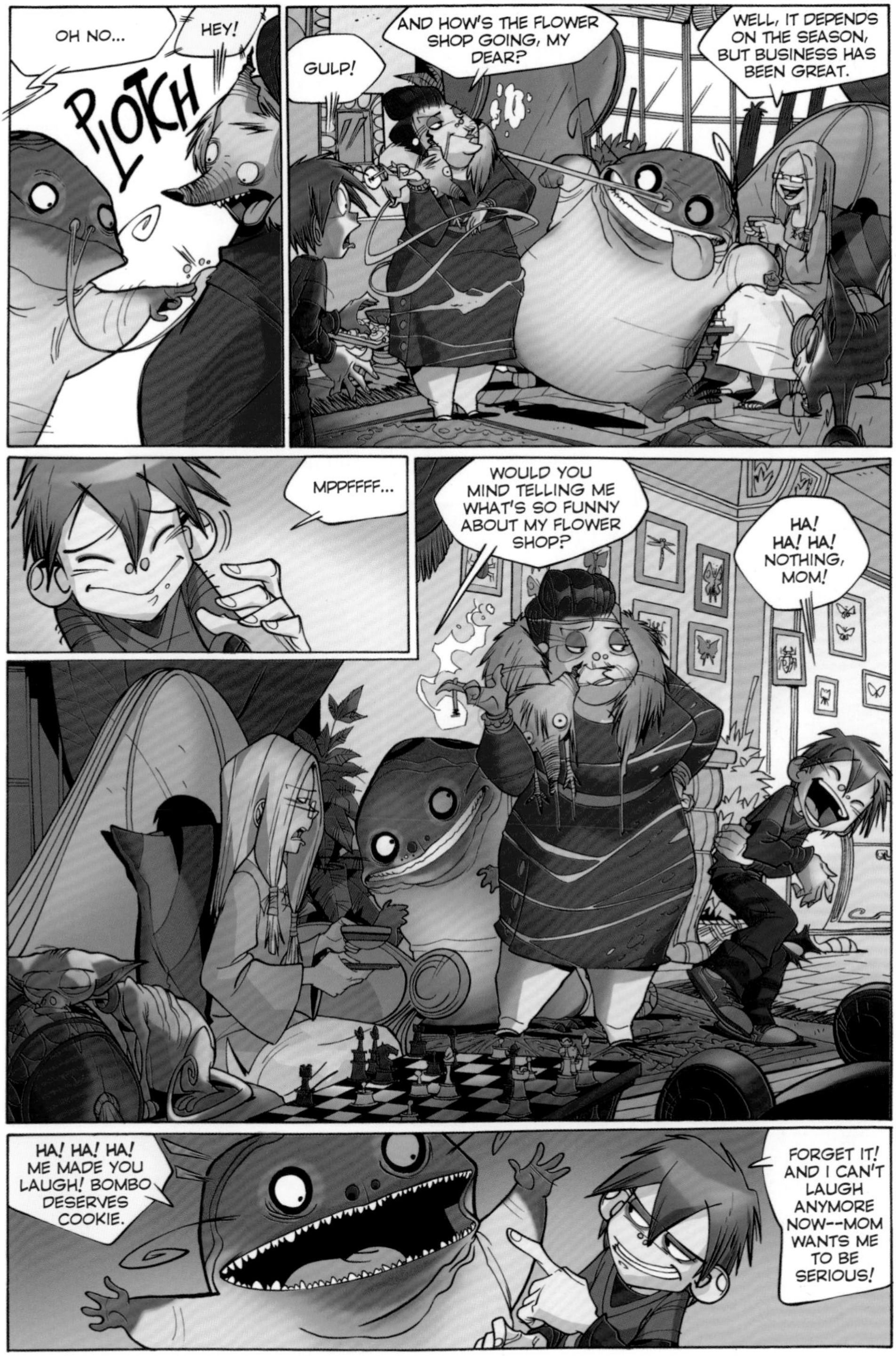
OH NO...
HEY!
PLOTCH
GULP!
AND HOW'S THE FLOWER SHOP GOING, MY DEAR?
WELL, IT DEPENDS ON THE SEASON, BUT BUSINESS HAS BEEN GREAT.
MPPFFFF...
WOULD YOU MIND TELLING ME WHAT'S SO FUNNY ABOUT MY FLOWER SHOP?
HA! HA! HA! NOTHING, MOM!
HA! HA! HA! ME MADE YOU LAUGH! BOMBO DESERVES COOKIE.
FORGET IT! AND I CAN'T LAUGH ANYMORE NOW--MOM WANTS ME TO BE SERIOUS!

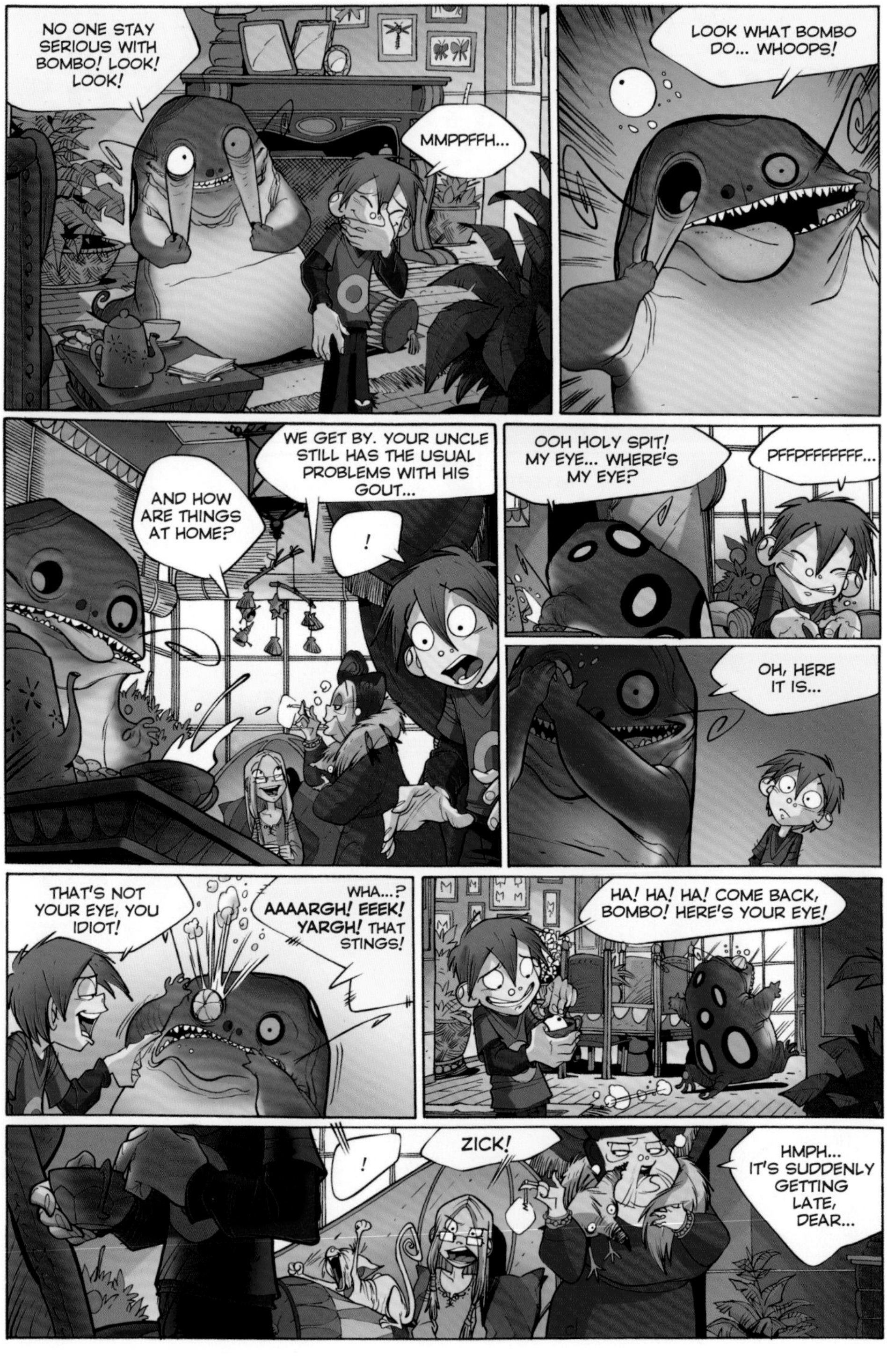
NO ONE STAY SERIOUS WITH BOMBO! LOOK! LOOK!
MMPPFFH...
LOOK WHAT BOMBO DO... WHOOPS!
AND HOW ARE THINGS AT HOME?
WE GET BY. YOUR UNCLE STILL HAS THE USUAL PROBLEMS WITH HIS GOUT...
!
OOH HOLY SPIT! MY EYE... WHERE'S MY EYE?
PFFPFFFFFFF...
OH, HERE IT IS...
THAT'S NOT YOUR EYE, YOU IDIOT!
WHA...? AAAARGH! EEEK! YARGH! THAT STINGS!
HA! HA! HA! COME BACK, BOMBO! HERE'S YOUR EYE!
!
ZICK!
HMPH... IT'S SUDDENLY GETTING LATE, DEAR...

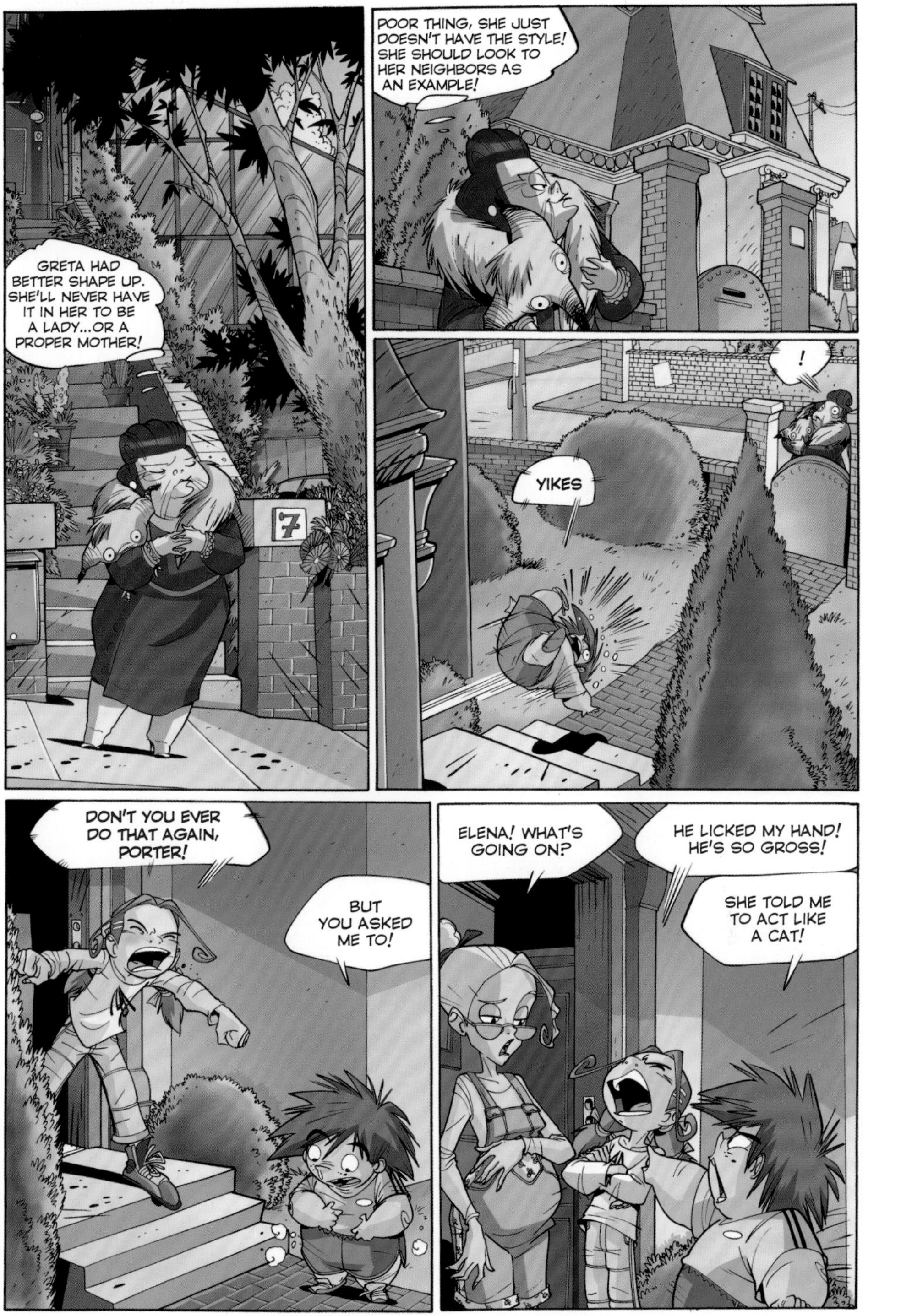
GRETA HAD BETTER SHAPE UP. SHE'LL NEVER HAVE IT IN HER TO BE A LADY...OR A PROPER MOTHER!
7
POOR THING, SHE JUST DOESN'T HAVE THE STYLE! SHE SHOULD LOOK TO HER NEIGHBORS AS AN EXAMPLE!
!
YIKES
DON'T YOU EVER DO THAT AGAIN, PORTER!
BUT YOU ASKED ME TO!
ELENA! WHAT'S GOING ON?
HE LICKED MY HAND! HE'S SO GROSS!
SHE TOLD ME TO ACT LIKE A CAT!

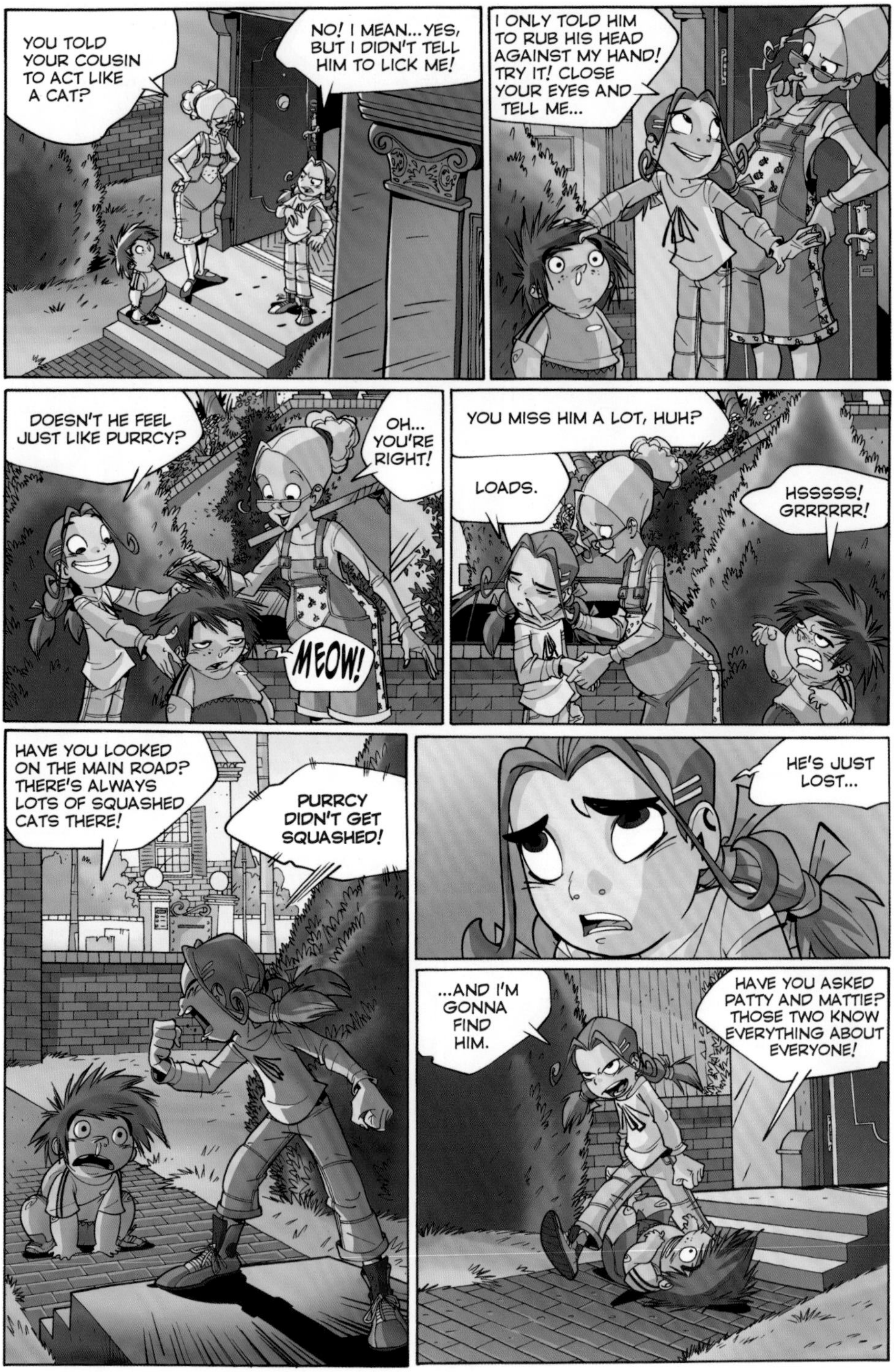
YOU TOLD YOUR COUSIN TO ACT LIKE A CAT?
NO! I MEAN...YES, BUT I DIDN'T TELL HIM TO LICK ME!
I ONLY TOLD HIM TO RUB HIS HEAD AGAINST MY HAND! TRY IT! CLOSE YOUR EYES AND TELL ME...
DOESN'T HE FEEL JUST LIKE PURRCY?
OH... YOU'RE RIGHT!
MEOW!
YOU MISS HIM A LOT, HUH?
LOADS.
HSSSSS! GRRRRRR!
HAVE YOU LOOKED ON THE MAIN ROAD? THERE'S ALWAYS LOTS OF SQUASHED CATS THERE!
PURRCY DIDN'T GET SQUASHED!
HE'S JUST LOST...
...AND I'M GONNA FIND HIM.
HAVE YOU ASKED PATTY AND MATTIE? THOSE TWO KNOW EVERYTHING ABOUT EVERYONE!

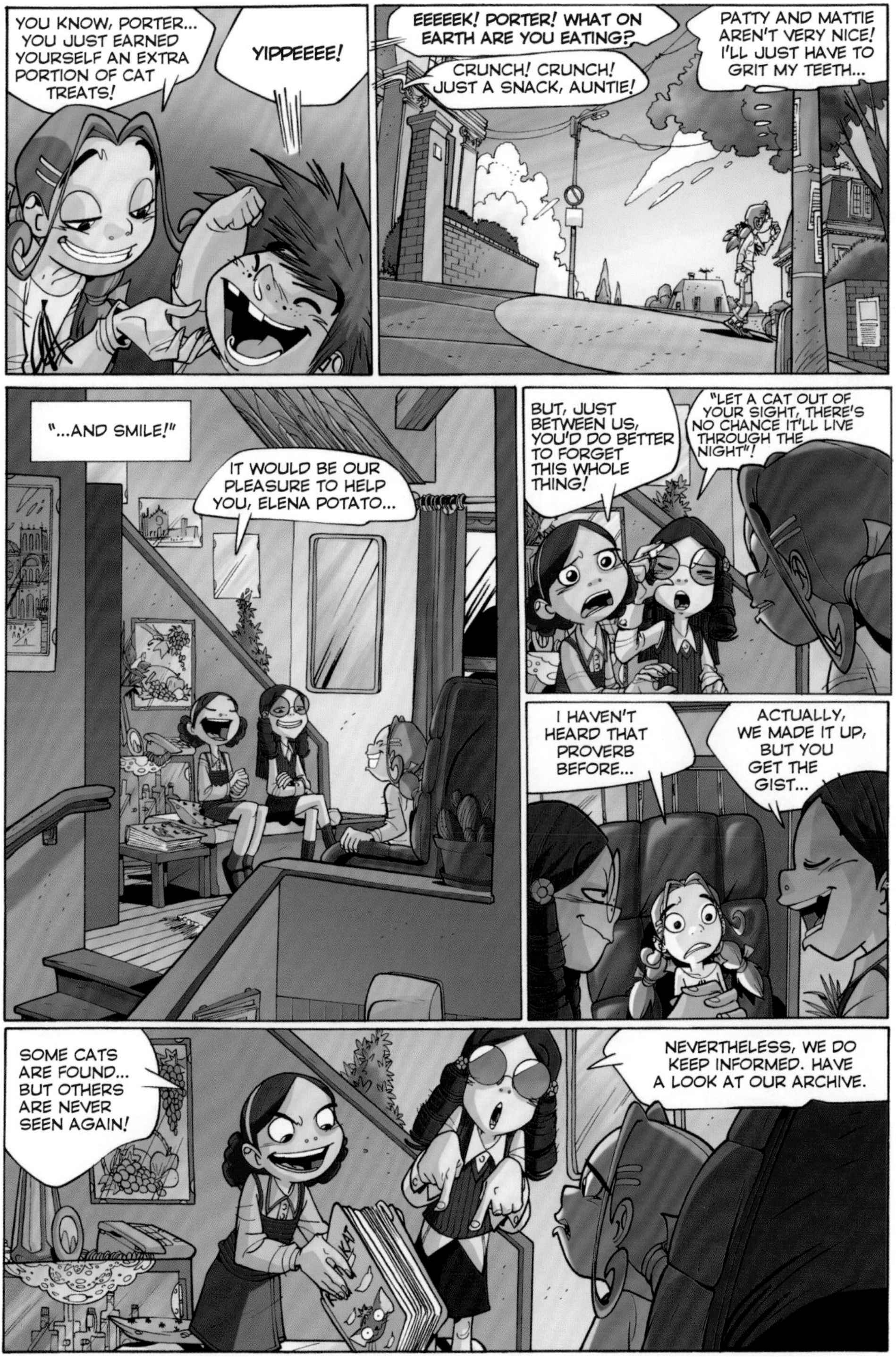
YOU KNOW, PORTER... YOU JUST EARNED YOURSELF AN EXTRA PORTION OF CAT TREATS!
YIPPEEEE!
EEEEEK! PORTER! WHAT ON EARTH ARE YOU EATING?
CRUNCH! CRUNCH! JUST A SNACK, AUNTIE!
PATTY AND MATTIE AREN'T VERY NICE! I'LL JUST HAVE TO GRIT MY TEETH...
"...AND SMILE!"
IT WOULD BE OUR PLEASURE TO HELP YOU, ELENA POTATO...
BUT, JUST BETWEEN US, YOU'D DO BETTER TO FORGET THIS WHOLE THING!
"LET A CAT OUT OF YOUR SIGHT, THERE'S NO CHANCE IT'LL LIVE THROUGH THE NIGHT"!
I HAVEN'T HEARD THAT PROVERB BEFORE...
ACTUALLY, WE MADE IT UP, BUT YOU GET THE GIST...
SOME CATS ARE FOUND... BUT OTHERS ARE NEVER SEEN AGAIN!
NEVERTHELESS, WE DO KEEP INFORMED. HAVE A LOOK AT OUR ARCHIVE.

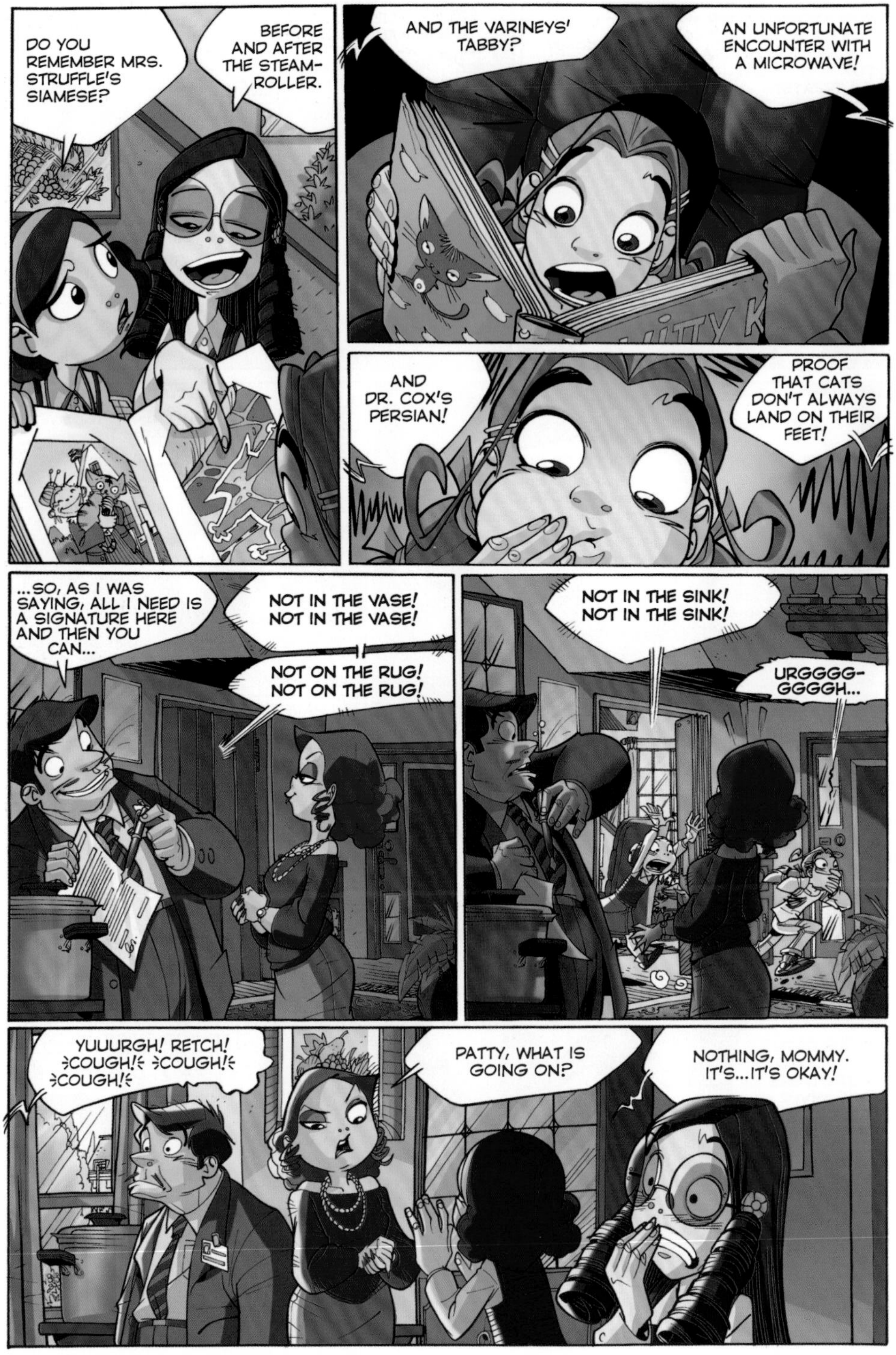
DO YOU REMEMBER MRS. STRUFFLE'S SIAMESE?
BEFORE AND AFTER THE STEAM-ROLLER.
AND THE VARINEYS' TABBY?
AN UNFORTUNATE ENCOUNTER WITH A MICROWAVE!
AND DR. COX'S PERSIAN!
PROOF THAT CATS DON'T ALWAYS LAND ON THEIR FEET!
...SO, AS I WAS SAYING, ALL I NEED IS A SIGNATURE HERE AND THEN YOU CAN...
NOT IN THE VASE! NOT IN THE VASE!
NOT ON THE RUG! NOT ON THE RUG!
NOT IN THE SINK! NOT IN THE SINK!
URGGGG-GGGGH...
YUUURGH! RETCH! COUGH! COUGH! COUGH!
PATTY, WHAT IS GOING ON?
NOTHING, MOMMY. IT'S...IT'S OKAY!

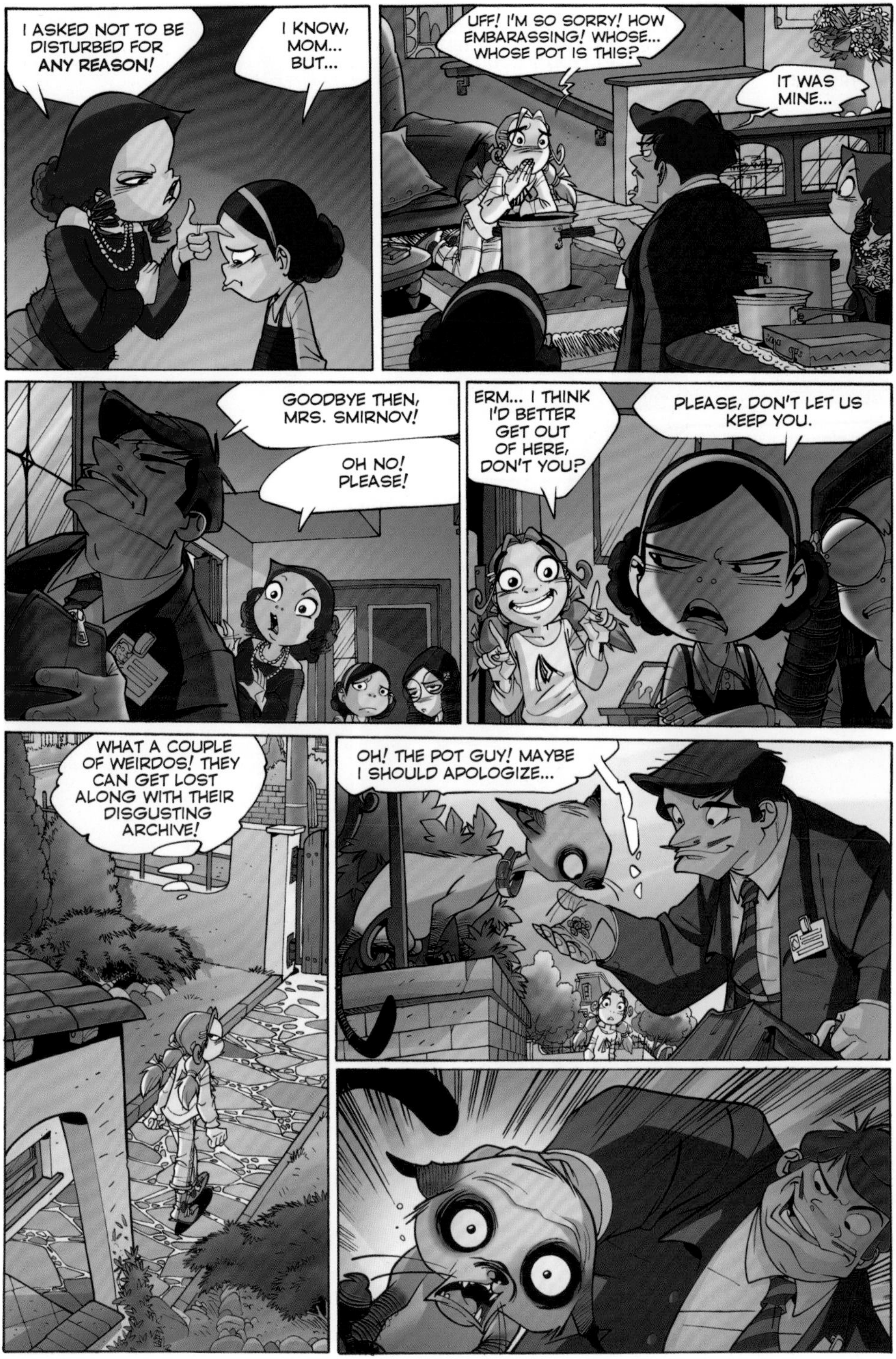
I ASKED NOT TO BE DISTURBED FOR ANY REASON!
I KNOW, MOM... BUT...
UFF! I'M SO SORRY! HOW EMBARASSING! WHOSE... WHOSE POT IS THIS?
IT WAS MINE...
GOODBYE THEN, MRS. SMIRNOV!
OH NO! PLEASE!
ERM... I THINK I'D BETTER GET OUT OF HERE, DON'T YOU?
PLEASE, DON'T LET US KEEP YOU.
WHAT A COUPLE OF WEIRDOS! THEY CAN GET LOST ALONG WITH THEIR DISGUSTING ARCHIVE!
OH! THE POT GUY! MAYBE I SHOULD APOLOGIZE...

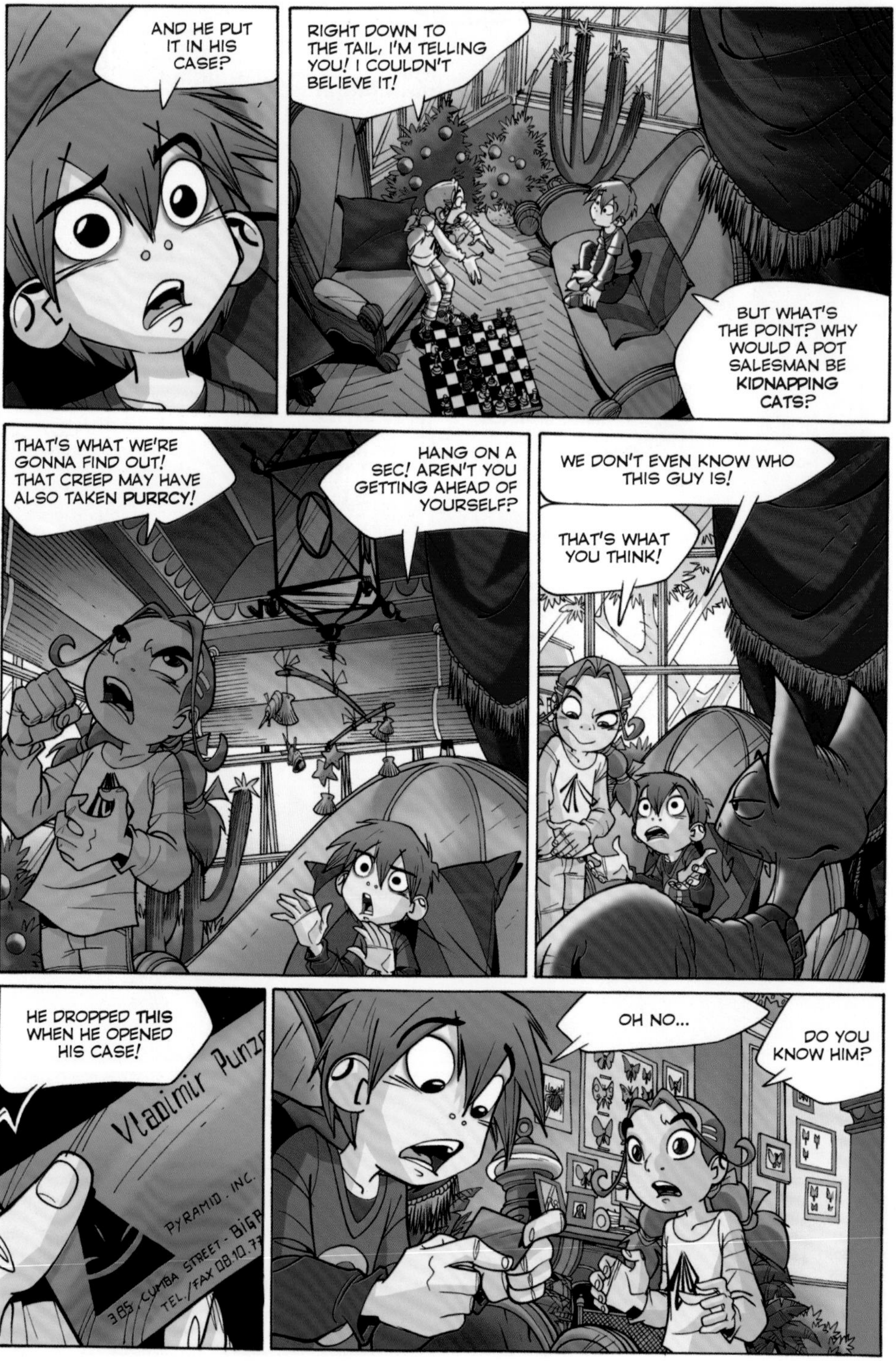
AND HE PUT IT IN HIS CASE?
RIGHT DOWN TO THE TAIL, I'M TELLING YOU! I COULDN'T BELIEVE IT!
BUT WHAT'S THE POINT? WHY WOULD A POT SALESMAN BE **KIDNAPPING** CATS?
THAT'S WHAT WE'RE GONNA FIND OUT! THAT CREEP MAY HAVE ALSO TAKEN **PURRCY**!
HANG ON A SEC! AREN'T YOU GETTING AHEAD OF YOURSELF?
WE DON'T EVEN KNOW WHO THIS GUY IS!
THAT'S WHAT YOU THINK!
HE DROPPED **THIS** WHEN HE OPENED HIS CASE!
Vladimir Punz
PYRAMID . INC.
3.65, CUMBA STREET - BIGR
TEL./FAX 08.10.77
OH NO...
DO YOU KNOW HIM?

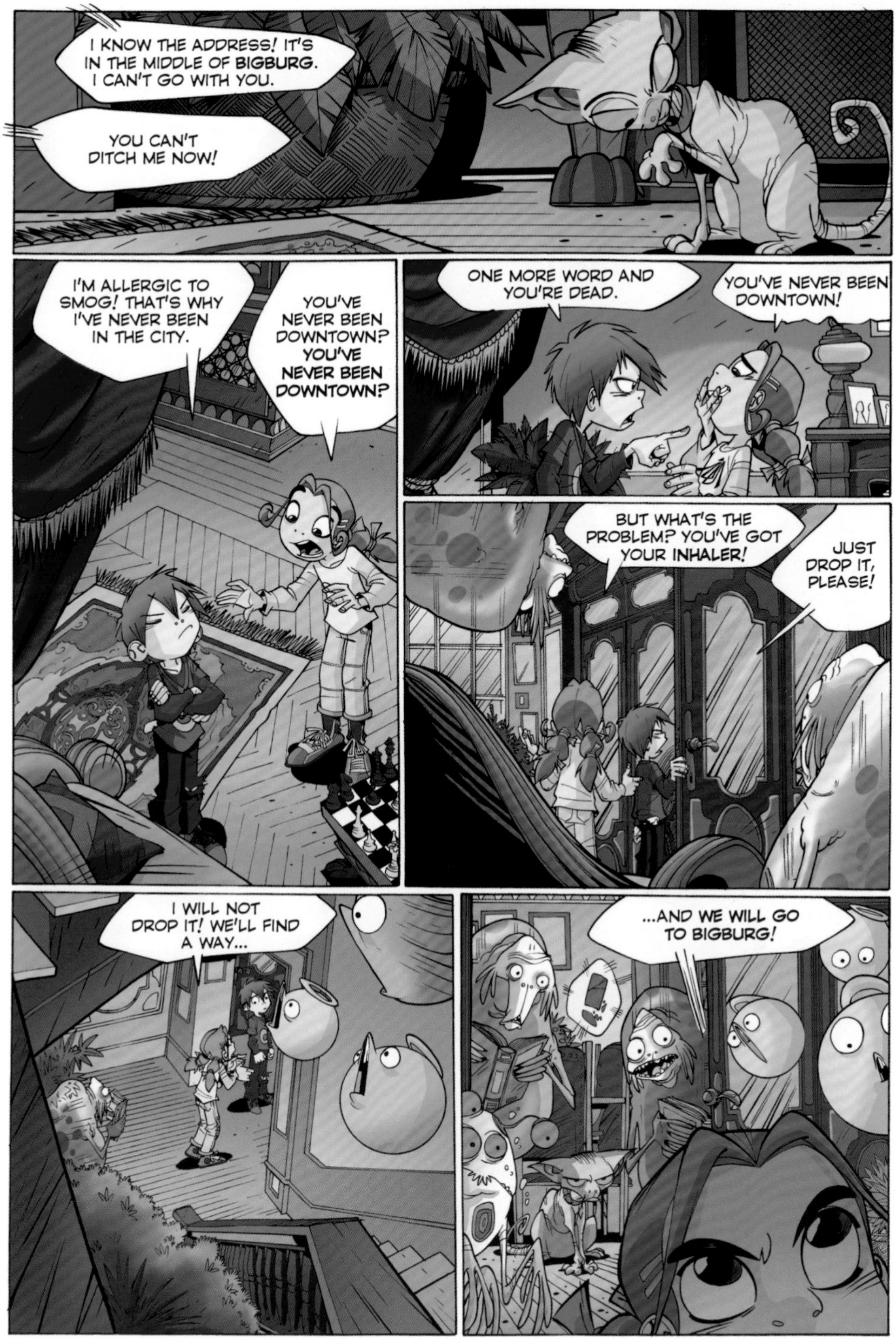
I KNOW THE ADDRESS! IT'S IN THE MIDDLE OF BIGBURG. I CAN'T GO WITH YOU.
YOU CAN'T DITCH ME NOW!
I'M ALLERGIC TO SMOG! THAT'S WHY I'VE NEVER BEEN IN THE CITY.
YOU'VE NEVER BEEN DOWNTOWN? YOU'VE NEVER BEEN DOWNTOWN?
ONE MORE WORD AND YOU'RE DEAD.
YOU'VE NEVER BEEN DOWNTOWN!
BUT WHAT'S THE PROBLEM? YOU'VE GOT YOUR INHALER!
JUST DROP IT, PLEASE!
I WILL NOT DROP IT! WE'LL FIND A WAY...
...AND WE WILL GO TO BIGBURG!

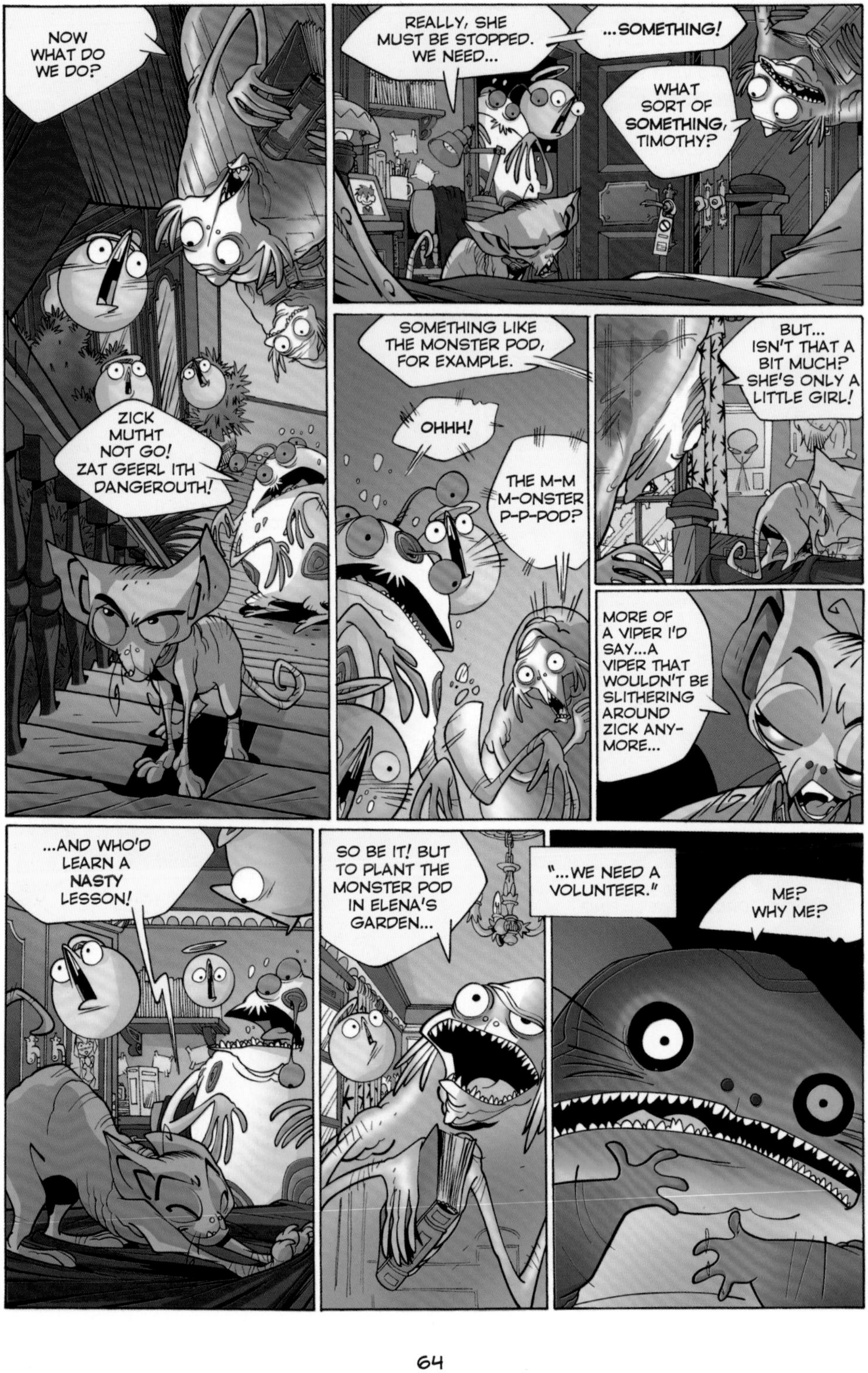
NOW WHAT DO WE DO?
ZICK MUTHT NOT GO! ZAT GEERL ITH DANGEROUTH!
REALLY, SHE MUST BE STOPPED. WE NEED...
...SOMETHING!
WHAT SORT OF SOMETHING, TIMOTHY?
SOMETHING LIKE THE MONSTER POD, FOR EXAMPLE.
OHHH!
THE M-M M-ONSTER P-P-POD?
BUT... ISN'T THAT A BIT MUCH? SHE'S ONLY A LITTLE GIRL!
MORE OF A VIPER I'D SAY...A VIPER THAT WOULDN'T BE SLITHERING AROUND ZICK ANY-MORE...
...AND WHO'D LEARN A NASTY LESSON!
SO BE IT! BUT TO PLANT THE MONSTER POD IN ELENA'S GARDEN...
"...WE NEED A VOLUNTEER."
ME? WHY ME?

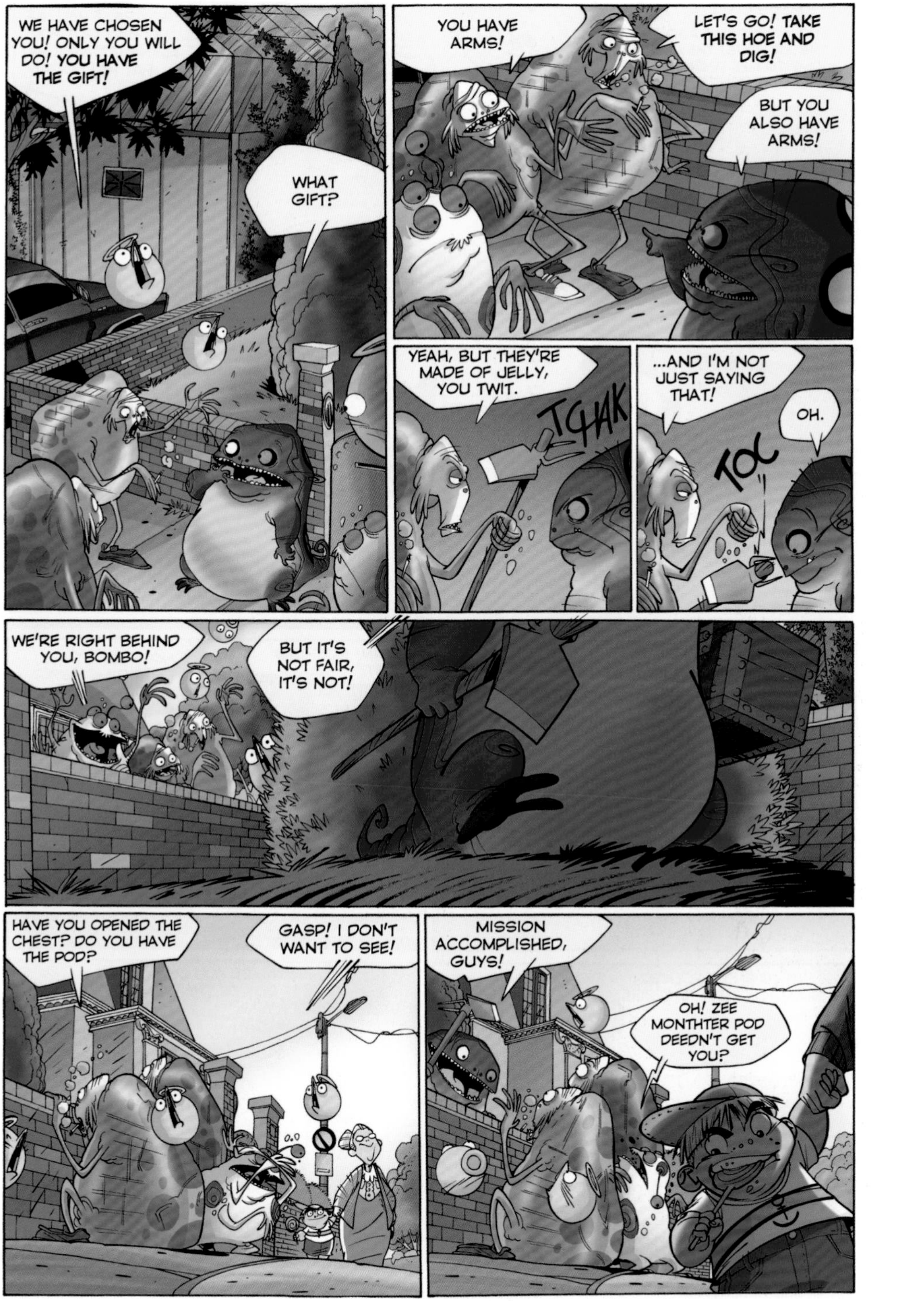
WE HAVE CHOSEN YOU! ONLY YOU WILL DO! YOU HAVE THE GIFT!
WHAT GIFT?
YOU HAVE ARMS!
LET'S GO! TAKE THIS HOE AND DIG!
BUT YOU ALSO HAVE ARMS!
YEAH, BUT THEY'RE MADE OF JELLY, YOU TWIT.
TCHAK
...AND I'M NOT JUST SAYING THAT!
OH.
TOC
WE'RE RIGHT BEHIND YOU, BOMBO!
BUT IT'S NOT FAIR, IT'S NOT!
HAVE YOU OPENED THE CHEST? DO YOU HAVE THE POD?
GASP! I DON'T WANT TO SEE!
MISSION ACCOMPLISHED, GUYS!
OH! ZEE MONTHTER POD DEEDN'T GET YOU?

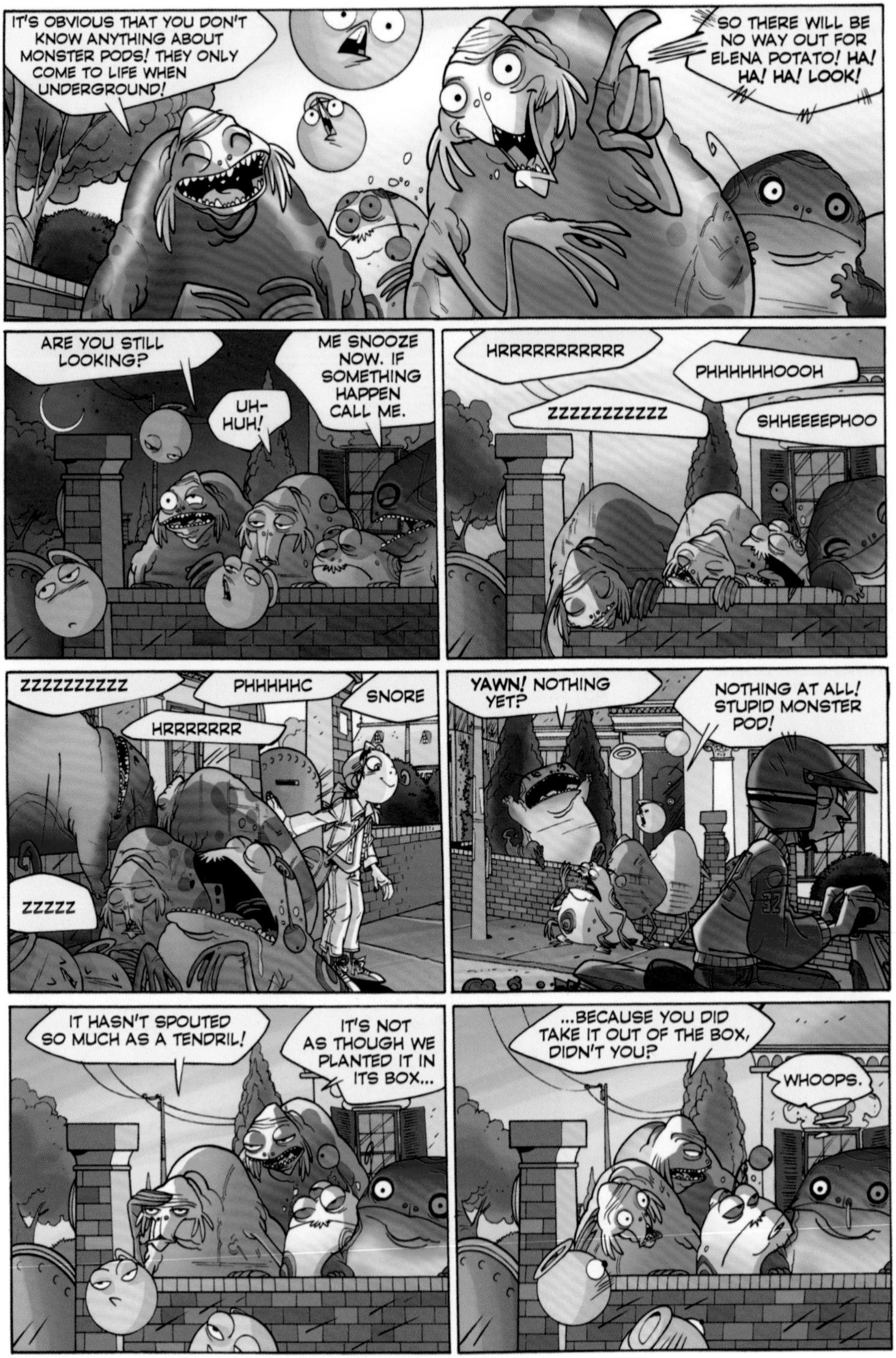
IT'S OBVIOUS THAT YOU DON'T KNOW ANYTHING ABOUT MONSTER PODS! THEY ONLY COME TO LIFE WHEN UNDERGROUND!
SO THERE WILL BE NO WAY OUT FOR ELENA POTATO! HA! HA! HA! LOOK!
ARE YOU STILL LOOKING?
UH-HUH!
ME SNOOZE NOW. IF SOMETHING HAPPEN CALL ME.
HRRRRRRRRRRR
PHHHHHHOOOH
ZZZZZZZZZZZ
SHHEEEEPHOO
ZZZZZZZZZZ
PHHHHHC
SNORE
HRRRRRRR
ZZZZZ
YAWN! NOTHING YET?
NOTHING AT ALL! STUPID MONSTER POD!
IT HASN'T SPOUTED SO MUCH AS A TENDRIL!
IT'S NOT AS THOUGH WE PLANTED IT IN ITS BOX...
...BECAUSE YOU DID TAKE IT OUT OF THE BOX, DIDN'T YOU?
WHOOPS.

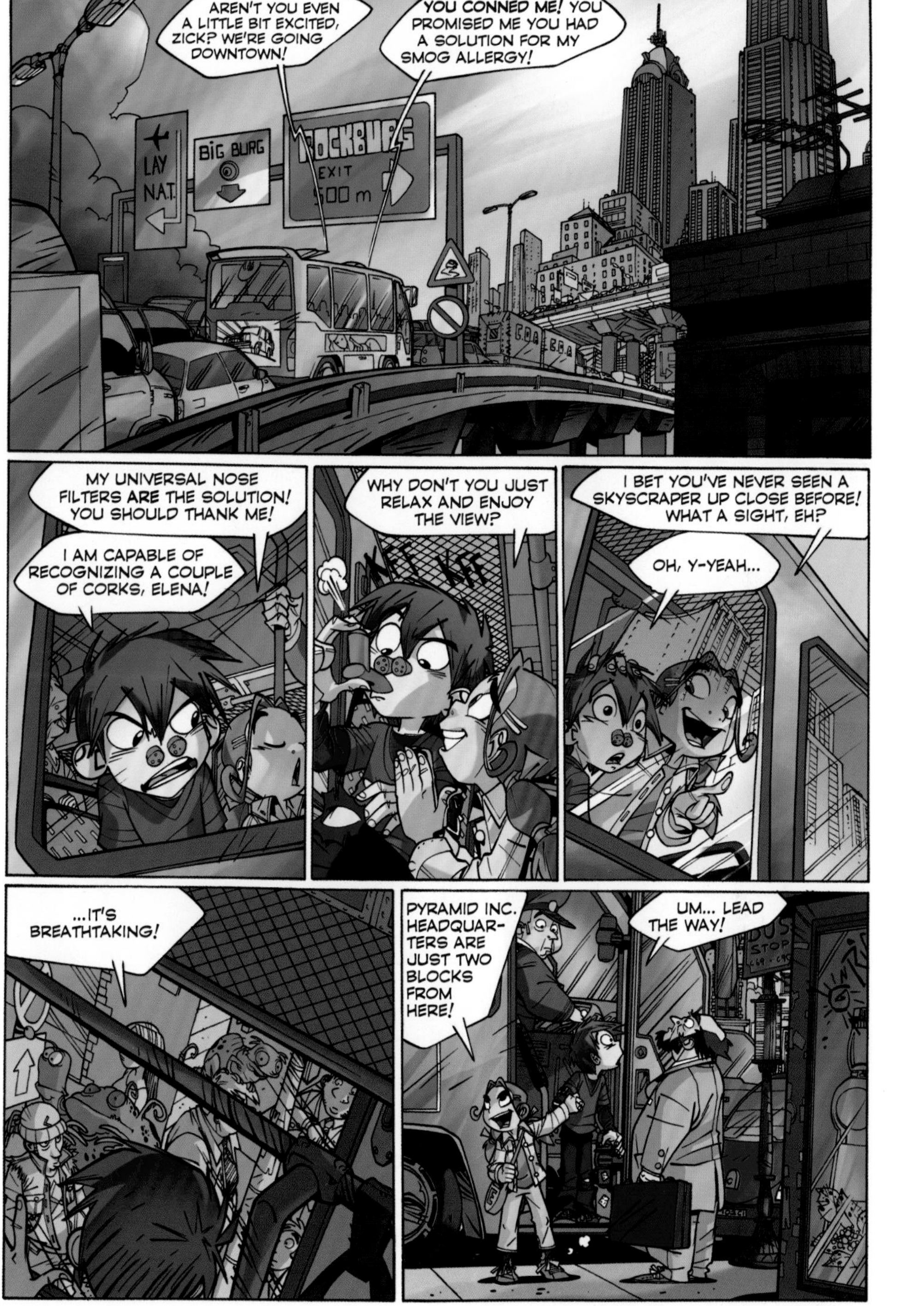

AREN'T YOU EVEN A LITTLE BIT EXCITED, ZICK? WE'RE GOING DOWNTOWN!
YOU CONNED ME! YOU PROMISED ME YOU HAD A SOLUTION FOR MY SMOG ALLERGY!
LAY N.A.T.
BIG BURG
EXIT
MY UNIVERSAL NOSE FILTERS ARE THE SOLUTION! YOU SHOULD THANK ME!
I AM CAPABLE OF RECOGNIZING A COUPLE OF CORKS, ELENA!
WHY DON'T YOU JUST RELAX AND ENJOY THE VIEW?
KFF KFF
I BET YOU'VE NEVER SEEN A SKYSCRAPER UP CLOSE BEFORE! WHAT A SIGHT, EH?
OH, Y-YEAH...
...IT'S BREATHTAKING!
PYRAMID INC. HEADQUARTERS ARE JUST TWO BLOCKS FROM HERE!
UM... LEAD THE WAY!
BUS STOP

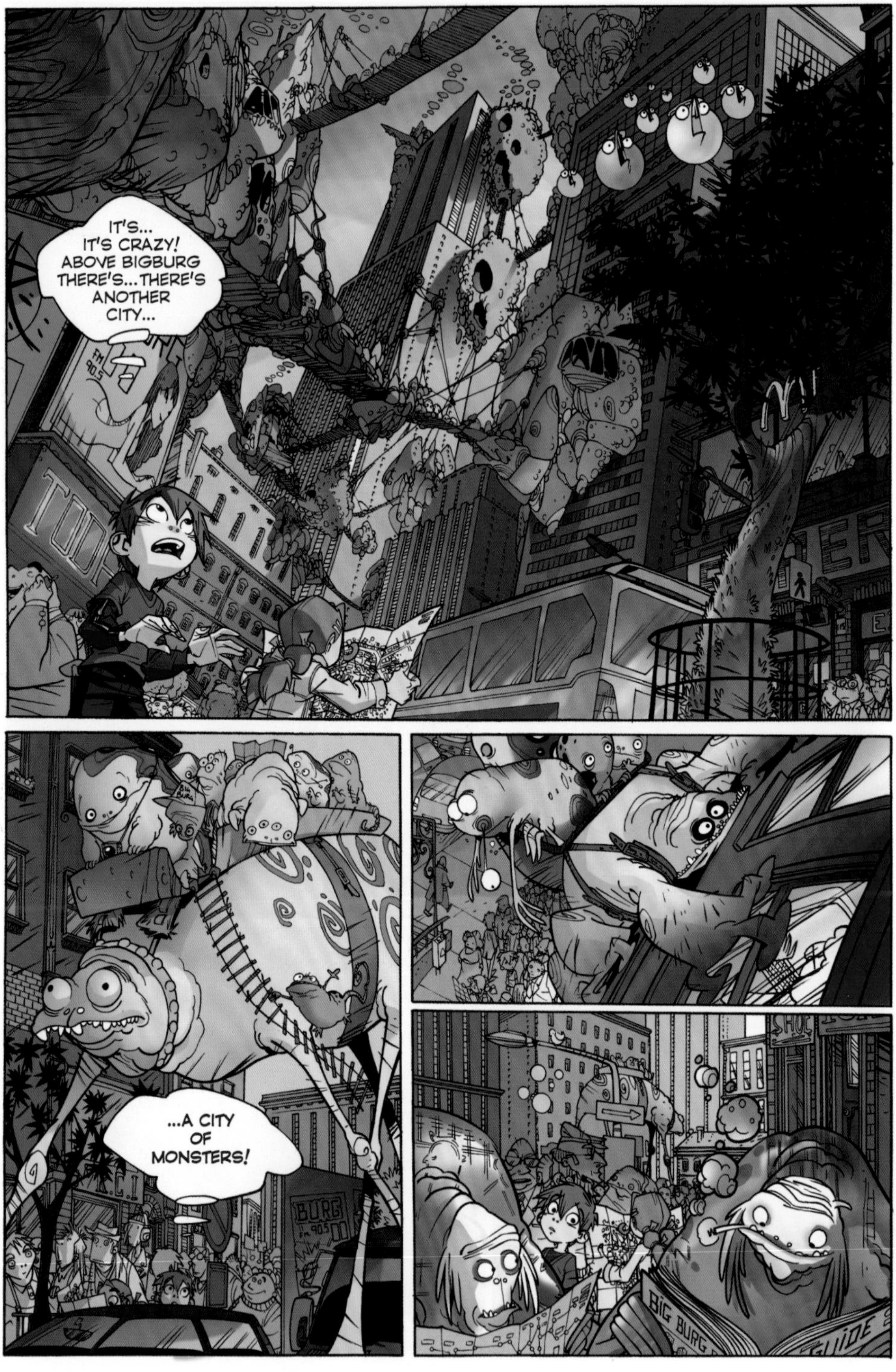
IT'S... IT'S CRAZY! ABOVE BIGBURG THERE'S...THERE'S ANOTHER CITY...
...A CITY OF MONSTERS!

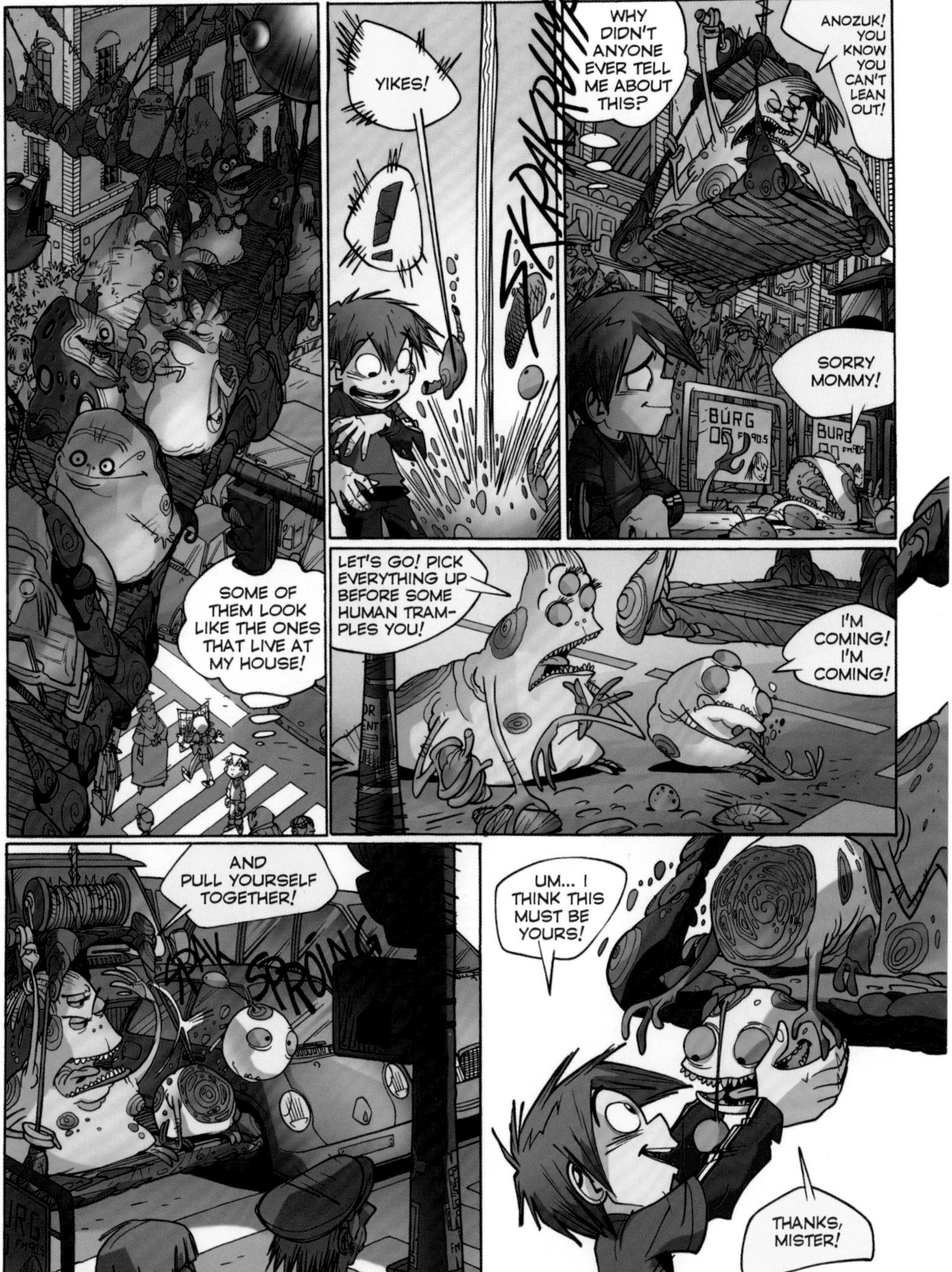
SOME OF THEM LOOK LIKE THE ONES THAT LIVE AT MY HOUSE!
YIKES!
!
WHY DIDN'T ANYONE EVER TELL ME ABOUT THIS?
ANOZUK! YOU KNOW YOU CAN'T LEAN OUT!
SORRY MOMMY!
BURG FM 90.5
LET'S GO! PICK EVERYTHING UP BEFORE SOME HUMAN TRAMPLES YOU!
I'M COMING! I'M COMING!
AND PULL YOURSELF TOGETHER!
SPROING
UM... I THINK THIS MUST BE YOURS!
THANKS, MISTER!

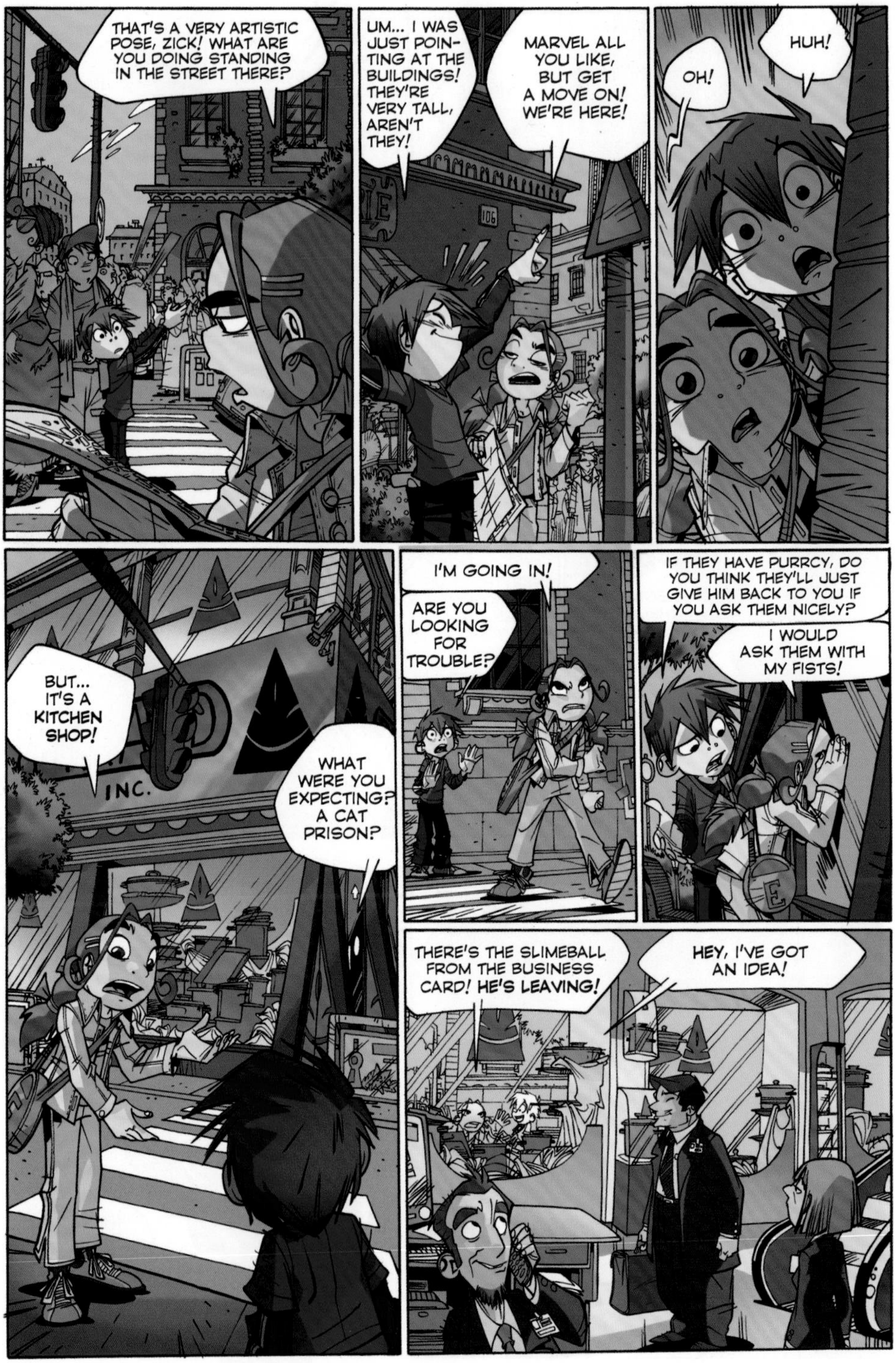
THAT'S A VERY ARTISTIC POSE, ZICK! WHAT ARE YOU DOING STANDING IN THE STREET THERE?
UM... I WAS JUST POINTING AT THE BUILDINGS! THEY'RE VERY TALL, AREN'T THEY!
MARVEL ALL YOU LIKE, BUT GET A MOVE ON! WE'RE HERE!
106
OH!
HUH!
BUT... IT'S A KITCHEN SHOP!
INC.
WHAT WERE YOU EXPECTING? A CAT PRISON?
I'M GOING IN!
ARE YOU LOOKING FOR TROUBLE?
IF THEY HAVE PURRCY, DO YOU THINK THEY'LL JUST GIVE HIM BACK TO YOU IF YOU ASK THEM NICELY?
I WOULD ASK THEM WITH MY FISTS!
THERE'S THE SLIMEBALL FROM THE BUSINESS CARD! HE'S LEAVING!
HEY, I'VE GOT AN IDEA!

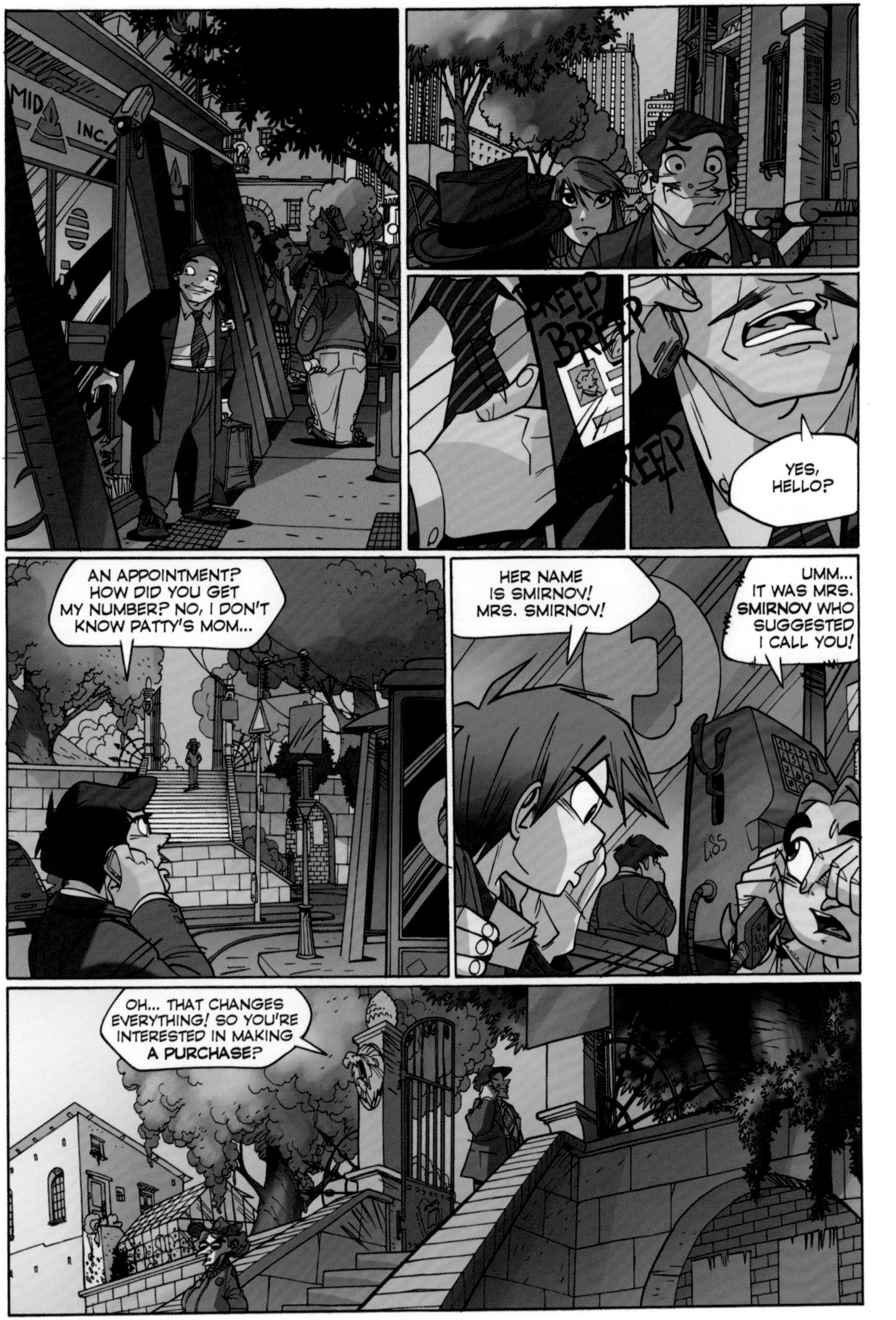
MID
INC.
BREEP
BREEP
BREEP
YES, HELLO?
AN APPOINTMENT? HOW DID YOU GET MY NUMBER? NO, I DON'T KNOW PATTY'S MOM...
HER NAME IS SMIRNOV! MRS. SMIRNOV!
UMM... IT WAS MRS. SMIRNOV WHO SUGGESTED I CALL YOU!
OH... THAT CHANGES EVERYTHING! SO YOU'RE INTERESTED IN MAKING A PURCHASE?

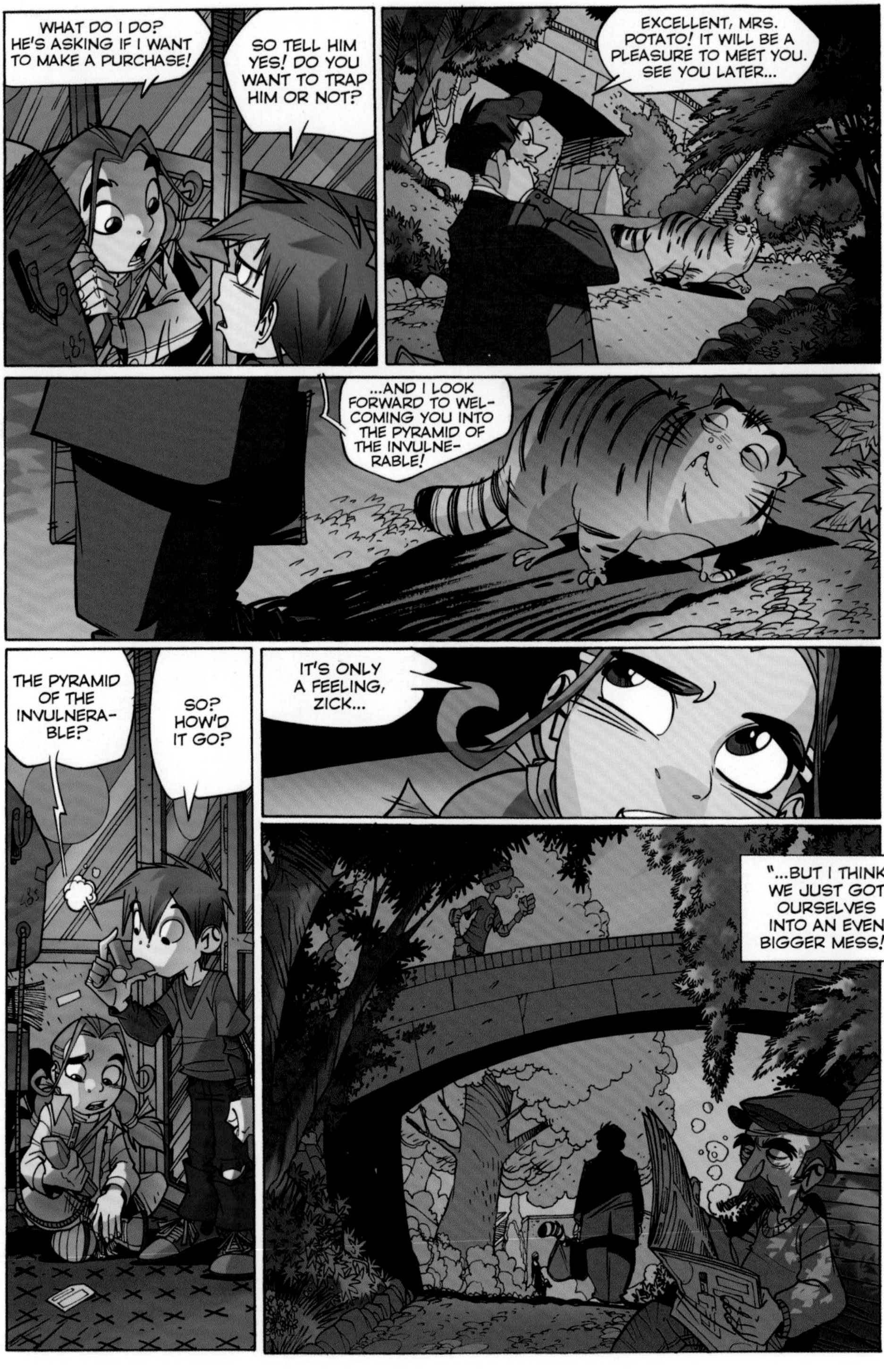
WHAT DO I DO? HE'S ASKING IF I WANT TO MAKE A PURCHASE!
SO TELL HIM YES! DO YOU WANT TO TRAP HIM OR NOT?
EXCELLENT, MRS. POTATO! IT WILL BE A PLEASURE TO MEET YOU. SEE YOU LATER...
...AND I LOOK FORWARD TO WELCOMING YOU INTO THE PYRAMID OF THE INVULNERABLE!
THE PYRAMID OF THE INVULNERABLE?
SO? HOW'D IT GO?
IT'S ONLY A FEELING, ZICK...
"...BUT I THINK WE JUST GOT OURSELVES INTO AN EVEN BIGGER MESS!"

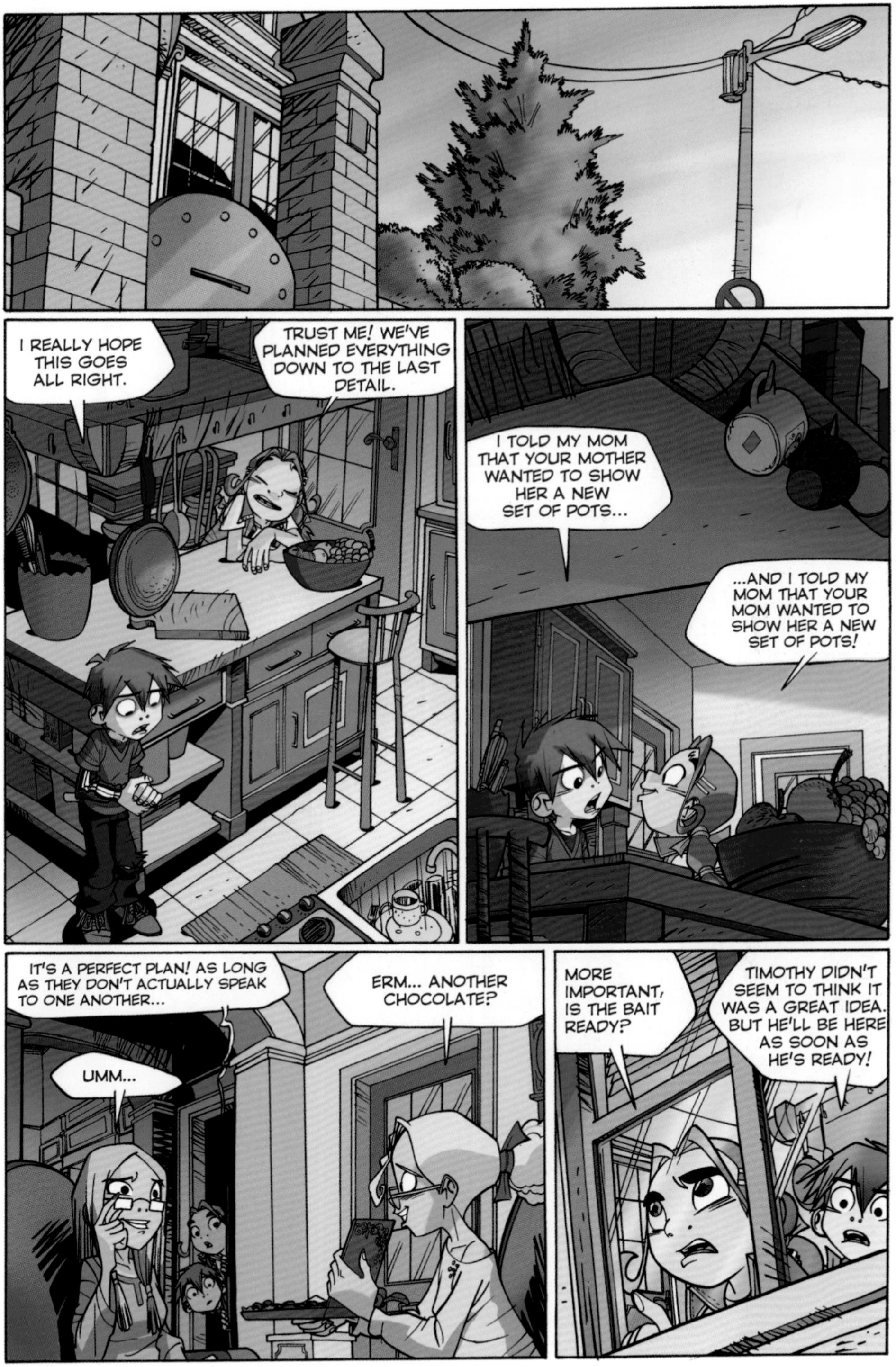
I REALLY HOPE THIS GOES ALL RIGHT.
TRUST ME! WE'VE PLANNED EVERYTHING DOWN TO THE LAST DETAIL.
I TOLD MY MOM THAT YOUR MOTHER WANTED TO SHOW HER A NEW SET OF POTS...
...AND I TOLD MY MOM THAT YOUR MOM WANTED TO SHOW HER A NEW SET OF POTS!
IT'S A PERFECT PLAN! AS LONG AS THEY DON'T ACTUALLY SPEAK TO ONE ANOTHER...
ERM... ANOTHER CHOCOLATE?
UMM...
MORE IMPORTANT, IS THE BAIT READY?
TIMOTHY DIDN'T SEEM TO THINK IT WAS A GREAT IDEA. BUT HE'LL BE HERE AS SOON AS HE'S READY!

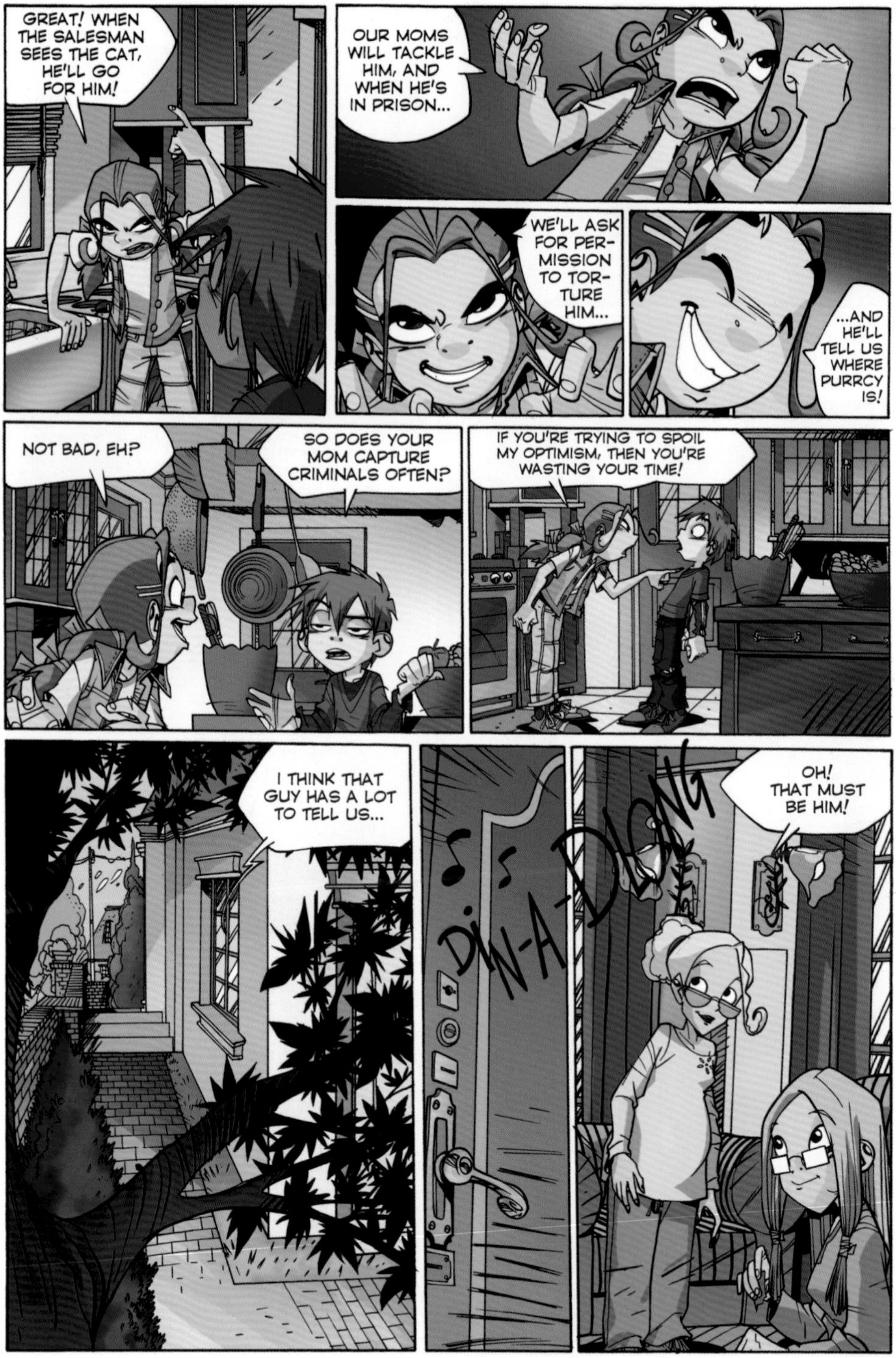
GREAT! WHEN THE SALESMAN SEES THE CAT, HE'LL GO FOR HIM!
OUR MOMS WILL TACKLE HIM, AND WHEN HE'S IN PRISON...
WE'LL ASK FOR PERMISSION TO TORTURE HIM...
...AND HE'LL TELL US WHERE PURRCY IS!
NOT BAD, EH?
SO DOES YOUR MOM CAPTURE CRIMINALS OFTEN?
IF YOU'RE TRYING TO SPOIL MY OPTIMISM, THEN YOU'RE WASTING YOUR TIME!
I THINK THAT GUY HAS A LOT TO TELL US...
DIN-A-DLONG
OH! THAT MUST BE HIM!

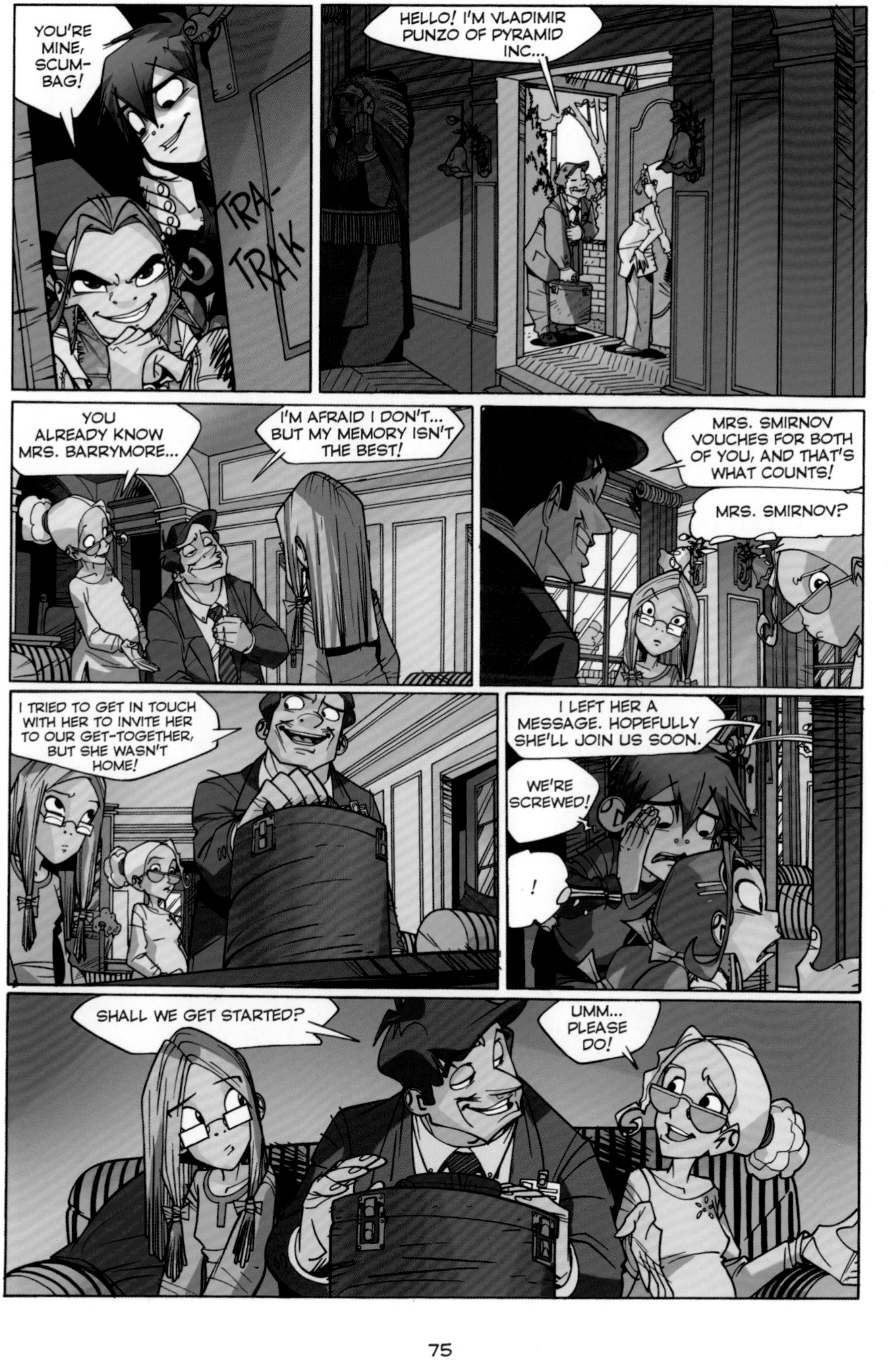
YOU'RE MINE, SCUM-BAG!
TRA-TRAK
HELLO! I'M VLADIMIR PUNZO OF PYRAMID INC...
YOU ALREADY KNOW MRS. BARRYMORE...
I'M AFRAID I DON'T... BUT MY MEMORY ISN'T THE BEST!
MRS. SMIRNOV VOUCHES FOR BOTH OF YOU, AND THAT'S WHAT COUNTS!
MRS. SMIRNOV?
I TRIED TO GET IN TOUCH WITH HER TO INVITE HER TO OUR GET-TOGETHER, BUT SHE WASN'T HOME!
I LEFT HER A MESSAGE. HOPEFULLY SHE'LL JOIN US SOON.
WE'RE SCREWED!
!
SHALL WE GET STARTED?
UMM... PLEASE DO!

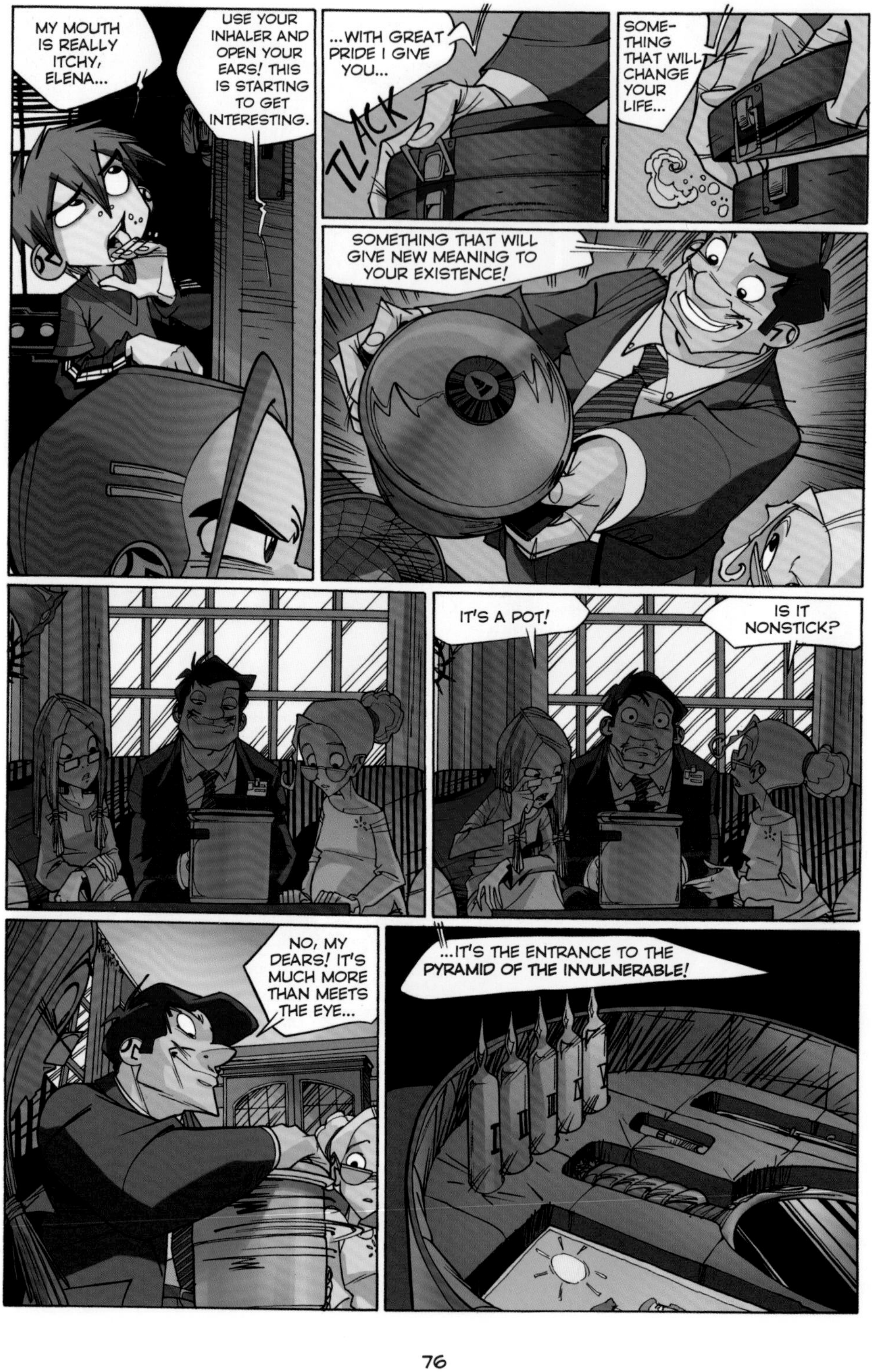

MY MOUTH IS REALLY ITCHY, ELENA...
USE YOUR INHALER AND OPEN YOUR EARS! THIS IS STARTING TO GET INTERESTING.
...WITH GREAT PRIDE I GIVE YOU...
TZACK
SOME-THING THAT WILL CHANGE YOUR LIFE...
SOMETHING THAT WILL GIVE NEW MEANING TO YOUR EXISTENCE!
IT'S A POT!
IS IT NONSTICK?
NO, MY DEARS! IT'S MUCH MORE THAN MEETS THE EYE...
...IT'S THE ENTRANCE TO THE PYRAMID OF THE INVULNERABLE!

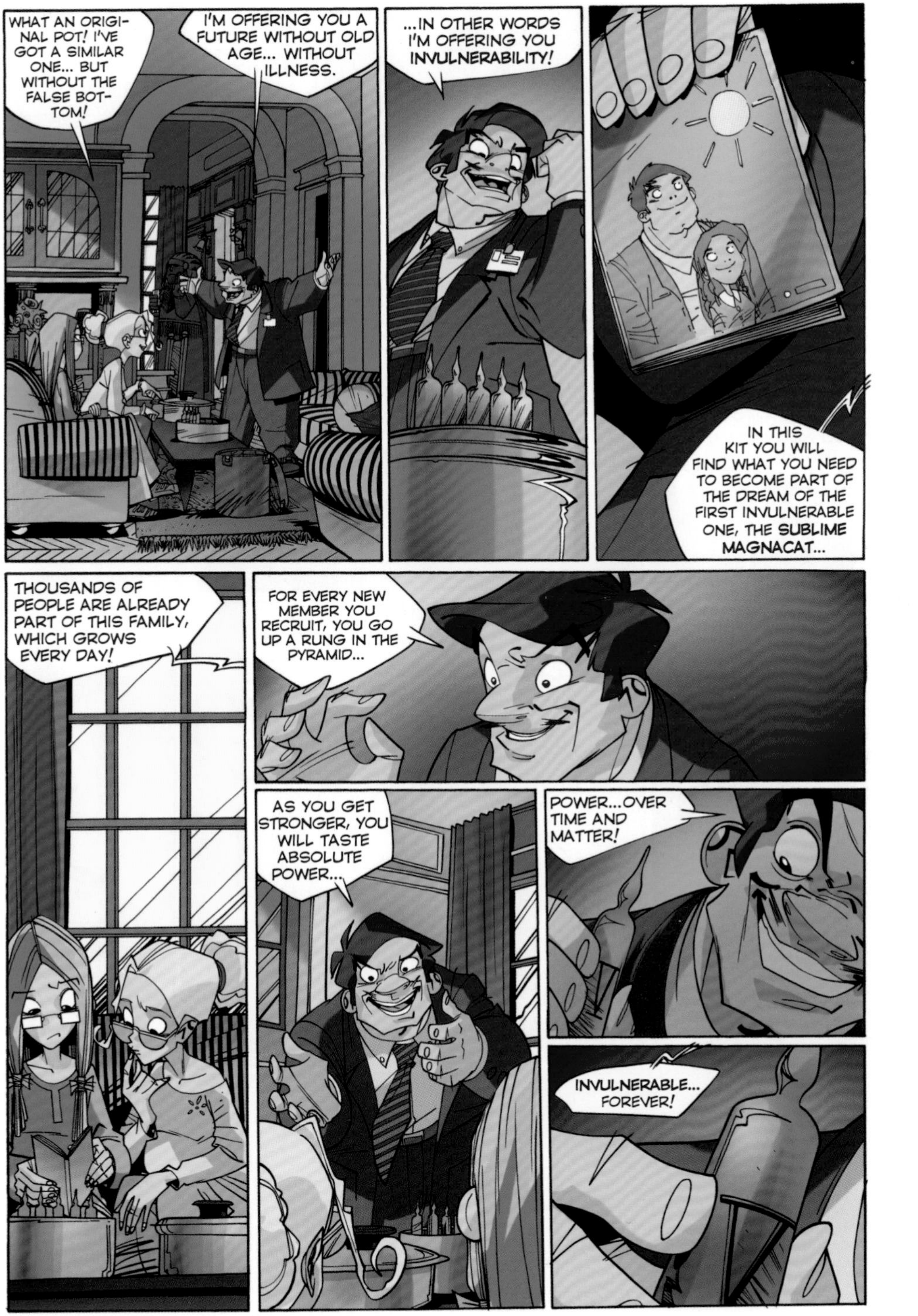
WHAT AN ORIGINAL POT! I'VE GOT A SIMILAR ONE... BUT WITHOUT THE FALSE BOTTOM!
I'M OFFERING YOU A FUTURE WITHOUT OLD AGE... WITHOUT ILLNESS.
...IN OTHER WORDS I'M OFFERING YOU INVULNERABILITY!
IN THIS KIT YOU WILL FIND WHAT YOU NEED TO BECOME PART OF THE DREAM OF THE FIRST INVULNERABLE ONE, THE SUBLIME MAGNACAT...
THOUSANDS OF PEOPLE ARE ALREADY PART OF THIS FAMILY, WHICH GROWS EVERY DAY!
FOR EVERY NEW MEMBER YOU RECRUIT, YOU GO UP A RUNG IN THE PYRAMID...
AS YOU GET STRONGER, YOU WILL TASTE ABSOLUTE POWER...
POWER...OVER TIME AND MATTER!
INVULNERABLE... FOREVER!

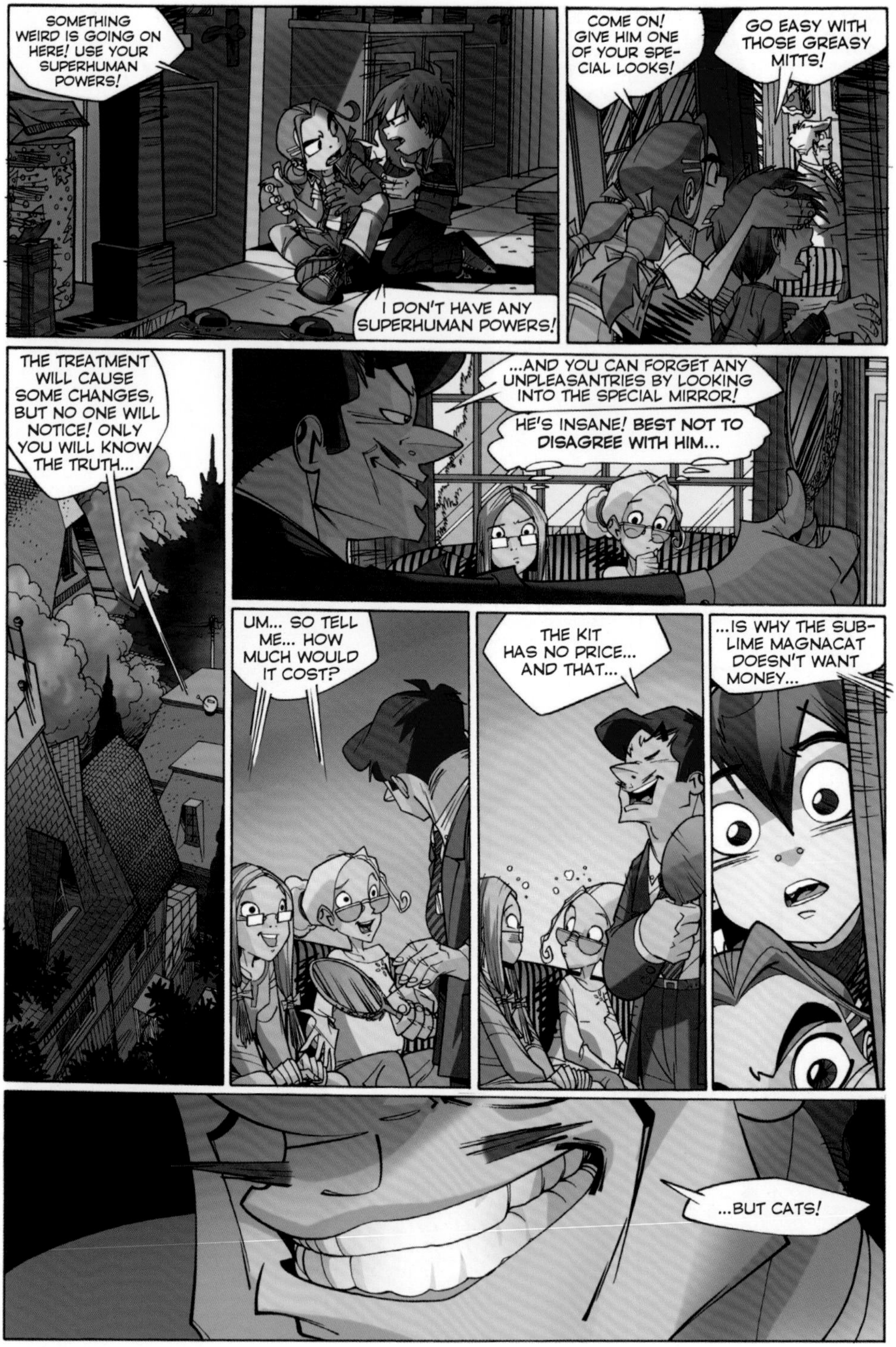
SOMETHING WEIRD IS GOING ON HERE! USE YOUR SUPERHUMAN POWERS!
I DON'T HAVE ANY SUPERHUMAN POWERS!
COME ON! GIVE HIM ONE OF YOUR SPE-CIAL LOOKS!
GO EASY WITH THOSE GREASY MITTS!
THE TREATMENT WILL CAUSE SOME CHANGES, BUT NO ONE WILL NOTICE! ONLY YOU WILL KNOW THE TRUTH...
...AND YOU CAN FORGET ANY UNPLEASANTRIES BY LOOKING INTO THE SPECIAL MIRROR!
HE'S INSANE! BEST NOT TO DISAGREE WITH HIM...
UM... SO TELL ME... HOW MUCH WOULD IT COST?
THE KIT HAS NO PRICE... AND THAT...
...IS WHY THE SUB-LIME MAGNACAT DOESN'T WANT MONEY...
...BUT CATS!

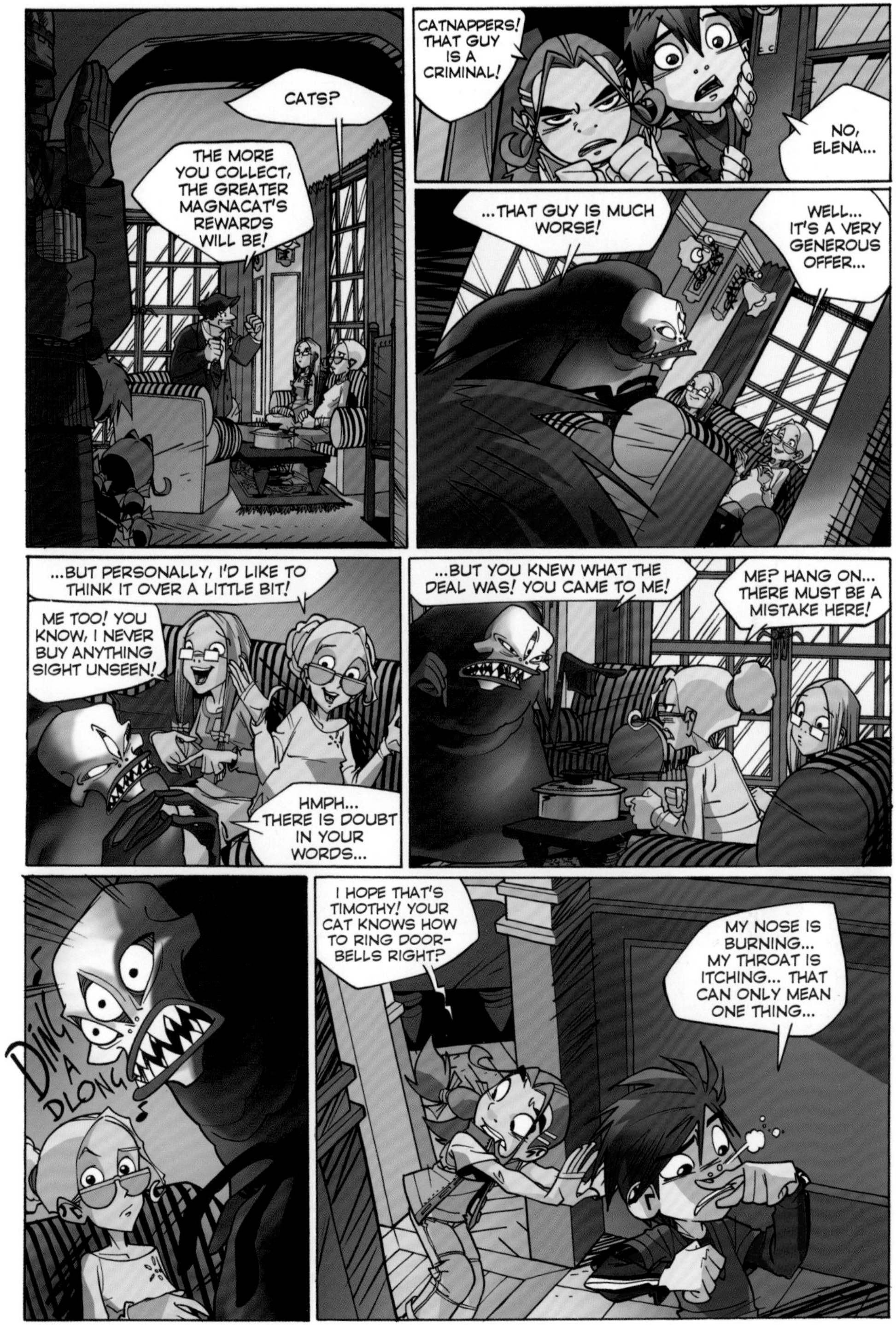
CATS?
THE MORE YOU COLLECT, THE GREATER MAGNACAT'S REWARDS WILL BE!
CATNAPPERS! THAT GUY IS A CRIMINAL!
NO, ELENA...
...THAT GUY IS MUCH WORSE!
WELL... IT'S A VERY GENEROUS OFFER...
...BUT PERSONALLY, I'D LIKE TO THINK IT OVER A LITTLE BIT!
ME TOO! YOU KNOW, I NEVER BUY ANYTHING SIGHT UNSEEN!
HMPH... THERE IS DOUBT IN YOUR WORDS...
...BUT YOU KNEW WHAT THE DEAL WAS! YOU CAME TO ME!
ME? HANG ON... THERE MUST BE A MISTAKE HERE!
DING A DLONG
I HOPE THAT'S TIMOTHY! YOUR CAT KNOWS HOW TO RING DOOR-BELLS RIGHT?
MY NOSE IS BURNING... MY THROAT IS ITCHING... THAT CAN ONLY MEAN ONE THING...

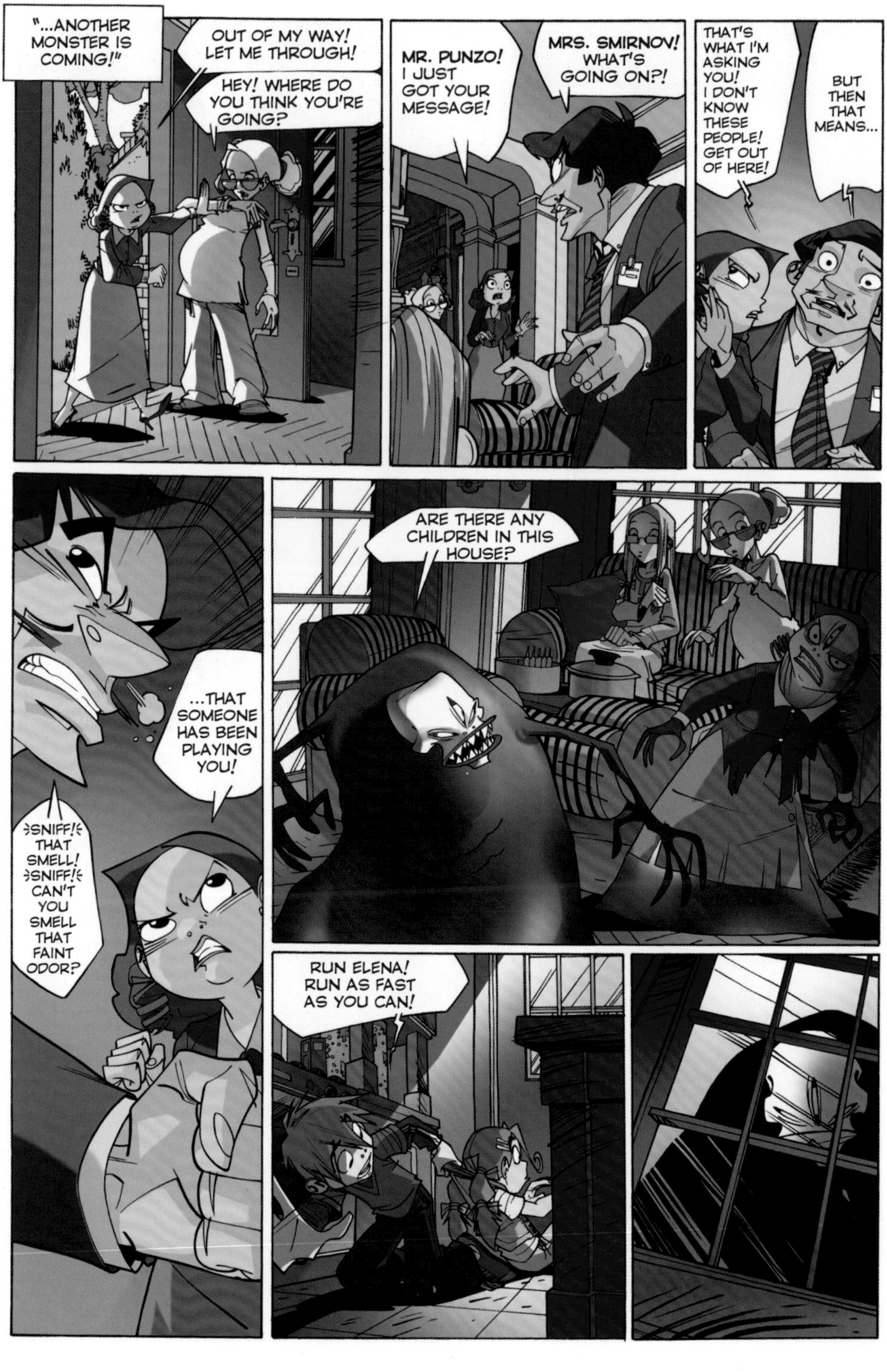
"...ANOTHER MONSTER IS COMING!"
OUT OF MY WAY! LET ME THROUGH!
HEY! WHERE DO YOU THINK YOU'RE GOING?
MR. PUNZO! I JUST GOT YOUR MESSAGE!
MRS. SMIRNOV! WHAT'S GOING ON?!
THAT'S WHAT I'M ASKING YOU! I DON'T KNOW THESE PEOPLE! GET OUT OF HERE!
BUT THEN THAT MEANS...
...THAT SOMEONE HAS BEEN PLAYING YOU!
SNIFF! THAT SMELL! SNIFF! CAN'T YOU SMELL THAT FAINT ODOR?
ARE THERE ANY CHILDREN IN THIS HOUSE?
RUN ELENA! RUN AS FAST AS YOU CAN!

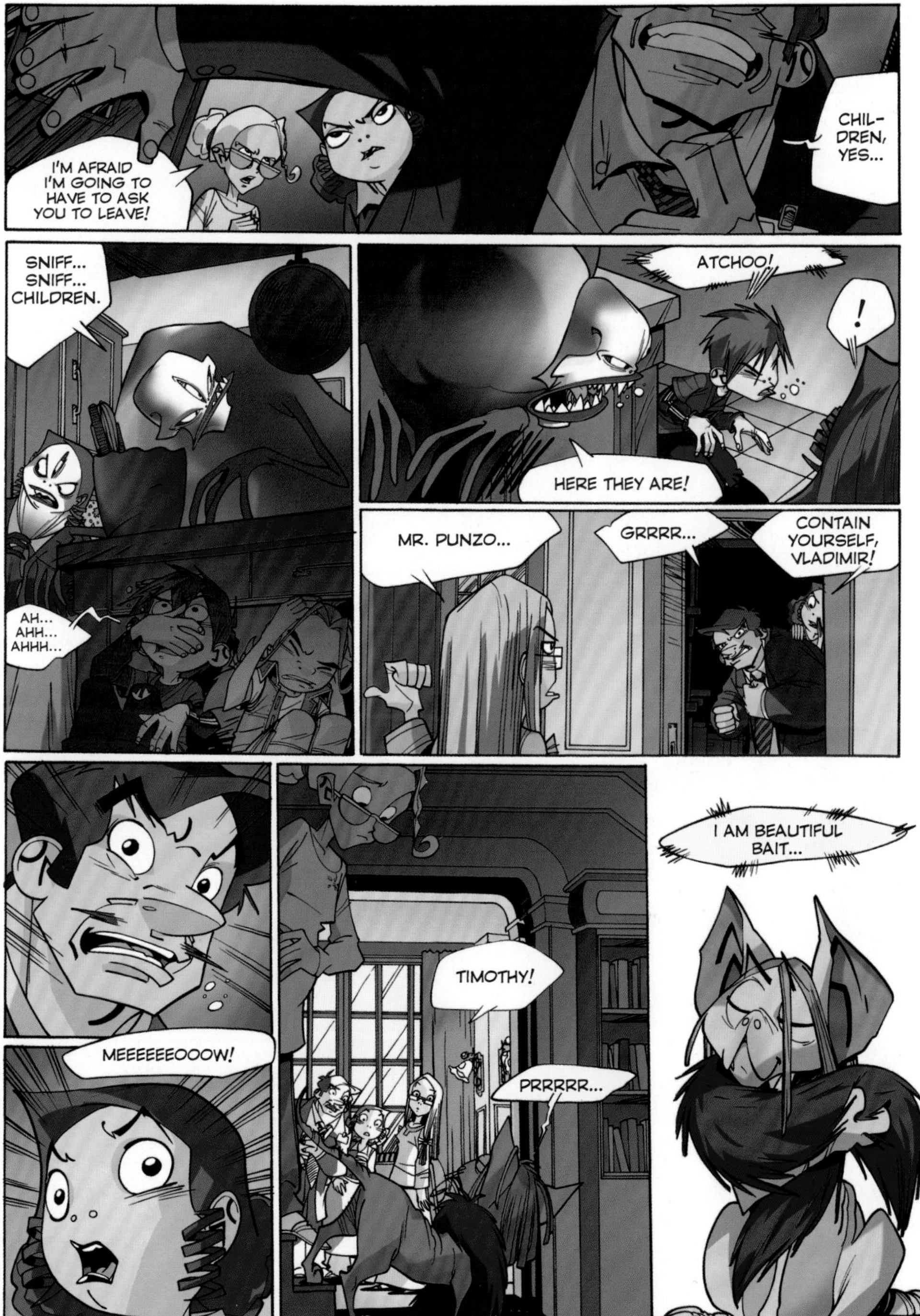
I'M AFRAID I'M GOING TO HAVE TO ASK YOU TO LEAVE!
CHIL-DREN, YES...
SNIFF... SNIFF... CHILDREN.
AH... AHH... AHHH...
ATCHOO!
!
HERE THEY ARE!
MR. PUNZO...
GRRRR...
CONTAIN YOURSELF, VLADIMIR!
MEEEEEEOOOW!
TIMOTHY!
PRRRRR...
I AM BEAUTIFUL BAIT...

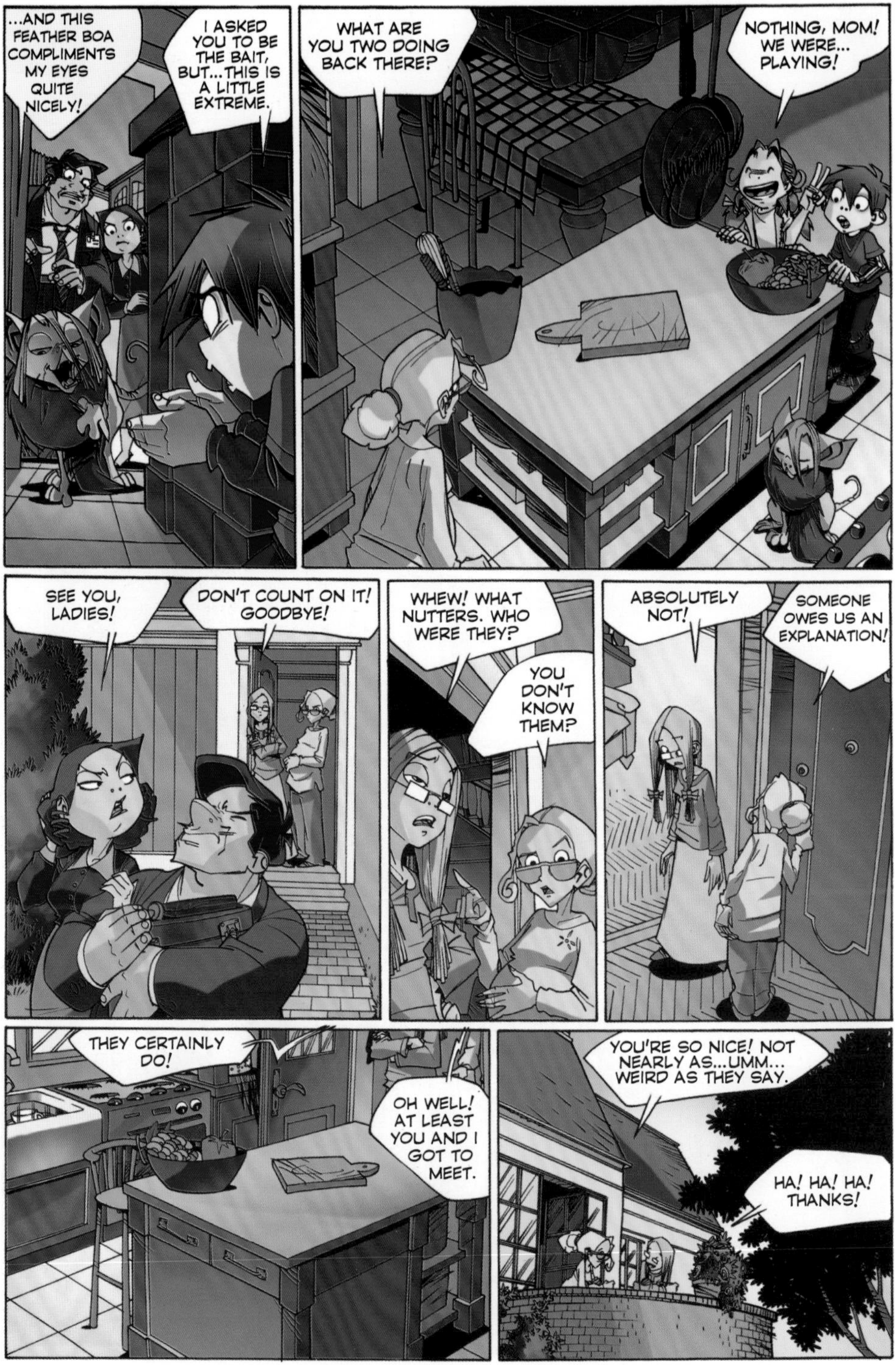
...AND THIS FEATHER BOA COMPLIMENTS MY EYES QUITE NICELY!
I ASKED YOU TO BE THE BAIT, BUT...THIS IS A LITTLE EXTREME.
WHAT ARE YOU TWO DOING BACK THERE?
NOTHING, MOM! WE WERE... PLAYING!
SEE YOU, LADIES!
DON'T COUNT ON IT! GOODBYE!
WHEW! WHAT NUTTERS. WHO WERE THEY?
YOU DON'T KNOW THEM?
ABSOLUTELY NOT!
SOMEONE OWES US AN EXPLANATION!
THEY CERTAINLY DO!
OH WELL! AT LEAST YOU AND I GOT TO MEET.
YOU'RE SO NICE! NOT NEARLY AS...UMM... WEIRD AS THEY SAY.
HA! HA! HA! THANKS!

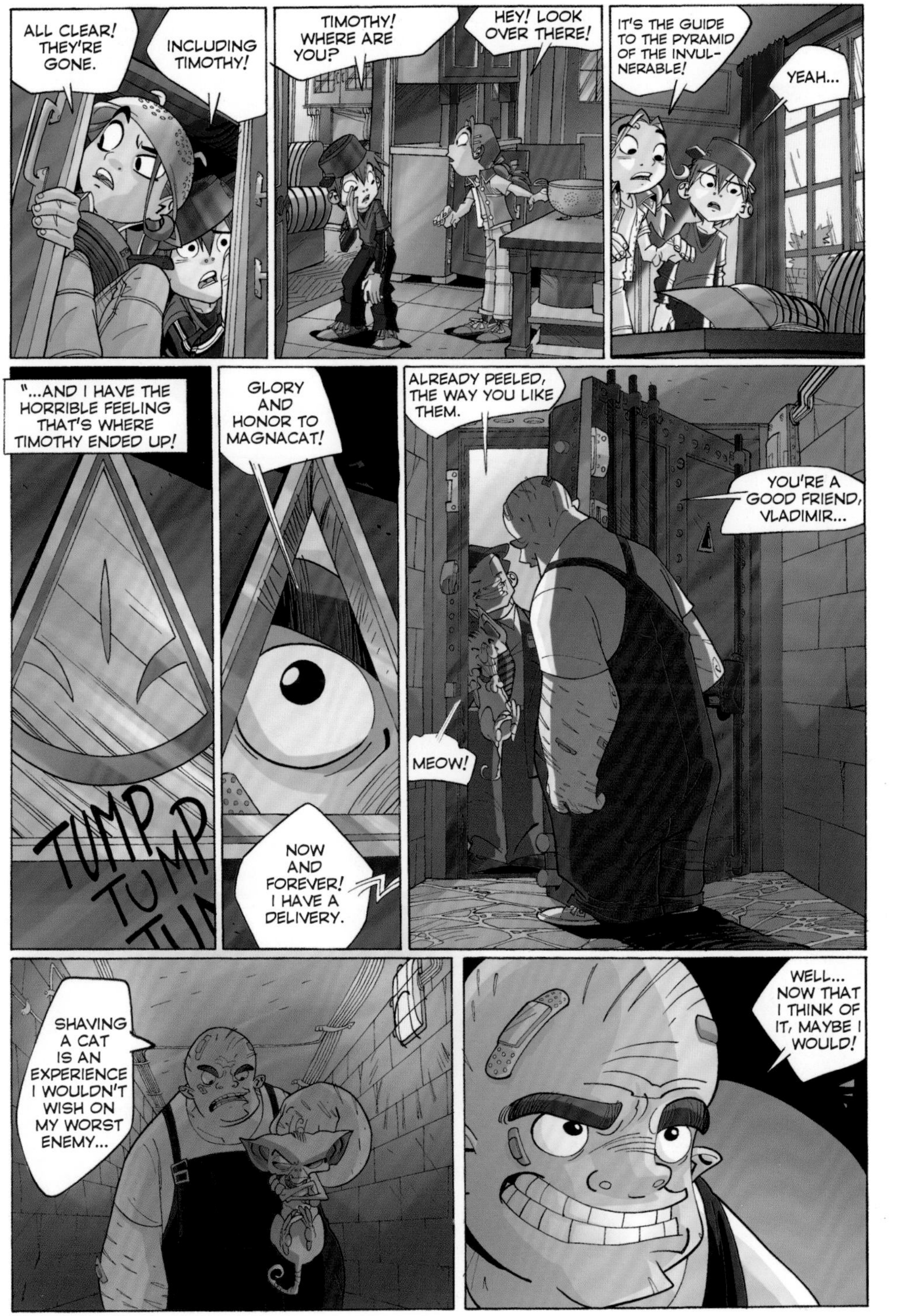
ALL CLEAR! THEY'RE GONE.
INCLUDING TIMOTHY!
TIMOTHY! WHERE ARE YOU?
HEY! LOOK OVER THERE!
IT'S THE GUIDE TO THE PYRAMID OF THE INVUL-NERABLE!
YEAH...
"...AND I HAVE THE HORRIBLE FEELING THAT'S WHERE TIMOTHY ENDED UP!
TUMP TUMP TUMP
GLORY AND HONOR TO MAGNACAT!
NOW AND FOREVER! I HAVE A DELIVERY.
ALREADY PEELED, THE WAY YOU LIKE THEM.
YOU'RE A GOOD FRIEND, VLADIMIR...
MEOW!
SHAVING A CAT IS AN EXPERIENCE I WOULDN'T WISH ON MY WORST ENEMY...
WELL... NOW THAT I THINK OF IT, MAYBE I WOULD!

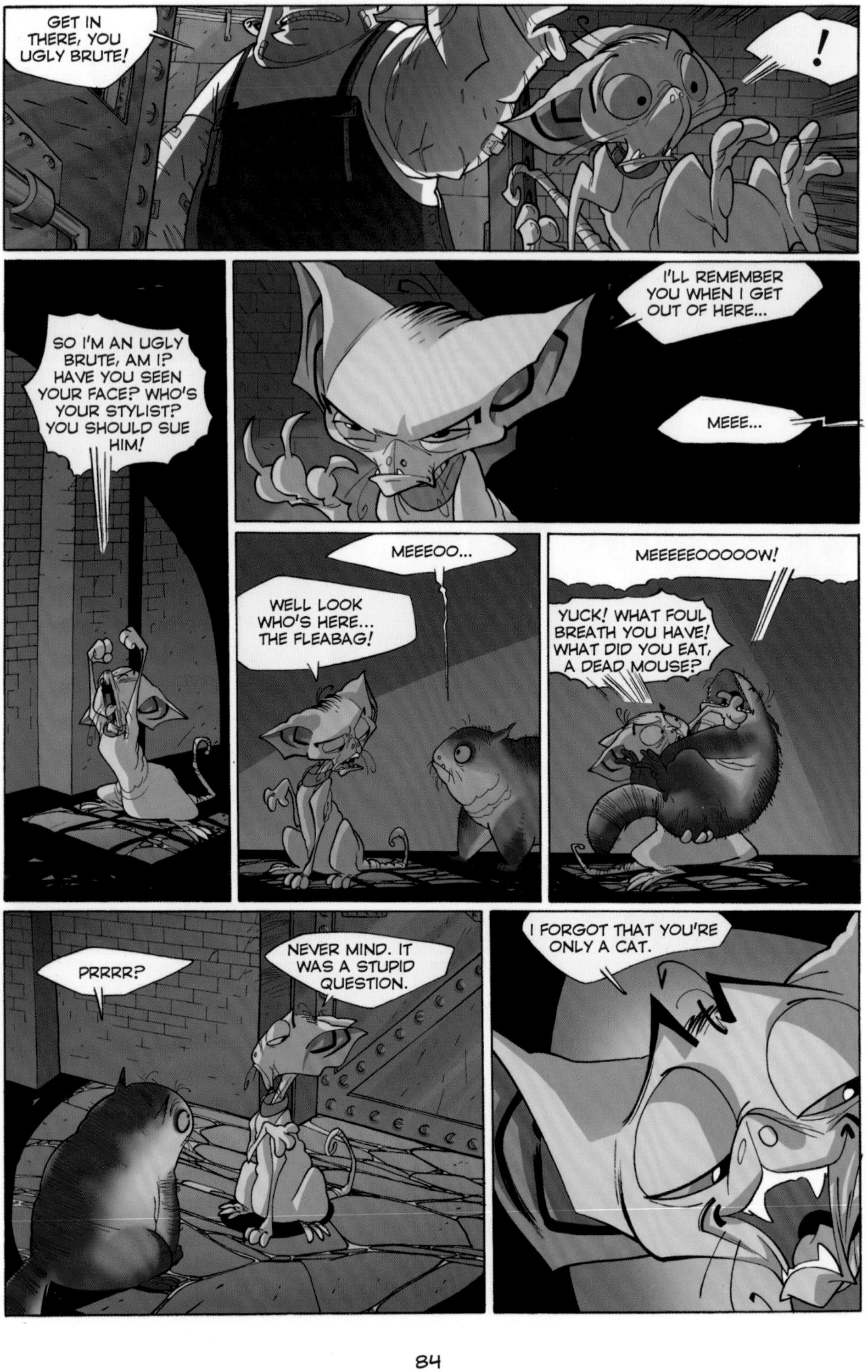
GET IN THERE, YOU UGLY BRUTE!
!
SO I'M AN UGLY BRUTE, AM I? HAVE YOU SEEN YOUR FACE? WHO'S YOUR STYLIST? YOU SHOULD SUE HIM!
I'LL REMEMBER YOU WHEN I GET OUT OF HERE...
MEEE...
MEEEOO...
WELL LOOK WHO'S HERE... THE FLEABAG!
MEEEEEOOOOOW!
YUCK! WHAT FOUL BREATH YOU HAVE! WHAT DID YOU EAT, A DEAD MOUSE?
PRRRR?
NEVER MIND. IT WAS A STUPID QUESTION.
I FORGOT THAT YOU'RE ONLY A CAT.

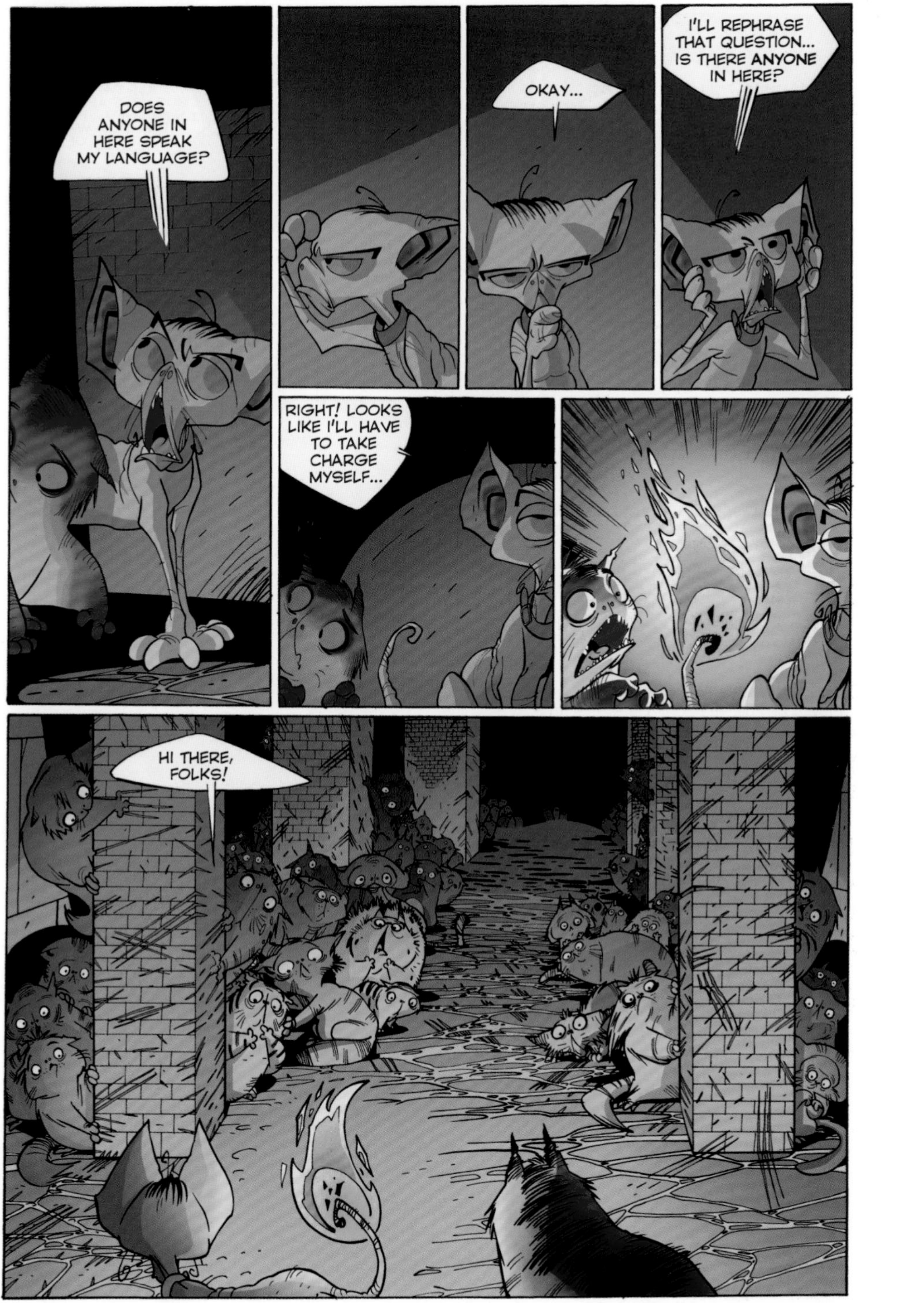
DOES ANYONE IN HERE SPEAK MY LANGUAGE?
OKAY...
I'LL REPHRASE THAT QUESTION... IS THERE ANYONE IN HERE?
RIGHT! LOOKS LIKE I'LL HAVE TO TAKE CHARGE MYSELF...
HI THERE, FOLKS!

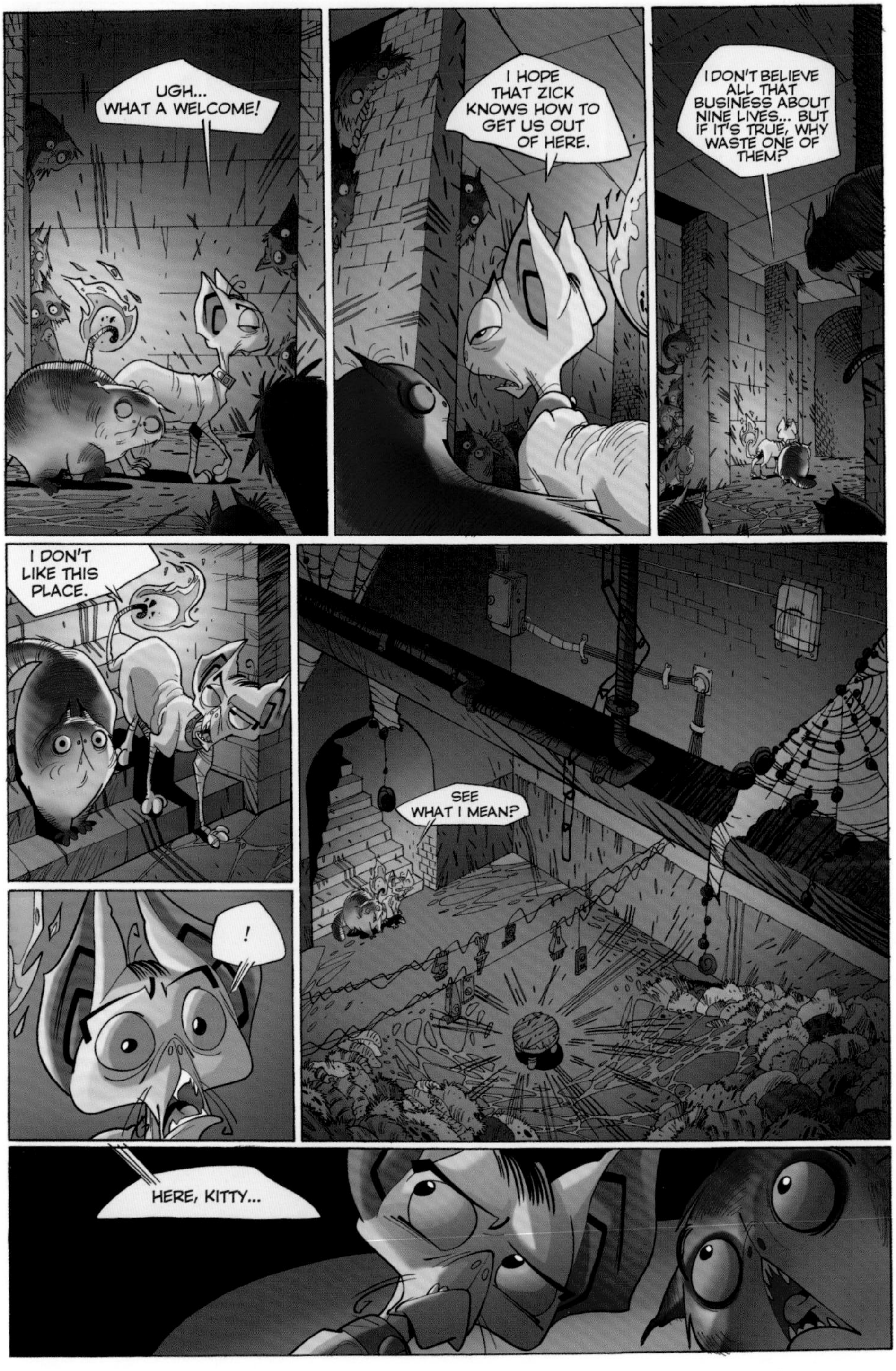
UGH... WHAT A WELCOME!
I HOPE THAT ZICK KNOWS HOW TO GET US OUT OF HERE.
I DON'T BELIEVE ALL THAT BUSINESS ABOUT NINE LIVES... BUT IF IT'S TRUE, WHY WASTE ONE OF THEM?
I DON'T LIKE THIS PLACE.
SEE WHAT I MEAN?
!
HERE, KITTY...

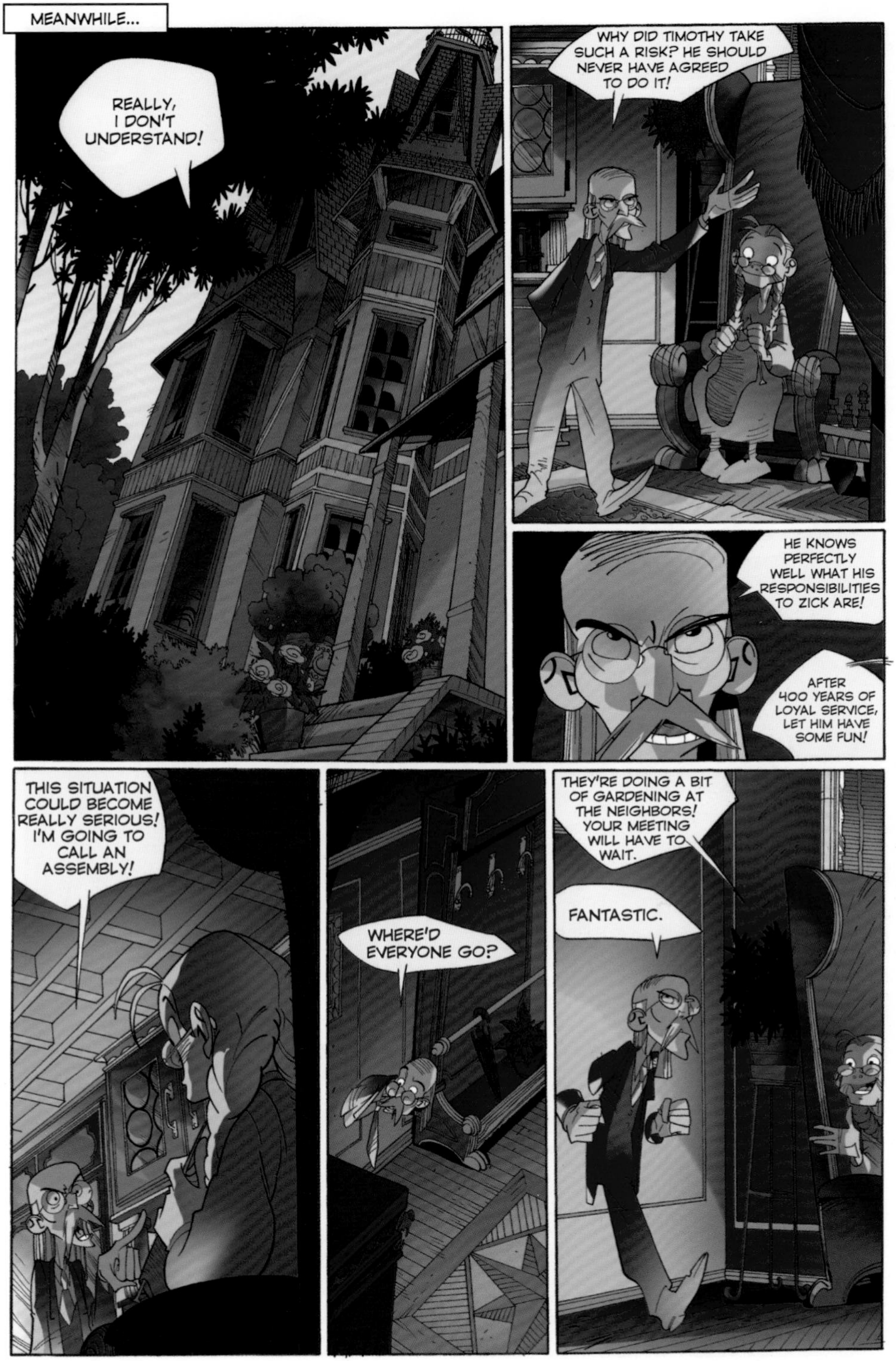
MEANWHILE...
REALLY, I DON'T UNDERSTAND!
WHY DID TIMOTHY TAKE SUCH A RISK? HE SHOULD NEVER HAVE AGREED TO DO IT!
HE KNOWS PERFECTLY WELL WHAT HIS RESPONSIBILITIES TO ZICK ARE!
AFTER 400 YEARS OF LOYAL SERVICE, LET HIM HAVE SOME FUN!
THIS SITUATION COULD BECOME REALLY SERIOUS! I'M GOING TO CALL AN ASSEMBLY!
WHERE'D EVERYONE GO?
THEY'RE DOING A BIT OF GARDENING AT THE NEIGHBORS! YOUR MEETING WILL HAVE TO WAIT.
FANTASTIC.

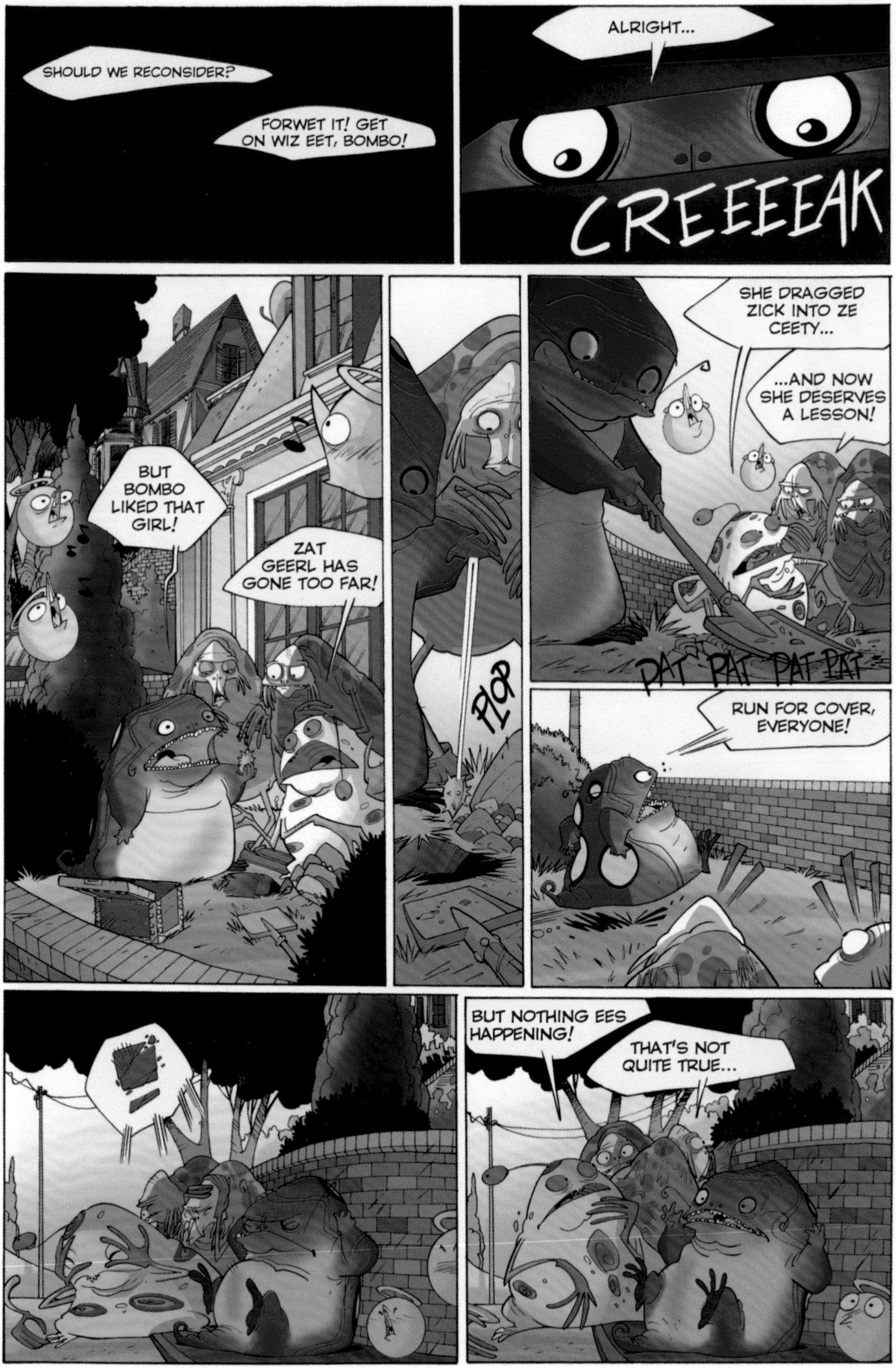
SHOULD WE RECONSIDER?
FORWET IT! GET ON WIZ EET, BOMBO!
ALRIGHT...
CREEEEAK
BUT BOMBO LIKED THAT GIRL!
ZAT GEERL HAS GONE TOO FAR!
PLOP
SHE DRAGGED ZICK INTO ZE CEETY...
...AND NOW SHE DESERVES A LESSON!
PAT PAT PAT PAT
RUN FOR COVER, EVERYONE!
BUT NOTHING EES HAPPENING!
THAT'S NOT QUITE TRUE...

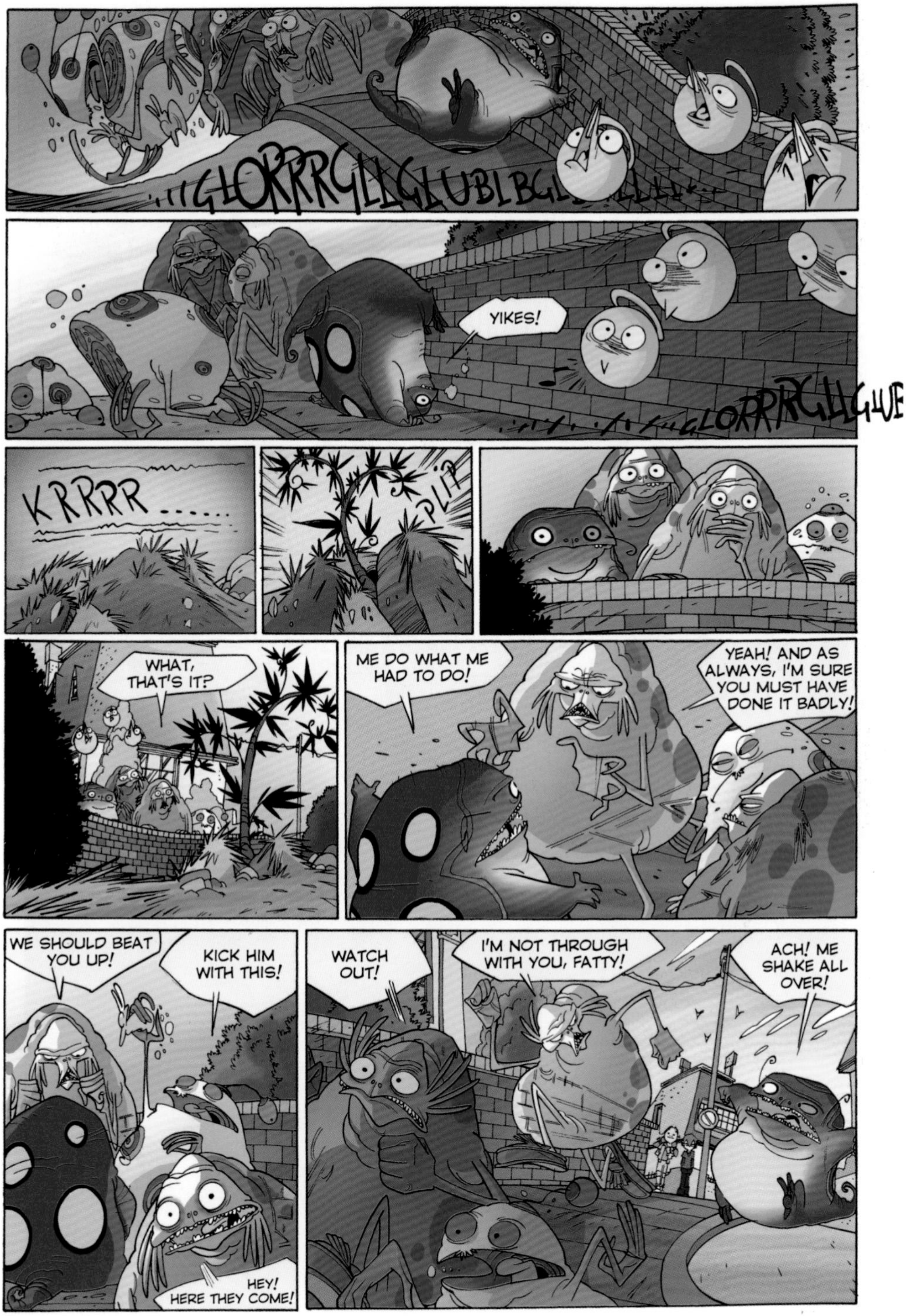
GLORRRGLLGLUBLBGL
YIKES!
GLORRRGLLGLUE
KRRRR
PLIP
WHAT, THAT'S IT?
ME DO WHAT ME HAD TO DO!
YEAH! AND AS ALWAYS, I'M SURE YOU MUST HAVE DONE IT BADLY!
WE SHOULD BEAT YOU UP!
KICK HIM WITH THIS!
HEY! HERE THEY COME!
WATCH OUT!
I'M NOT THROUGH WITH YOU, FATTY!
ACH! ME SHAKE ALL OVER!

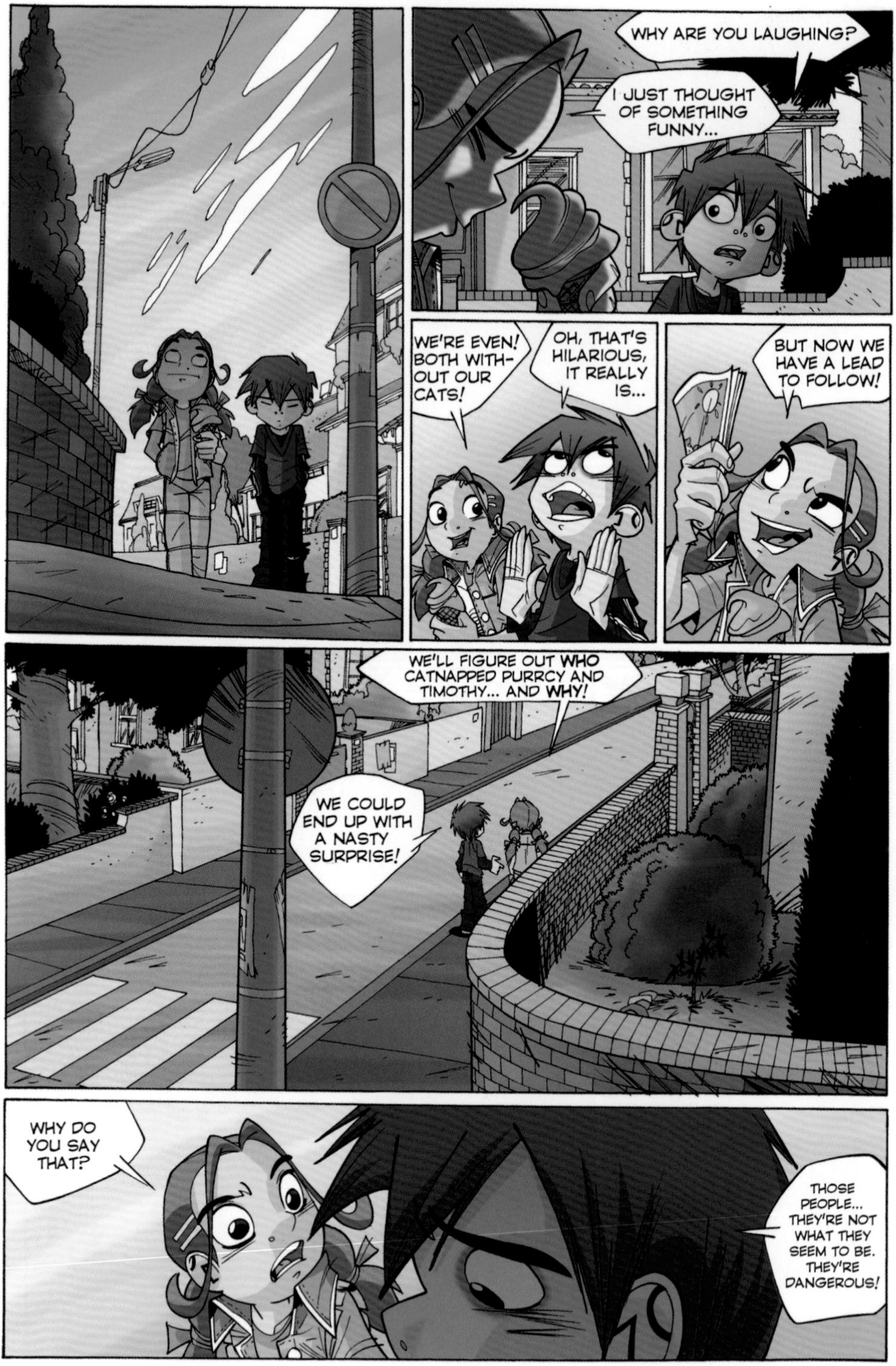
WHY ARE YOU LAUGHING?
I JUST THOUGHT OF SOMETHING FUNNY...
WE'RE EVEN! BOTH WITH-OUT OUR CATS!
OH, THAT'S HILARIOUS, IT REALLY IS...
BUT NOW WE HAVE A LEAD TO FOLLOW!
WE'LL FIGURE OUT WHO CATNAPPED PURRCY AND TIMOTHY... AND WHY!
WE COULD END UP WITH A NASTY SURPRISE!
WHY DO YOU SAY THAT?
THOSE PEOPLE... THEY'RE NOT WHAT THEY SEEM TO BE. THEY'RE DANGEROUS!

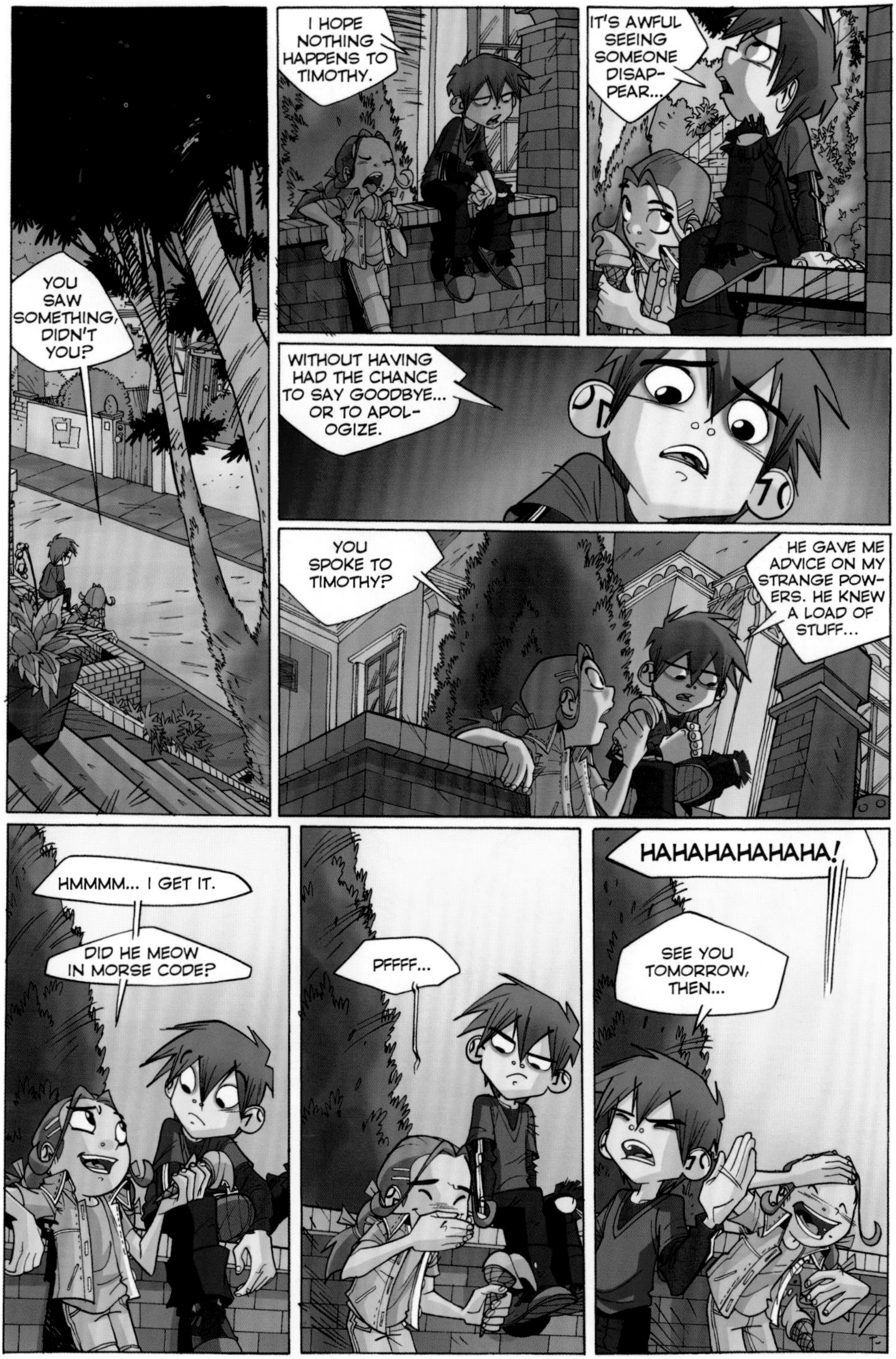
YOU SAW SOMETHING, DIDN'T YOU?
I HOPE NOTHING HAPPENS TO TIMOTHY.
IT'S AWFUL SEEING SOMEONE DISAP-PEAR...
WITHOUT HAVING HAD THE CHANCE TO SAY GOODBYE... OR TO APOL-OGIZE.
YOU SPOKE TO TIMOTHY?
HE GAVE ME ADVICE ON MY STRANGE POW-ERS. HE KNEW A LOAD OF STUFF...
HMMMM... I GET IT.
DID HE MEOW IN MORSE CODE?
PFFFF...
HAHAHAHAHAHA!
SEE YOU TOMORROW, THEN...

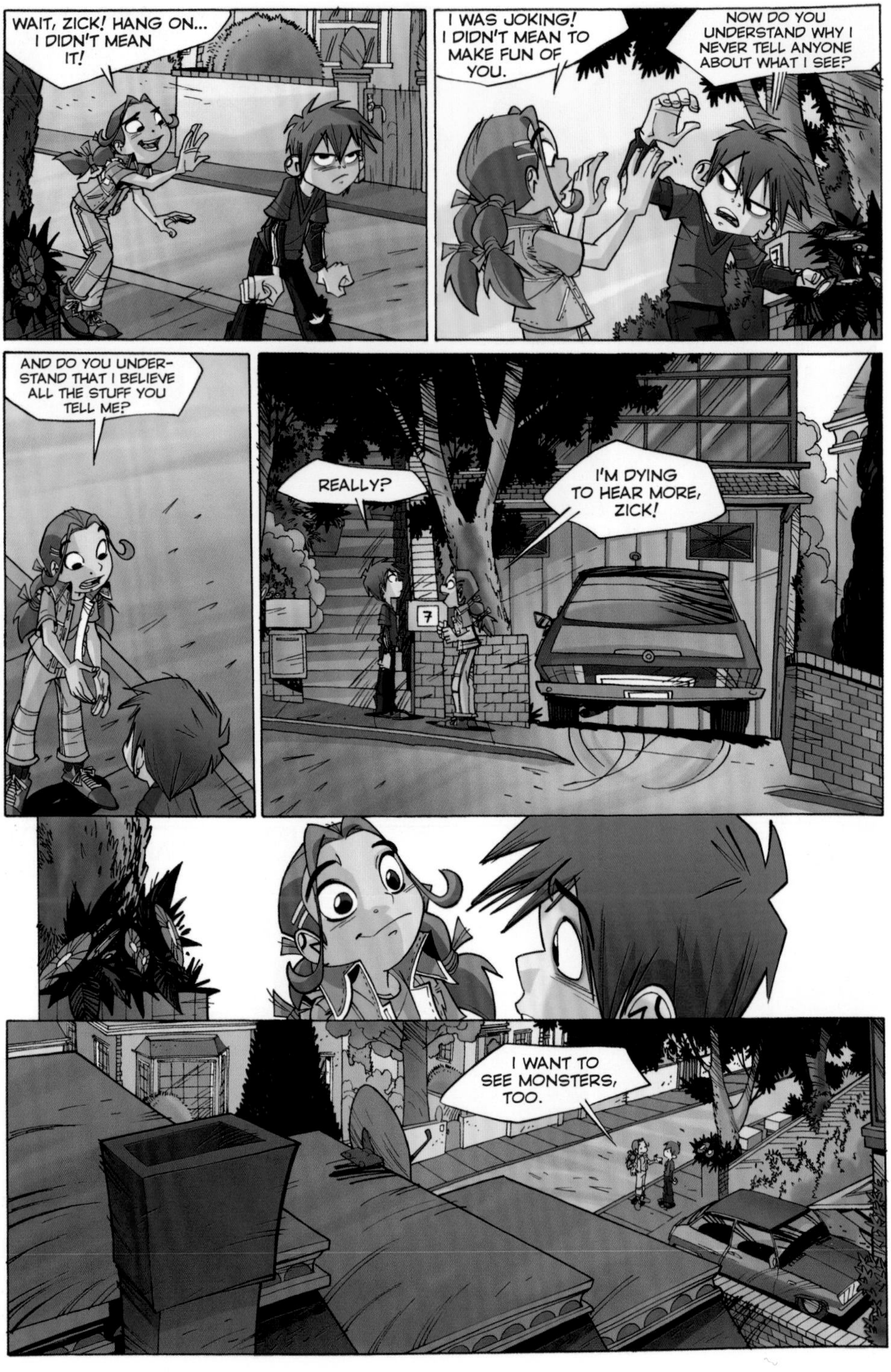

WAIT, ZICK! HANG ON... I DIDN'T MEAN IT!
I WAS JOKING! I DIDN'T MEAN TO MAKE FUN OF YOU.
NOW DO YOU UNDERSTAND WHY I NEVER TELL ANYONE ABOUT WHAT I SEE?
AND DO YOU UNDER-STAND THAT I BELIEVE ALL THE STUFF YOU TELL ME?
REALLY?
I'M DYING TO HEAR MORE, ZICK!
7
I WANT TO SEE MONSTERS, TOO.

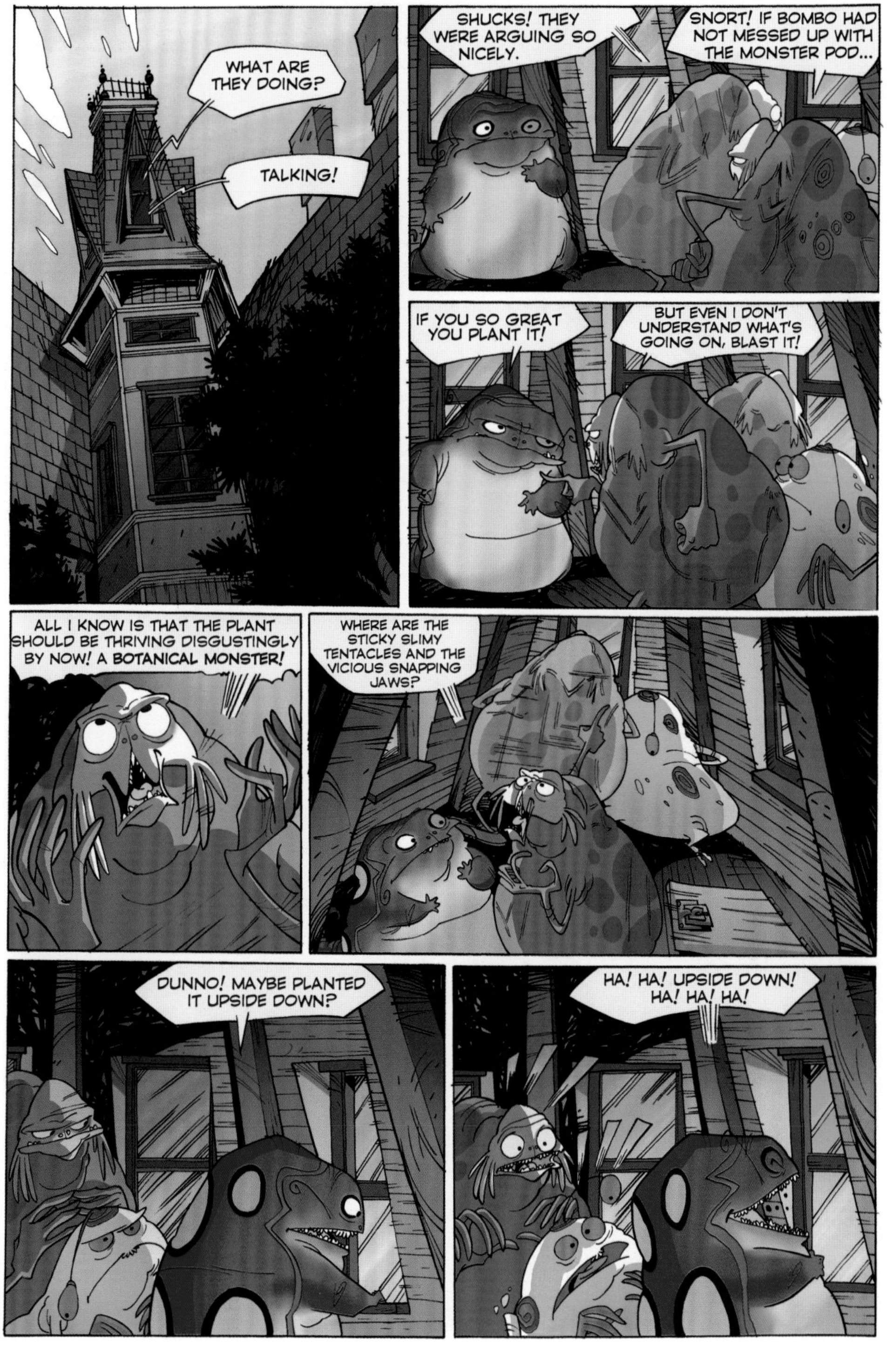
WHAT ARE THEY DOING?
TALKING!
SHUCKS! THEY WERE ARGUING SO NICELY.
SNORT! IF BOMBO HAD NOT MESSED UP WITH THE MONSTER POD...
IF YOU SO GREAT YOU PLANT IT!
BUT EVEN I DON'T UNDERSTAND WHAT'S GOING ON, BLAST IT!
ALL I KNOW IS THAT THE PLANT SHOULD BE THRIVING DISGUSTINGLY BY NOW! A BOTANICAL MONSTER!
WHERE ARE THE STICKY SLIMY TENTACLES AND THE VICIOUS SNAPPING JAWS?
DUNNO! MAYBE PLANTED IT UPSIDE DOWN?
HA! HA! UPSIDE DOWN! HA! HA! HA!

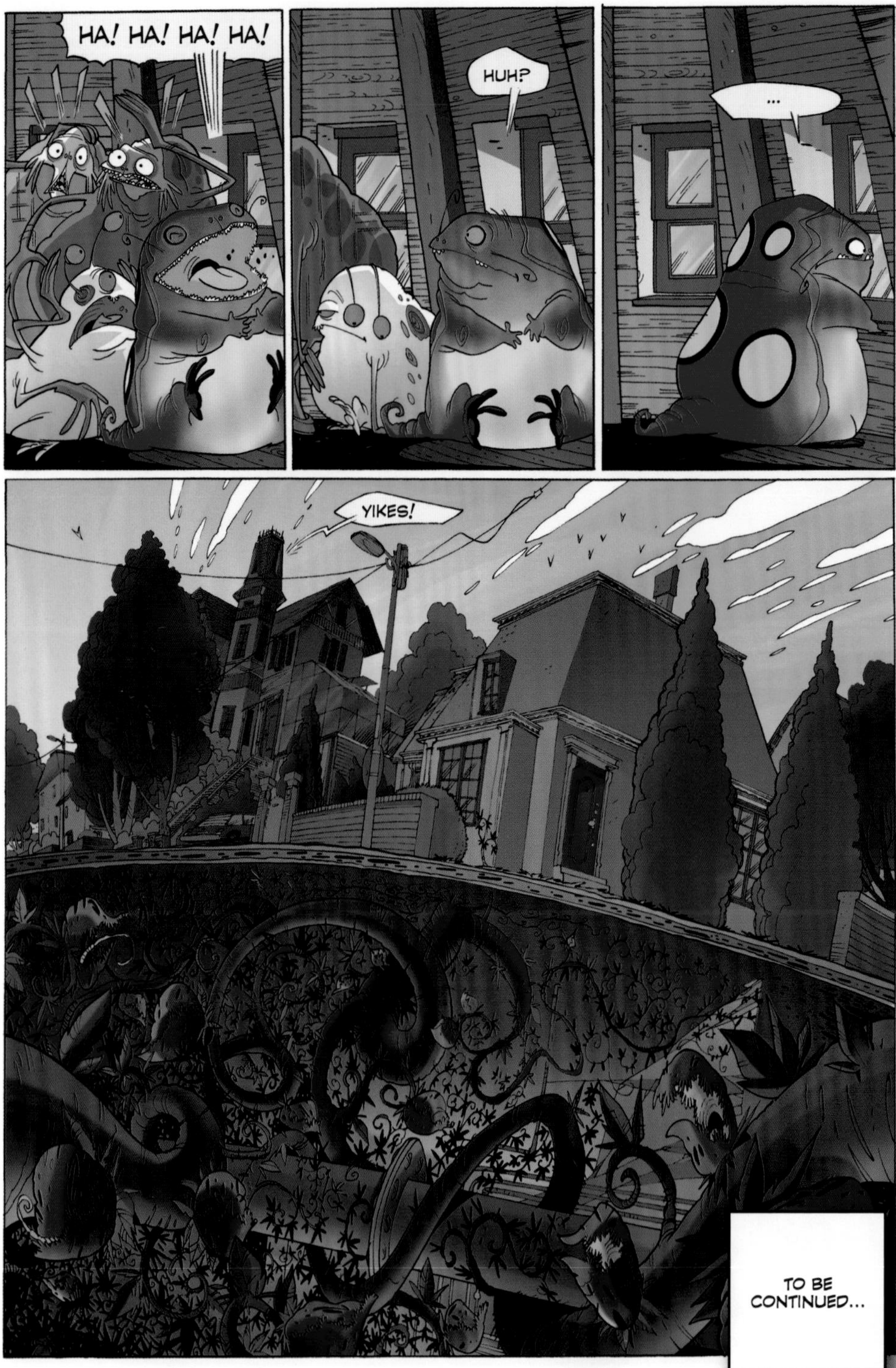
HA! HA! HA! HA!
HUH?
...
YIKES!
TO BE CONTINUED...

An Imprint of Insight Editions
PO Box 3088
San Rafael, CA 94912
www.insightcomics.com

Find us on Facebook:
www.facebook.com/InsightEditionsComics

Follow us on Twitter:
@InsightComics

Follow us on Instagram:
Insight_Comics

Published in the United States in 2019 by Insight Editions. Originally published in Italian
as *Monster Allergy Collection Vol. 1* by Tunué, Italy, in 2015.

Library of Congress Cataloging-in-Publication Data available.

ISBN: 978-1-68383-540-0

Publisher: Raoul Goff
Associate Publisher: Vanessa Lopez
Design Support: Brooke McCullum
Executive Editor: Mark Irwin
Assistant Editor: Holly Fisher
Senior Production Editor: Elaine Ou
Senior Production Manager: Greg Steffen

ROOTS of PEACE

Insight Editions, in association with Roots of Peace, will plant two trees for each tree used in the manufacturing of this book.
Roots of Peace is an internationally renowned humanitarian organization dedicated to eradicating land mines worldwide
and converting war-torn lands into productive farms and wildlife habitats. Roots of Peace will plant two million
fruit and nut trees in Afghanistan and provide farmers there with the skills and support necessary for sustainable land use.

Manufactured in China by Insight Editions

10 9 8 7 6 5 4 3 2